wait
for
me

Books by Jody Hedlund

Waters of Time Series
Come Back to Me
Never Leave Me
Stay With Me
Wait For Me

Knights of Brethren Series
Enamored
Entwined
Ensnared
Enriched
Enflamed
Entrusted

The Fairest Maidens Series
Beholden
Beguiled
Besotted

The Lost Princesses Series
Always: Prequel Novella
Evermore
Foremost
Hereafter

Noble Knights Series
The Vow: Prequel Novella
An Uncertain Choice
A Daring Sacrifice
For Love & Honor
A Loyal Heart
A Worthy Rebel

The Colorado Cowboys
A Cowboy for Keeps
The Heart of a Cowboy

To Tame a Cowboy
Falling for the Cowgirl
The Last Chance Cowboy

The Bride Ships Series
A Reluctant Bride
The Runaway Bride
A Bride of Convenience
Almost a Bride

The Orphan Train Series
An Awakened Heart: A Novella
With You Always
Together Forever
Searching for You

The Beacons of Hope Series
Out of the Storm: A Novella
Love Unexpected
Hearts Made Whole
Undaunted Hope
Forever Safe
Never Forget

The Hearts of Faith Collection
The Preacher's Bride
The Doctor's Lady
Rebellious Heart

The Michigan Brides Collection
Unending Devotion
A Noble Groom
Captured by Love

Historical
Luther and Katharina
Newton & Polly

WATERS OF TIME #4

wait for me

JODY HEDLUND

 NORTHERN LIGHTS PRESS

© 2023 by Jody Hedlund
Jody Hedlund Print Edition

Published by Northern Lights Press

Printed in the United States of America

ISBN: 979-8-9852649-5-1

Cover design by Roseanna White Designs
Cover Images from Shutterstock

~ 1 ~

June 11

DAWSON HUXHAM LET THE COLD SOIL slip through his fingers down onto the coffin. It thudded against the solid oak with a finality that echoed in his empty heart.

A part of him wanted to follow the dirt into the dark chasm in front of him and die with his sister. But something held him back—the same something that had held him back since he'd been injured.

Strong fingers clamped his left shoulder, the thumb pressure extra hard. The particular grip belonged to Acey. As did the cologne—a mixture of old leather and spicy-sweet tobacco. Slightly uneven breathing. Sniffing from allergies.

Another hand patted his right shoulder. Baxter. The pressure points from all his fingers even and tempered. No cologne. Instead, a faint waft of dark-roast coffee lingered on his breath. Controlled breathing. Controlled movements. Controlled everything.

Dawson resisted the urge to toss off both hands. His friends meant well. Had stayed by his side for the past two weeks since Sybil had been found unconscious and nearly dead under the stairs at Reider Castle.

But now, after battling to save her life . . . it was over. His sister was gone. Really gone.

He opened his hand all the way, tipped it over, and let the rest of the dirt fall. A second later, the soft patter was barely audible over the whisper of the wind in the long grass of the cemetery.

His chest tightened, and a part of him wished he could release the tension by roaring with rage. He wanted to throw something. Or punch, or kick.

But his uncontrolled anger was what had gotten him into this situation, had pushed Sybil away from him so that she'd taken him up on his rash declaration . . .

"I loathe your visits. I wish you'd gone missing instead of Mum."

A wave of grief slammed into him, and he wavered. He'd killed her. Maybe not directly. But during the last conversation he'd had with her, he'd been worse than a viper in the venom he'd spewed her way. The truth was, he'd planted land mines all around his life. She'd dodged them for years. But stepping on one had been inevitable, especially because he'd become an expert at allowing everything to bother him.

With weakening legs, he let himself sink to the ground. The cushion of grass underneath his knees was damp from a recent rain, and the moisture soaked through the dress slacks. He'd lost Baxter's hold, but Acey's grip remained. Firm. Unyielding.

"You guys get on." Dawson cleared his throat, trying to get rid of the lump of sorrow that made his voice wobbly. "I need a few minutes alone."

Baxter's presence shifted away. "No problem—"

"You sure?" Acey didn't release his shoulder clamp.

"I can find the car when I'm done here." Dawson rested his elbow on his upturned knee and buried his face into his hand.

From the silence all around, Dawson could tell the rest of the guests—the few who had come out to the graveside from the church—had already started walking back to their vehicles. Except for Acey's fiancée, Chloe. She waited a dozen paces away, politely giving the three of them a moment.

Even though Dawson's right eye was completely blind, his left had some vision remaining. While the nerve damage was severe, he had the ability to see light, faint distinctions in color, and general shapes of bigger items. That meant he could make out a darkish form where Chloe stood, but he couldn't distinguish what she looked like, not even when she was but a few inches away. She was fuzzy. So were Baxter and Acey. And everyone and everything else.

He'd been told too many times to count that he ought to be thankful he could at least see the outlines, that he could maneuver on his own to a degree, that the world wasn't totally black.

But every time someone reminded him of the slim eyesight he retained, he wanted to shout out that they didn't have to miss seeing the low clouds rolling over the hills beyond the church, the ivy winding up the window lattice, or the moss staining the cracked headstones.

They didn't know what it was like, couldn't understand.

He lived in a dark and broken world. And now with Sybil gone, he'd lost the last of any light with her.

God, please . . . His attempt at prayer fell flat as it had every other time he'd tried to reason with heaven. Instead, the overwhelming need for nicotine, alcohol, or something stronger pulsed into his blood.

He hadn't touched any substances since the day he'd learned she was dying. Not even the Oxycontin he'd used occasionally to temper the pain from his wounds. He didn't have numerous scars the same way Acey did. In fact, the doctors had claimed that he was lucky he'd walked away without any facial disfigurement. Even so, fine slivers of shrapnel remained embedded in his body and caused him excruciating pain at times.

He'd kept vigil at her bedside at the hospital for the past couple of weeks as she'd lain in a coma, and the detox had been his penance, his way of asking her to forgive him. Maybe if she knew he was finally giving up substances the way she'd wanted, she'd decide to give him a second chance. Maybe it had even been his way of bargaining with God to bring Sybil out of her coma.

But now that she was in the grave, what reason did he have for staying clean?

His two friends hesitated a moment longer before their footsteps began to lead them away. Acey's had the extra *thunk* of his cane that aided his prosthesis. From the slowness and heaviness of their tread, he could tell they were reluctant to leave him. But they would. They always gave him the space he wanted, even if it was to his detriment.

A humid breeze swelled and lifted a strand of his hair off his forehead—as Sybil used to. For a second, he could imagine her beside him, comforting him. The way she had when they'd had the funeral for their mum. At this church. In this very spot. Mum's headstone was already there. And Sybil's would go next to hers.

He bowed his head, the words inside him churning. "I'm sorry." He'd already apologized a hundred times, but all the apologizing in the world wouldn't bring her back.

If only he'd known she was suicidal. But he hadn't been thinking about anyone except himself. He'd been so selfish, so wrapped up in his own pain, that he hadn't paid attention to hers.

Her ex-boyfriend had been the one to discover her in the closet where she'd apparently hidden before attempting to kill herself. They hadn't been able to figure out exactly what she'd ingested. The bottle they'd found next to her had been empty, and the lab tests of the residue had proven it to be nothing more than water.

They'd begun to speculate that maybe she tried to asphyxiate herself instead of overdosing. But they'd found nothing to validate that theory either.

Whatever the case, Sybil hadn't wanted to live. That much was clear. There was no other explanation for why she'd hidden away in the closet.

And he blamed himself . . .

"If only . . ." he whispered. If only what? If only he hadn't lost himself when he'd lost his eyesight?

A strange sense of foreboding prickled his skin. A strange sense that someone was watching him. He glanced behind him, an instinctual reaction. But, of course, he couldn't see anything. The landscape that he knew was there—Canterbury's sprawling hills and heathland—was nothing but a blur of lights and darks.

Even so, he peered into the distance, needing to discover who was spying on him. It was the same feeling he'd had after Mum's disappearance . . . the feeling that he wasn't alone, that he was being followed, that his every move was being calculated.

He hadn't experienced the sensation in over two years.

A man cleared his throat from his left. An unfamiliar throat-clearing. One that didn't belong to Acey or Baxter. One that didn't belong to anyone from his vision impairment support group. One that didn't belong to the reverend. One that didn't belong to Sybil's workmates or chums—at least those he'd met.

Still on his knees in the grass, Dawson shifted to face the fellow. Immediately, he could sense a kind soul—unlike the threatening vibe from whoever else was out there watching him.

"Dawson Huxham?" The pitch of the man's voice wasn't too old or young. From the clipped, almost elegant tone as well as the waft of an expensive aftershave, Dawson guessed this was a man of some means.

"I'm Harrison Burlington." The man spoke again solemnly. "Sybil . . . she was . . . well, she was my private investigator for the past year and helped me tremendously."

Harrison Burlington. As in *the* Lord Burlington of Chesterfield Park?

"I'm so sorry for your loss. Sybil was exceptional, truly brilliant."

6

Dawson pushed himself up so that he was standing. The local news had been full of reports when Lord Burlington had been kidnapped in May of last year. Recently, Lord Burlington had been in the news again when his girlfriend—or maybe his wife—had also been abducted. Apparently, the two had experienced recovery from long-lasting illnesses as a result of an experimental—but extremely dangerous—drug that had been in the developmental stages at Mercer Pharmaceutical Company.

Even in the days before his blindness, Dawson had never met Lord Burlington, but he'd known that the wealthy nobleman had suffered from a tragic car accident as a child, one that had left him paralyzed and wheelchair-bound. If the recent rumors were true, then Lord Burlington was walking again. From the faint dark outline, Lord Burlington appeared to be standing alone.

"I would have come to visit her—and you—at the hospital," Lord Burlington continued, his voice laden with regret, even self-deprecation, "but I didn't hear about all that had happened to Sybil until last evening after returning from my honeymoon."

"She wouldn't have known you were there." Dawson stuffed his hands into his pockets, trying to squelch the nervous pinch in his chest. Though he'd never been in the presence of the queen or any of the royal family, he guessed it felt a little bit like this chasm—an ordinary bloke like him from a working-class family in the presence of a titled aristocrat who had a rich history of nobility and wealth.

Lord Burlington was silent, sorrow radiating off him in

waves. He must have gotten close to Sybil over the past year.

Dawson strained to see past the fuzziness but couldn't observe anything more than Lord Burlington's silhouette—which was of average height and size. He'd seen Lord Burlington's picture once in the newspaper before he left for Afghanistan—before the accident. From what he remembered, the lord had been an intelligent-looking man.

"So she was in a coma?" Lord Burlington's question was an anguished whisper.

"She was unconscious when she was found, and she never recovered."

"And there was a small bottle beside her?"

How had Lord Burlington known such a private detail of the investigation? Maybe he had close connections at Sybil's workplace and had already gained information on her case. "Yes, but it wasn't related to her death. The investigators believe it was just an old relic left in the closet."

Lord Burlington seemed to be shaking his head. "If my suspicions are correct, then the contents of the bottle contributed to her death."

Something ominous in the man's tone set Dawson's nerves on edge—more than they already were. "The bottle had traces of water in it. That's all."

"I'm not sure how much Sybil shared with you about the nature of her work for me." Lord Burlington spoke hesitantly. "But she was investigating ancient holy water on my behalf."

Ancient holy water? Everything within Dawson slowed to a halt except for his thoughts, which whirred into high speed. The last time Sybil had visited his flat, she'd brought him what she'd called "medicine," claiming it would heal him. During their angry exchange, she'd used those exact words: *ancient holy water*. And she'd been secretive, had told him not to tell anyone else about it.

"I can tell you know about it," Lord Burlington said.

Her claim that she'd found a cure for him had made him feel inadequate, as if he could never be good enough for her. So he'd done his best to forget about the so-called medicine. He honestly didn't know if she'd left the holy water somewhere in his room before she stormed out. Even if she had, he wouldn't have noticed it. His place was a terrible mess—as cluttered and full of rubbish as his life was.

Maybe she'd taken her offering of the ancient medicine with her after leaving his flat. And maybe she'd thought to heal herself of some disease. But obviously, she'd been wrong about its curative abilities. If she'd consumed it, as Lord Burlington implied, then it had killed her.

"Did Sybil mention where she found the bottle of holy water?" Lord Burlington asked. "I venture she discovered it during her investigations at Reider Castle . . ."

Dawson shrugged. "She didn't say anything about that."

Harrison was quiet for a beat. "But she did say something."

How much should he reveal to Lord Burlington? What would it hurt to share a little more? "She wanted me to drink it." He lifted a hand and half-heartedly motioned toward his eyes. "She thought it would cure my blindness."

Dawson could sense Lord Burlington studying him more carefully. Maybe the man hadn't realized he was visually impaired. After all, he didn't look like a blind person—not that there was a particular look. But someone passing by wouldn't guess he was blind, especially when he was standing or sitting.

"I should've drunk it like she wanted." Dawson couldn't keep the regret from lacing his voice. "Then I'd be dead instead of her."

"That's not how the holy water works."

Dawson didn't know what to think of this conversation. It was among the strangest he'd ever had.

"I can assure you, the holy water does provide a cure for those in need of one." Lord Burlington's voice dropped to a whisper.

Was this man insinuating the holy water had healed him? Was that how he'd been able to walk again? Was the *extremely dangerous drug* developed by Mercer Pharmaceuticals just a cover?

Dawson wanted to shake his head but remained immobile, unwilling to reveal his doubts—at least, not yet. Not until he'd heard Lord Burlington out.

"If a person who isn't in need of healing drinks the holy water, it has the power to put them into a coma . . ." Lord Burlington paused, but from the way he left his last word hanging, Dawson knew he had more to say. "Once in a coma, the person has the ability to travel into the past."

"What?" A scoffing half laugh slipped out.

"I realize I sound like a deluded lunatic, but I guarantee that I'm not fabricating this. It's entirely possible Sybil is still alive in the past, perhaps having gained a connection to the year 1382 as a result of the other overlaps before her."

Lord Burlington was more than a deluded lunatic. He was

genuinely out of his mind. Dawson wished he could stalk off. Instead, he awkwardly shuffled away from the open grave far enough that he wouldn't accidentally fall in. Then he started to make his way in the direction of the parking lot.

"Wait." Lord Burlington fell into step with him, which wasn't hard to do since his pace was slow and cautious.

"Beg your pardon, Lord Burlington." Dawson aimed away from the dark blob that formed the outline of the church. "I don't know what you've got to gain from messing with my mind like this. But I—"

"I'm not messing with your mind. I debated not divulging anything at all. But with what happened to Sybil, I won't be the only one to suspect she had access to the holy water."

"She's gone. So it doesn't matter now, does it?" Dawson couldn't keep the edge from his tone.

"Dangerous people are after the holy water, and they'll stop at nothing to get information about it. Believe me, I should know."

Was that why Lord Burlington had been kidnapped? Because of the holy water? Dawson released another scoffing sound. "Leave me out of this."

"I just wanted to warn you to be careful and to look after yourself."

"Can't you tell?" Bitterness filled Dawson's words too easily. "I'm *looking* after myself just fine."

Lord Burlington stopped, but Dawson kept walking in the direction of the few remaining cars lined up on the side of the road. He braced himself for more of Lord Burlington's nonsense, but the man remained where he was.

Dawson's hands clenched into fists. What a lot of nerve. Taking him for a fool. Bothering him on a day like today, in such a private, sacred moment. Maybe the lord had filled Sybil's head with tales of healings and miracles, so much so that she'd convinced herself she should drink the water.

If so, then Lord Burlington was at fault for Sybil's death.

As Dawson drew nearer the voices and outlines of his friends, he was tempted to turn around and shout blame upon Lord Burlington. But even as the need arose, so did the reminder that ultimately he'd been the one to send Sybil away, to tell her he wished she'd died instead of their mum.

No matter how much he wanted to shift the responsibility for her death, it would always come back to rest solely upon his shoulders. He was the one who'd killed his sister. And he'd have to live with that guilt the rest of his life.

~ 2 ~

DAWSON SKIMMED HIS HAND across the bedside table. His fingers had become his eyes over the years, and they were showing him that the top of the table was nearly as cluttered as the rest of his bedroom.

He picked up a wad of sticky napkins and dumped them into the plastic bag that was full of all the other rubbish he'd collected off his floor, bed, and the half bookshelf that sat below the window, now open and letting in a breeze to clear out the mustiness.

How long had it been since he'd opened the window? Maybe never?

And how long had it been since he'd cleaned his flat? Possibly the same answer as the previous question.

During the drive back into old Canterbury after the funeral, his mind had replayed the conversation with Lord Burlington at least half a dozen times. He'd finally asked Baxter to drop him off at home instead of joining the others for a meal at the pub. Baxter had suggested getting takeaway so they could be with him. But Dawson had begged out of participating, insisting that his friends go on without him.

He didn't feel guilty about skipping out. His friends were

used to his antisocial tendencies and knew he was stubborn and wouldn't give in to their efforts to include him, no matter how much they pressured him.

He drifted to the next items on the bedside table: a pill bottle and a vape pen. His fingers hovered above them, need welling up within him—the need to lose himself in oblivion and forget about everything . . .

But had he ever really been able to forget all the losses he'd suffered? Maybe the drugs provided a short break from thinking about his problems. But when the high wore off, he always fell even lower. High highs and low lows. A body wasn't meant to swing back and forth like that.

Besides, with how he'd treated Sybil, hadn't he learned his lesson? He needed to find an equilibrium, wanted to be steadier and more levelheaded. And now that he was through the worst of his headaches and chills and cravings, he couldn't go back to that.

With a frustrated growl, he swiped up the last of the drugs and tossed them into the bag with the rest of the rubbish.

He most certainly wasn't cleaning his room because he wanted to check if Sybil had left holy water for him.

But even as he tried to deny his motivation, the nagging wouldn't leave him alone. The truth was, as intense as Sybil had always been, she wouldn't have asked him to drink the holy water or insisted it would heal him if she hadn't been certain of its capability. And the other truth was, she wouldn't have offered it to him and then taken it away and used it on herself. In spite of how he'd lashed out at her, Sybil was too unselfish and giving and caring to take back a gift. She would have left it for him, hoping he'd change his mind and drink it.

His guess was that if she had really ingested holy water, she'd likely had an additional bottle. Which meant the original bottle might be in his room. Or perhaps at her flat among her belongings.

He was banking on it being somewhere here among the chaos.

What would he do if he found it? He'd mulled that over, too, since the meeting with Lord Burlington. Clearly the man believed in the power of the holy water. While he hadn't come right out and said it, he'd alluded that the water had healed him.

Dawson bent and patted the floor beside his bed, his fingers connecting with dirty clothes. He tossed them onto a pile he'd started, then sat back on his heels.

What if the holy water really could heal? If it harmed him or put him in a coma, as apparently it had done to Sybil, then what did he have to lose? Not much. Not anymore after already losing so much.

Whatever the case, he owed it to her to give it a go. It was the least he could do to make up for being so rude to her, not just during the last couple of visits but during the last couple of years.

He'd been a terrible brother. When was the last time he'd asked her about her life? About her work? Or even about how she was doing without Mum in their lives?

Breathing out a sigh laden with remorse, he finished sweeping his hand over the floor before standing. "I was a first-class jerk, Sybil," he whispered. "And I didn't love you the way you needed or deserved."

With the rubbish bag in hand, he shuffled across the room toward his chest of drawers. As his fingers made contact with one of the open drawers, he shoved it closed along with another that was sticking out. Then he traced a hand to the top, to the stack of folded socks he vaguely remembered Sybil telling him she'd washed for him. Had he ever thanked her for helping him?

He gave an angry shake of his head. He'd probably yelled at her and told her to leave him alone, the same way he had that last time.

Carefully—so he didn't topple the neat pile—he skimmed his fingers along the smooth surface of the chest of drawers until they brushed up against an unfamiliar object. A glass bottle. Small. Oddly shaped. A cork wedged in tightly.

His pulse hopped. This had to be it.

He picked it up and rubbed his fingers around the bulbous middle, then the thinner neck before going to the flat bottom. It certainly felt like an antique, wasn't familiar enough for his mind to picture.

He shook it slightly, feeling the swish and hearing the slosh of the liquid inside.

What should he do with it? Pop the cork off and drink it here and now?

At the slight opening squeal of the back door of the flat, he stuffed the bottle down into the rubbish bag, then loosely tied the top flaps closed. He didn't want any of his friends to come into his room, see the bottle, and start to question him about it, especially where he'd gotten it and what it contained. No doubt it was an unusual-looking bottle and would attract attention and unwanted questions.

At the creak of footsteps entering the flat, he placed the bulging bag against the chest of drawers, then pretended to be busy putting the socks into the top drawer.

A second pair of steps followed the first into the kitchen. Both were too soft, not like Acey's uneven, thumping gait or Chloe's carefree patter or even Baxter's thudding, determined tread. These were most definitely not his friends, who would have called out to him or to each other as they entered.

Lord Burlington's recent warning dinged in his head. *"Dangerous people are after the holy water, and they'll stop at nothing to get information about it."*

Dawson's muscles tensed, and he fumbled to find the bottom drawer where he kept his illegal gun. After all that he'd experienced in Afghanistan, he hadn't been able to relinquish the need to have a way to protect himself. Acey had a gun too. While they'd never needed the weapons, having them close at hand had kept them both sane through the nightmares that had plagued them since the war had ended.

His fingers finally found the handle, but as he tugged at the drawer, it stuck.

The footsteps veered toward his room. Yes, unfamiliar footsteps.

Adrenaline shot through him, and he yanked on the drawer. It scraped open another inch, enough that he could slip his hand inside and dig around at the bottom beneath T-shirts.

His fingers gripped at the handle of his Glock. In the same moment, his arm spasmed with a burst of pain from the unlocated shrapnel. He bit back a curse and closed his eyes to ward off the agony.

The steps paused at the door of his bedroom and then lengthened as they crossed toward him.

He struggled to wedge the gun through the crack in the drawer. Before he could pull it free, something slammed into his back. The force was so hard and painful, he arched against it. Before he could move again, the same something—a metal baton—came down against his arm with such punishing strength he had no choice but to release the gun.

As he straightened, he tried to focus on the dark shape of someone just a foot away. He took a swing but only managed to punch at the air. As he attempted another punch, the bar came down across his arm again, easily blocking him.

Frustration and anger boiled up swiftly inside. This was one of many reasons he loathed his blindness. Intruders had entered his home, and he was too clumsy to defend himself. What kind of man had he become that he could no longer fight?

The baton thwacked against his stomach, doubling him over. The moment he bent, the other intruder was behind him, wrenching his arms up and slipping a zip tie around his wrists.

"Who are you?" Dawson gasped through the pain. "And what do you want?"

One of the men wrenched open the bottom drawer, sliding it out all the way. A moment later came the thud of contents hitting the floor.

"We want information on your sister," said Baton Man, still a blurry outline in front of Dawson.

Dawson didn't need for them to spell things out any further. They wanted information on the holy water. Should he give them the bottle, tell them what he knew, and get them off his case? Or should he play ignorant?

"Where did she get the holy water?" The question was tinged with a slight accent.

"I don't know what you're talking about—"

The baton crashed against his ribs.

Pain sliced through him, and he grunted and bent to protect his chest. At the same time, he could hear the other intruder emptying another drawer. One thing was clear—these men were professionals. But professionals at what?

"Did your mother supply her with the water?"

"My mother?" The question was so unexpected that Dawson straightened.

Baton Man pressed the tip against Dawson's chest. "Where did Cecilia leave the water and how much?"

This time the accent was more pronounced. The man was from the Middle East. Dawson had been deployed long enough to recognize it. Did they have connections with his mum? And if so, how?

"I thought my mum was dead."

The baton against Dawson's chest didn't waver. "If not her, then who supplied Sybil with the holy water?"

More dumping behind Dawson was followed by the tossing of the drawer. "What do you know about my mum? Is she still alive?"

Baton Man pulled back. Before Dawson could protect himself, the metal bar whacked his chest again, cracking another rib.

He couldn't hold back a cry of pain. "I don't know anything! I swear it!" The holy water was more important than he'd realized—enough that these intruders wouldn't hesitate to kill him over it. And strangely, somehow, both Sybil and his mum had gotten involved in the holy water dealings.

"Did Sybil go back into the past too?"

"I don't know what you're going on about."

"Is she supplying you now?"

"Sybil's dead, you moron! I just got home from her funeral."

The baton slammed into Dawson again. Before he could protect himself, the man brought the bar down repeatedly until Dawson found himself on the floor, gasping for breath, blood pooling in his mouth, agony radiating throughout his body.

The other intruder was still on a rampage in his room, and Baton Man joined him—slashing pillows, flipping over his mattress, tearing apart his closet, and searching through every item—except the rubbish.

One of them sliced open the top of the bag and poked around, but a moment later backed away and left it undisturbed. No doubt the odor had repelled him.

Dawson hadn't moved, not even to release a breath of relief, not until they'd exited and started ransacking the rest of the flat. From the sounds of crashing, he could tell that one was in the kitchen and the other was in Acey's room. No doubt they were seeking holy water, believed he had a stash of it someplace in the flat, a stash they assumed his mum and now Sybil were delivering to him from the past.

The very idea was as crazy as Lord Burlington's time-traveling declaration earlier ... except this time, Dawson couldn't make himself scoff, not even a little. The fact that these two thugs talked as though time crossing was real made the possibility much more valid than when Lord Burlington had brought it up.

His mum had always been silent about her job in the country's counterterrorism agency. She'd had an office in the London headquarters. But shortly after Dad had abandoned them, her work had brought them to Canterbury.

After Dawson's deployment to Afghanistan, Mum had taken an assignment in Norfolk and bought a town house in Fakenham. Sybil had stayed in Kent for police training. Once he'd been discharged from the military hospital and transported to the UK, he'd learned that Mum had returned to Canterbury to be close to him and help him through his recovery and rehab.

He was ashamed to admit that he'd been too self-absorbed to pay much attention to the changes in her work, had never thought to ask more.

Clearly he should have.

A text dinged on Dawson's mobile, the sound coming from several feet away. Not surprisingly, his mobile had ended up on the floor with everything else. He stretched out his arm but then gasped as agony shot through him. How many of his ribs were broken?

Drawing in a breath and steeling himself, he activated the device with his voice and a command: "Text Acey. H E L P."

A moment later, footsteps veered toward the bedroom. His intruders had heard him. In the next instant, a boot planted into the middle of his back against a painful scar. "We'll be watching you. And if you get holy water, there is no way you can hide it from us."

Before he could respond, the baton bashed against his head, and all went black.

~ 3 ~

"I'M FINE," DAWSON GROUSED as Acey held on to his arm and led him into the flat.

After a week in the hospital, Dawson was feeling a hundred times better than the day of Sybil's funeral when he'd been assaulted. He'd suffered a concussion, six cracked ribs, a bruised spleen, and so many bruises across his back and stomach that Baxter had been afraid of blood clots.

The police had visited with him in an attempt to discover more about his attackers. But, of course, Dawson hadn't been able to give them any information other than vague descriptions. With so little to go on, there was practically no way to investigate the case. At the end of all the questioning, Dawson felt as inadequate and humiliated as always.

"Let's get you to bed," Acey said without releasing his hold on Dawson, his cane tapping a steady rhythm.

The ride home from the hospital had exhausted Dawson, and he wanted nothing more than to stretch out on his own bed in his own room and have blessed quiet.

But first . . . he had to find the bottle of holy water he'd tossed into the rubbish. Thank the hand of God that had allowed him a brief few seconds to stash the bottle before the thugs made it inside.

When Acey had indicated that he wasn't allowed to touch anything until the Canterbury investigative unit went through the flat and gathered any evidence, Dawson still hadn't wanted to take any chances. He'd asked Acey to put the rubbish bag into a safe location where no one would be able to throw it out or tamper with the contents.

Acey's hesitant response had been normal enough. His friend probably assumed the beating had rattled a few things in Dawson's head, that he wasn't fully functioning or rationally thinking. Why else would he request saving a bag of garbage?

Dawson put out a hand and grabbed on to the nearest kitchen chair. "Hold on, Acey."

"What's up?" Acey paused beside him.

Chloe closed the door behind them, bringing with her the scent of chicken chimichanga takeaway from their favorite taco restaurant. As a professor of architectural conservation at the University of Kent, her work hours were flexible, and she'd spent a lot of time at the hospital over the past week with him. Acey taught British history at a local secondary school. He'd just resumed summer term after a short break but still had made a point of coming to the hospital in his every spare moment.

Even this evening, Acey had been the one to help him with signing the discharge papers, wheeling him out to the car, and driving him home. Dawson wouldn't have been able to do it without his friend—or at least do it half as smoothly.

In the past, the lack of independence and the helplessness had embarrassed and frustrated Dawson, making him moody and causing him to lash out at everyone around him—including Acey.

But for a reason Dawson couldn't explain, tonight he was overwhelmed with gratitude rather than the usual irritation. Maybe his loss of Sybil made him realize how much Acey was doing in her absence. Maybe his own brush with death during the attack had made him realize he wasn't ready to let go of life yet.

He'd thought long and hard about it over the past couple of days that he'd lain in the hospital bed, and he'd come to the conclusion it was past time to show Acey his appreciation for all his support. It was past time to set his friend free from having to bear the burden of caring for him. And it was past time to do a better job of learning the life skills he needed to become more independent.

He'd only gone to his vision-impairment support group for a couple of years when Mum was alive, when she'd encouraged—and nagged—him to go. But now he needed to give the group a real try, stop feeling sorry for himself and start living—the way he should have been doing all along.

He pulled out the kitchen chair and lowered himself into it, biting back a groan from pain and weariness.

"You don't want to eat in your bed?" Acey's question rose with disbelief.

Dawson could only see the faint outline of his friend's giantlike frame. He tried to picture Acey's face, the boyish expression behind the curly red beard, but it had been over eight years since he'd seen any faces, including his own. The fact was, Dawson could hardly remember what he looked like anymore either.

With dark-brown hair and lean features, he'd been considered handsome and garnered plenty of attention from women. He'd once even been approached by a modeling agent who told him he had classic lines, perfectly proportioned features, and a sexy, brooding look—whatever all that meant. He'd been quick to reject the agent's interest—maybe too quick, considering that if he'd taken up a career in modeling, he wouldn't have lost his eyesight.

He still attracted women . . . until they learned he was blind, after which came the pity, silence, excuses—it was all too much to bear. And so he usually spurned female attention.

At times, he could admit he was lonely for a woman's companionship. Especially whenever he was around Acey and Chloe and listened to the way they interacted. The two loved each other. Though their lives weren't perfect, they were perfect for each other.

They deserved to be together without him always present.

"I want to eat in here tonight." Dawson motioned to the table. "Sit down and join me."

The cessation of activity told him his request was unexpected. Perhaps he had to amend his ways and stop ordering people around. "Please." He cleared his throat. "I'd appreciate you both joining me."

The pause dragged on for another moment. Their surprise hung in the air every bit as much as the humidity of the wet June evening.

He reached for the dark blur on the table, which he guessed was the takeaway. His fingers connected with the paper bag, and he fumbled to pull out the first carton.

He could feel Chloe reaching out to assist him. After all, he couldn't read the initials on each box that indicated which one had the extra guacamole that Acey always ordered or the chimichanga without cheese for Chloe, who was lactose intolerant.

His muscles began to tighten. Under normal circumstances he would have lashed out, maybe said something cutting or rude, then slunk off to his room to eat alone.

But he wouldn't tonight. Tonight he wanted to choose to handle the situation with gratefulness instead of bitterness. He had to do that now while his resolve remained strong.

Before Chloe could take the container out of his hand, he popped the lid up and then sniffed it. "No cheese, extra rice. This is yours, Chloe." He held it out in her direction.

He popped open the lid on the next box and breathed in the rich aromas again of the grilled chicken, spicy enchilada sauce, and the deep-fried tortilla shell. "Mine."

He skimmed his fingers over the lid of the last carton. "That means this one is yours, Acey." He picked it up and handed it toward the fuzzy, blurred form of Acey, still standing beside the table. Unmoving.

Neither Acey nor Chloe responded to his unusual actions. Instead, he could feel their gazes upon him, likely full of questions.

He extended Acey's box farther. "You planning to stand there all night?"

After a moment more, his friend took the food and slowly lowered himself into a chair. Chloe did the same. As they unwrapped their plastic forks, he took a deep breath and pushed forward with what was long overdue. "You're both better friends than I deserve. By quite a lot, I'd say."

Acey's crinkling fork wrapper grew silent. "Don't say that—"

"It's true. I've been dreadful to live with, and you've been a saint to put up with me."

"That's what friends do."

"Don't let me off the hook. You should have chucked me out long ago."

Chloe sniffled. Was she starting to cry?

Dawson hurried. "I've decided it's time for me to move out and learn to be on my own."

"No, man. Chloe and me, we talked this week, and we're planning to look for a bigger place where we can live after we get married, but we want it to have room for you."

Emotion crowded into Dawson's throat. Words wouldn't be able to express his appreciation. He wished, instead, he could look Acey in the eyes and let him see his gratitude for all he'd done. He missed sharing meaningful looks—there was so much a person could see and learn through eye contact. He hadn't realized it until he could no longer experience it.

"I've made up my mind." Dawson slipped out his fork and plunged it into his chimichanga. "And I've decided to move to Fakenham and live in my mum's town house."

After Mum's disappearance, he and Sybil had clung to the hope that she'd show up and need it again. But as the years had passed without any word from her, they'd forgotten about the place—or at least he had. Only a month or so ago, Sybil had mentioned she was thinking about putting it on the market.

Two days ago in the hospital, he'd phoned the caretaker of the complex and learned Sybil hadn't gotten around to listing it. He'd let the fellow know he intended to come and stay there for a while.

He hadn't yet met with the family lawyer to transfer ownership of everything he and Sybil had jointly shared, including the savings Mum had left for them. It wasn't a lot, but along with his war disablement pension, it would be enough to get by.

"You know you don't have to move out." Acey still hadn't touched his food, which told Dawson more than anything how much he was rattling his friend.

Dawson swallowed his first mouthful. "That's just it. I have to do this. For me." He should have done it long ago. But he supposed it had taken the stripping away of everything else in his life for him to see how pathetic he truly was.

"I respect that." Acey's voice dropped a notch. "But someone clearly has it out for you."

They hadn't talked much about the attack. Whenever Acey had started to question him at the hospital, Dawson insisted they wait to discuss everything in private. After the thugs' final warning that they would be watching him, Dawson hadn't wanted to take any chances. The investigative unit had located and removed several spy bugs from their flat. But that feeling of being watched was back now all the time.

Acey paused as though he sensed that feeling too. "Maybe you oughta wait until the police catch your attackers—"

"You and I both know that won't happen, not when I can't give them more details."

"At least here, you won't be alone."

"If I stay, there's a risk I'll be putting you and Chloe in danger."

At the beat of silence, Dawson guessed the couple was exchanging silent communication, reassuring each other that they were willing to face danger for him.

Before Acey could protest any further, Dawson flipped on a playlist and turned up the volume. If the investigators had missed any bugs, he didn't want anyone hearing the upcoming conversation.

"Can you bring me that rubbish bag you set aside?" Now that he'd informed his friends of his plans, he also had to let them know about the holy water and the real reason he'd been targeted.

Acey pushed up, disappeared outside, then returned a minute later and set the bag down beside Dawson's chair. The foul odor was all the evidence Dawson needed to determine that this was indeed the same rubbish he'd collected the day of the attack.

"Hid it in the shed behind some gardening tools." The shed—likely once an old privy—now served as a storage unit for the building's few occupants.

"I appreciate it." Dawson half wanted to wait to dig around in the trash until after he'd eaten, but he'd already put Acey off long enough and suspected his friend wouldn't rest until he had a sense of what was going on.

He slipped his hand through the slash the thugs had made. The stench rose powerfully, forcing him to breathe through his mouth instead of his nose. He dug through refuse, his fingers providing the sight he needed as usual. He bypassed old takeaway containers, pill bottles, vape pens, pizza crusts, and sticky cans.

After one pass through and no sign of the small bottle, his pulse accelerated. Had one of the thugs searched through the rubbish? Maybe after they'd knocked him out?

He shifted in his chair, bending and digging deeper. This time as his fingers touched the bottom of the bag, he connected with the smooth, rounded middle of the bottle and released a short huff of relief.

As he pulled the bottle out, he concealed it in the pocket of his hoodie. "Is everything closed up? Windows? Curtains?"

Chloe and Acey stood and began moving from room to room, making sure they were alone. Dawson tied up the rubbish bag tightly to diminish the stench, and then he washed his hands before he returned to the table. As he sat, so did Chloe and Acey.

"So?" Acey said.

"So, what I'm about to tell you will make me sound completely mad . . ."

"Go on, then."

Dawson pulled the bottle out and placed it on the table. He waited for a reaction from his friends, but they responded with only silence.

"And . . .?" Acey finally asked, as if he was expecting more than an ancient-looking bottle.

"I think this is what my attackers were after."

"It doesn't appear to be of any particular value." With Chloe's background in history and architectural conservation, she was more knowledgeable of historical artifacts than the average person.

"It's not the bottle itself." Dawson lowered his voice to a whisper. "It's what's inside."

Acey's blurry outline leaned in. "It seems empty."

"If you shake it, you'll be able to tell there's a tiny amount of liquid in it."

Chloe picked up the bottle first and shook it. Then Acey. When the bottle was back at the center of the table, Dawson took another bite of his now-lukewarm chimichanga.

"Well?" Acey asked.

"It's possible this bottle contains ancient holy water."

Acey released a snort of disbelief, but Chloe seemed to be nodding.

"Everything I'm about to tell you . . . well, it needs to stay confidential."

"Right," Acey said.

"Of course," Chloe added.

While they ate, Dawson shared the details of all that had happened, starting with Sybil showing up a few days before her coma and insisting that he drink the holy water so it would cure him, to the bottle found beside her at Reider Castle. He relayed everything Lord Burlington had explained to him at the graveside along with what he'd learned from his attackers.

"I'm flabbergasted." Dawson pushed away the last few bites of his meal. "I don't know what to think."

"The ancient history books"—Chloe spoke with an undercurrent of excitement—"and even the windows of Canterbury Cathedral attest to miracles associated with holy water."

"Yes," Acey interjected, "but don't most people believe the miracles were invented in order to draw more pilgrims to the shrines? After all, the more pilgrims, the more income the Church generated."

"That is one theory, yes," Chloe answered. "But there are too many recorded healings for all of them to have been fabricated. Besides, the Church didn't need to make up stories about healings to draw people. The relics of the saints brought swarms of pilgrims regardless of the promise of miracles."

Dawson's blood thrummed faster. "So you believe holy water could heal diseases?"

"I have no reason to doubt the historical accounts of miracles any more than I have a reason to question other recorded history." Chloe spoke as confidently as she always did whenever she talked about history and old architecture.

Dawson could admit he'd contemplated what it would be like to drink the holy water from the bottle on the table. Sybil had given it to him to help revive his eyesight. It was his. Wasn't it?

But the question that had nagged him over the past days and hadn't gone away, the same question his attackers had asked—where had Sybil gotten the bottles of holy water? The one she'd delivered to him as well as the one she'd had under the stairs. The ramblings about time crossing from both Lord Burlington and his attackers didn't have merit, did they? There had to be a more plausible explanation for where the holy water had come from.

His fingers made contact with the small bottle, and he drew it closer. "Does anyone know where the source of the holy water is located?" Maybe a secret well existed someplace that contained the special water.

And for that matter, what made the holy water different from any other water?

"I suppose one way to narrow down potential sources is to review the records of miracles." Chloe seemed to have her head bent over her mobile. Was she already researching?

"What are you going to do, man?" Acey asked. "You planning to drink this water and see what happens?"

"It killed Sybil."

"Unless Lord Burlington is right, and it made her travel to the past." Acey's tone held a hint of humor. Clearly he didn't believe in traveling through time any more than Dawson did.

If the concept was so ludicrous, why had the thugs brought it up? Why had they insinuated that his mum was in the past? Almost as if they'd sent her there on a mission. Almost as if they'd received holy water from her. Almost as if they now believed Sybil intended to do the same thing for him.

His attackers hadn't found any humor in the matter. They'd been deadly serious. They'd almost destroyed the flat in their attempt to find the holy water that supposedly Sybil, or his mum, was delivering to him—from the past.

They could have killed him, but they'd probably allowed him to live because they still had use of him. And now they were watching him closely. Why would anyone go to such great lengths if the holy water was a farce?

"For now, until we understand more, it's best if I keep the bottle hidden." Dawson stuffed the container back into his sweatshirt pocket. "The less anyone else knows about it, the safer we'll all be."

Amidst the uncertainty, one thing was clear... he intended to keep investigating what had happened to his mum and Sybil. But the last thing he wanted to do was cause more problems for Acey and Chloe. All the more reason to move away from them. As soon as possible.

~ 4 ~

DAWSON BREATHED IN THE MUSTINESS of Reider Castle. From the moment he'd stepped through the front door, chills had raised his flesh and hairs. Something about the castle was different, eerie.

He wasn't a believer in ghosts or spirits or haunted houses. But . . .

With a shiver, he shuffled along the underground passageway, away from the medical lab that Sybil had raided when she'd brought an end to the kidnapping of the woman who had become Lord Burlington's wife.

Since then, the Kent Police—and apparently Sybil—had been working at the site of the crime to track the criminals involved in the kidnapping. But no one had made any headway on the case, and after Sybil's body had been discovered, the investigation had been suspended.

Dawson wished to have his keen eyesight back so he could solve for himself the mystery surrounding Sybil's death. The keen eyesight that had earned him his expert position in the military intelligence unit of the army. The keen eyesight that had elevated him to the position of lance corporal of his section. The keen eyesight that had helped him in countless missions and had saved countless lives during his time serving in Afghanistan.

The keen eyesight that had been ripped from him when he'd failed to pay attention and had gotten distracted for mere seconds by women passing by, smiling and waving at them. That was all the time it had taken for him to miss seeing the partially detonated explosive among the munitions they were disposing of.

He pressed a hand against his shirt and felt the outline of the dog tags he still wore underneath. Losing his vision had been fair payment for letting his gaze wander where it shouldn't have. He'd always struggled with the temptation of admiring beautiful women. It had been one of his weaknesses. And it had turned out to be a deadly one. In addition to his injuries, Acey had lost his leg from the knee down and three privates had died from their wounds.

Yes, as difficult as his blindness was, he'd deserved the punishment for his mistake. Even so, this visit to Reider Castle would have been easier if he'd been able to assess the lab and the closet under the stairway for himself, instead of relying upon Chloe, who'd graciously given up her afternoon to accompany him.

"Ready to head back up?" she asked as they stopped in the small room at the base of the stairway.

He held the bottle that had been found with Sybil. Isaac—Sybil's ex-boyfriend and the investigator who'd let them into the castle—had given it to him. The fellow hadn't needed much persuading to hand it over since it wasn't important to the investigation anymore and wasn't of much value even as an antique.

"Don't let me rush you." Isaac paused at the bottom step. "You can take all the time you need. I'll just head up and wait outside."

Dawson nodded his thanks. Isaac hadn't been the right man for Sybil—Dawson hadn't needed eyesight to see that. But the guy was still a nice bloke.

As soon as Isaac's footsteps reached the top and faded away, Chloe touched the bottle in his hands. "It's nearly identical to the one you already have."

Dawson's fingers had already told him that much. "If it contained holy water, then the question is, where did she get two bottles?"

"The original holy water was sold in containers called ampullae, each having only about a tablespoon of the water." Chloe had become a walking encyclopedia over the past week since the night he'd come home from the hospital and shown his friends the bottle. "But clearly someone stored this holy water differently, although yours appears to still just have a tablespoon amount."

"You're certain the bottle was made in the 1300s?"

"My friend was just going off the pictures I gave him of your bottle. I can't be certain unless I can have it examined."

"No."

She sighed.

He wasn't giving his bottle to anyone else. It was like a partially detonated explosive, ready to discharge at any time. He'd had the sensation several times over the past week that he was being watched, and he guessed it was only a matter of time before he got another visit from the same thugs. During the next altercation, he might not escape alive. And if the thugs got wind that Chloe was testing a bottle, then they'd focus on her.

As it was, he'd hesitated to bring her along today to Reider Castle. He could have come alone with Isaac. But she'd insisted on accompanying him, hadn't taken no for an answer. Dawson had only given in because he was moving tomorrow. His boxes and bags were packed, and he'd soon be far away where he wouldn't be able to endanger Acey or her.

In spite of his hesitations in associating with her, he could admit he was relieved she was there and was able to add her knowledge to the situation.

He rubbed his thumb across the bottle. "You really think it's possible the holy water came from the 1300s?"

"From everything I found about the miraculous cures attributed to the holy water, they seemed to happen earlier, in the 1100s. Historical records indicate that monks of Christ Church collected blood from Saint Thomas Becket and mixed it with water drawn from a nearby wellspring. Shortly after that, they began to record accounts of numerous healings. Interestingly, I was able to trace another slew of healings to the latter part of the 1300s, most of them in and around Canterbury."

"Lord Burlington mentioned the year 1382. Maybe that's when the holy water made a comeback."

"It's very possible."

Miraculous cures. Were the tales a bunch of nonsense as he'd always believed? Or was there a hint of truth to them?

"The twin wells in Walsingham were also believed to cause miracles. So my guess is that the water in both places was somehow special, although I haven't worked out how."

Another strange sensation seemed to swirl in the damp air of the dark room. Though they both had the torches on their mobiles lit, only a faint glow touched the outer circle of his vision. The rest was dark and indistinguishable.

Regardless, he had the distinct feeling they weren't alone. "Maybe we should head up."

"Before we do, I want to take another peek at the nook in the closet under the stairs." Chloe moved away from him, and a moment later the closet door squeaked open. "Sometimes architects had the nooks made in order to hide jewels and money they pilfered during the building stages." Her voice grew muffled as she crawled back into the closet where Sybil's body had been discovered.

He'd already gone in, and once was enough for him. The tight quarters had only caused his body to react to the shrapnel and brought spasms of pain. Besides, the place was creepy. He couldn't understand why Sybil had chosen that spot to die. He still hadn't ruled out the possibility that someone had harmed her, then hidden her body there. He had no proof, and none of the clues pointed to foul play, but now, after his own attack, he wouldn't discount the possibility that the thugs who'd assaulted him had been involved in her death somehow.

"Yes," came Chloe's voice. "This nook was likely an original aspect of the castle."

Dawson held up Sybil's bottle and sniffed at the rim. Without sight, he'd honed his other senses and could often detect even the slightest of scents. But there wasn't a trace of anything. He tipped it over, but nothing came out. He stuck his pinky into the mouth and wiggled it around. The interior was mostly dry now. Even so, he lifted his finger to his tongue. His sense of taste was extra strong now too. If there was something in the bottle, he'd be able to tell.

As he licked at his finger, a strange rushing swirled around him. The blurriness that filled his vision lifted away like a rising mist, and he found himself staring at two women in an underground cavern. Both were wearing long medieval gowns, like the kind he'd seen at jousting reenactments when he'd been a kid. Both had dark hair. One had her hair wound into an elaborate coil and covered with a sheer veil. The other wore her hair loosely.

Was he having a hallucination?

Not only could he see them, he also had no trouble hearing their conversation. "Hamin Sahaba have discovered several places for the transport of the holy water in Walsingham, and I have had access to those hiding places, especially now as Lady Wilkin." The voice of the woman wearing the veil sounded like his mum. "None quite so hidden as this spot."

"Yes, it's safe," the other woman said, and as she did so, Dawson froze. It was Sybil. Her voice was clipped, distinct, and as no-nonsense as always.

What was happening? How was he seeing her? How was he seeing anything?

He waited for the world to turn black and fuzzy again, but everything remained visible—the damp walls, the mildew along the edges, what appeared to be bloodstains on the floor, a torch in a sconce, a set of old-fashioned keys hanging next to an arched door.

The women faced away from him as they bent and peered into the closet under the stairs. Even so, he hungrily took in the sight of Sybil's brown hair, her slender frame, the strength in her bearing.

"Nicholas didn't even know about it until recently," she said.

"You cannot use this place again. Not unless you know Dawson will check it."

He startled at the sound of his name falling from the other woman's lips. Who was she? As she shifted, he caught sight of her profile, and this time he couldn't keep from sucking in a sharp breath.

"Mum?" The word escaped before he could hold it in.

Both women swiveled.

Dawson's gaze fixed first upon the weapon in Sybil's hand—a dagger like none he'd ever seen. Then his sights lifted to reveal Sybil's beautiful face, the delicate lines of her features, thinly arched brows above green eyes, lips open in a surprised *o*.

This was crazy. Was he having some sort of vision?

Everything assaulted his senses at once: the earthiness of the cavern, the chill in the air, the flickering shadows moving too precisely to be anything but real.

In the next instant he took in his mum. After all the years of not being able to see her, he still recognized her even though her face had aged. It contained lines in her forehead and crow's feet that hadn't been there before he'd left for the war. Her hair had lighter silver threads woven in with the dark brown. But overall, she was still as pretty as always.

"Dawson?" Sybil spoke tentatively, as if she wasn't sure

what kind of reception she'd receive from him. He didn't blame her after their horrible last parting, and he took full blame for it. "Can you see me?"

Speechless, he could only nod.

"Then you drank the holy water and were cured?"

Was he seeing ghosts, or were they real? He opened his mouth and tried to force words out, but in the next instant someone else was ducking out of the closet, someone slightly heavier with medium-length blond hair, wearing capris and a loose, flowery shirt.

"Chloe?"

Since Acey had met her after returning from Afghanistan, Dawson hadn't ever seen her. He'd only been able to speculate certain aspects based upon his other senses. Now as she straightened, he got a clear view of a broad, sturdy face and brown eyes.

Could his mum and Sybil see Chloe the same way they could see him? He glanced to where they'd been standing a moment ago, but they were gone. Completely.

Frantically he searched the shadows for them, but everything began to turn blurry.

"Dawson? Something up?"

As Chloe's voice registered in his mind, the light faded, as if smoke had blown in and clouded his ability to see anything.

He blinked, trying unsuccessfully to clear the blurriness. He rubbed at his eyes, praying desperately that when he took his hands away, his vision would be clear. But as he attempted to peer at the spot where he'd seen his mum and Sybil, the smoke remained.

It wasn't quite as thick, was it? And what was that? Was the darkness gone from his right eye?

He closed his left lid and braced a hand over it. As he peered out his right eye, a strange tremor of awe coursed through him. Chloe's outline was distinguishable across the room. It was hazy, certainly not clear. But he could see something where there had previously been nothing.

How had this happened?

His fingers tightened around the empty bottle he still held. Had his taste of the residue brought about a slight amount of healing? He dropped his other hand to the inner pocket of his jacket where he'd stored the bottle Sybil had given him. If a miniscule amount could start to work changes and heal him, what would happen if he drank the full tablespoon?

An overwhelming need rose within him. He'd gotten a glimpse at all that he was missing by not having his sight. He'd had thirty seconds, maybe a little longer, to view the people and world around him. And it wasn't enough. He wanted more.

He dug his hand into the pocket and clasped the bottle.

"What happened, Dawson?" Chloe approached, and when she stood in front of him, she was more than just a dark blob. She was like an answer that had been smudged on a piece of paper. He couldn't see her features or even the color of her hair, but he could see more of her than he ever had before.

He swayed, a wave of exhaustion hitting him.

She grabbed his arm.

He had an overwhelming need to lie down on the floor and fall asleep. But he fought against the urge. He had to stay awake and find out what had just happened. And try to see Sybil and Mum again.

His knees wobbled, and he leaned into Chloe.

"Let's get you home, champ." She tugged him toward the stairs. "This trip was too much too soon for you. And it's proof you're not ready to leave tomorrow either."

He let her lead him to the stairwell. Once at the bottom, he started to lower himself, not wanting to leave. "Give me a minute more, Chloe. If I rest for a spell, maybe I'll catch a second wind."

She didn't protest as he sat on the second-to-last stair. He'd figured she wouldn't. Unlike Acey, Chloe almost always went along with his plans. In fact, she settled on the step below him as if she, too, wasn't ready to leave the haunted hallways of Reider Castle.

He strained to see around the small room, hoping for another sighting of Sybil and his mum. But there was nothing. And no one.

Had he really seen them? Or had his mind merely played tricks on him?

"You saw something, didn't you?" Chloe finally said quietly.

"I think so."

"Did you try a little bit of the holy water?"

"Barely any. But the miniscule amount must have been enough."

"From all the stories I researched this past week, I've concluded it's very powerful."

"Does it cause hallucinations?"

"Maybe. People in the Middle Ages wouldn't have called them that. They would have referenced having visions."

"Visions?"

"There is one well-known vision that happened in Walsingham during the eleventh century. A woman named Lady Richeldis was supposedly taken back to Nazareth and beheld the original house where Mary, the Holy Mother, received her news from the archangel Gabriel that she would conceive Christ."

"I've heard a little of the history." He'd always considered the stories of visions—like the healing miracles—to be exaggerated accounts.

"What if it wasn't a vision?" Chloe's voice again took on an excited edge. In spite of the inherent danger, she was clearly enjoying exploring all the historical elements, was actually quite the expert at all of this. "What if this talk of the time travel Lord Burlington and the attackers mentioned is real? What if Lady Richeldis didn't just have a vision? What if she actually traveled back in time?"

He hadn't wanted to believe it was possible. But after what he'd just seen, how could he scoff any longer? What if he'd traveled to the Middle Ages for a brief visit?

If it had been just a vision—hallucination—then why had he seen Chloe so clearly when he'd returned to the present time? He wouldn't have hallucinated seeing her.

And if it had been just a vision, his mum and Sybil wouldn't have been able to see him, would they? Which they had. Sybil had spoken to him, said his name, asked him if he'd drunk the holy water.

"This blows my mind, Chloe." He pressed his hands to his temples, that same strange tiredness seeping through every muscle and limb in his body. Was the tiredness a side effect of the time traveling?

"It blows my mind too." She cast a glance up the stairs as though to make sure they were alone.

He was still holding the ancient bottle in his palm. "Should I try it again? See if I can talk to them and find out more information?" The truth was, the need to see them again welled up so strongly that he didn't wait for Chloe's response. Instead, he dipped his pinky into the bottle, rubbed it around as far as he could reach, then stuck his finger into his mouth.

He searched for the sensations he'd experienced last time. But he felt nothing . . . except the overwhelming need to sleep.

"Anything?" Chloe whispered after a moment, realizing he'd tried to cross time again.

He shook his head. "Maybe it only works once."

"There could be any number of factors at play—"

"What if you try it?" He held the bottle out to her.

She pushed it back at him. "I can't."

"We need to learn more about this. If you connect with them, you can ask questions." He offered the bottle to her again.

This time she tentatively took it. "Like what?"

"Like how does the time traveling work? How much holy water does a person need to drink? How long do they stay in the past? Can they return to the present?"

Chloe was silent for a long moment. "Alright. I'll give it a go."

"Good, then."

He could hear her fidget around with the bottle. Then she tensed and grew silent.

He wished he could watch her, see her expression and reactions. But he didn't want to say anything or even move just in case it interfered with her time-crossing experience.

"It's not working for me, Dawson," she whispered after long seconds.

"You're sure?"

"Quite positive."

"Maybe you didn't get enough of the holy water."

"I made certain I did."

His mind whirred, trying to grasp everything. But the haze of exhaustion clouded his thoughts so he couldn't think anymore. "Alright." He pushed himself up but then swayed.

She stood, grabbed his arm, and steadied him. "You need to rest. We can sort this all out later."

He was too tired to argue and allowed her to lead him up the stairs. But with each step he took away from the underground area, the feeling that he was leaving a piece of himself behind increased.

~ 5 ~

HIS MUM'S FAKENHAM TOWN HOUSE was bugged—probably from when she'd lived there. And maybe it even had secret cameras positioned in different rooms.

Dawson couldn't see the bugs or cameras, but he had the sensation that his every move, every sound, every emotion was being carefully monitored. So he reclined on the sofa, trying to appear as he always had in the past—uncaring and depressed.

After a week in his new place, he'd done a sufficient job of making it messy. The curtains were drawn, the TV blared, dirty clothes were strewn across the floor, and half-eaten cartons of takeaway sat on the coffee table.

Causing chaos wasn't hard to do. What was hard—excruciatingly so—was waiting for Acey and Chloe's visit and the information they'd hopefully been able to collect.

As much as he'd wanted to phone them up or even text, he managed to refrain—for their safety more than his. He couldn't risk bringing attention their way, at least not any more than he already had by their association with him.

He didn't think Chloe had suffered as a result of going to Reider Castle. Regardless, he hadn't communicated with her since she'd dropped him off at his Canterbury flat that day, had known she'd be safest if he didn't reach out to her in case she was bugged too.

The only thing he'd done was whisper a request to her as she'd helped him into the flat—a request to secretly arrange and secretly meet with Lord Burlington and try to get more information.

The next morning, he'd left with Acey for Fakenham, and they'd refrained from saying anything related to the holy water. Acey had likely suspected—as Dawson had—that the car might be bugged. And his friend had probably also decided the more normal they acted, the safer they'd all be.

After Acey had helped him settle in and returned to Canterbury, Dawson had kept his texts to his friend to a minimum, and Acey had been brief too, letting him know he and Chloe would visit on the weekend to check how he was doing.

Now, as Dawson waited for their arrival, he was going mad with the need to get up and pace. The truth was, he couldn't go on like this much longer. All week, he'd replayed what had happened to him in Reider Castle, the short span he'd been with Mum and Sybil. He'd dissected each word they'd spoken and attempted to piece them back together in a way that made sense.

His mum had called herself Lady Wilkin. That had been strange. But the more he'd thought about it, the more he guessed that if she really was alive in the past, she'd probably taken an alias, some cover in order to survive.

Another line his mum had spoken had played through his head more than the others: "*Hamin Sahaba have discovered several places for the transport of the holy water in Walsingham.."*

From his time working in military intelligence, he was well aware who the Hamin Sahaba were—an elite terrorist group with ties to some of the wealthiest Arabians living in Qatar. Extremely dangerous, even lethal, willing to do anything for their billionaire patrons.

Dawson guessed his mum had been tracking the Hamin Sahaba and their threats within the UK. She must have gotten caught by them, and they'd done something to her. Did it all have to do with the holy water? Maybe that's why the group was in the UK to begin with, because they knew about the historical presence of the holy water in Canterbury and Walsingham and were attempting to get their hands upon any remnants.

From what his mum had said about "the transport of the holy water," Dawson guessed that the holy water was no longer readily available in the present, that the original sources had dried up long ago. Was it possible someone in the past was able to stow the water in places that had survived through the ages so that people in the present could find it? Was that what his mum and Sybil had been discussing?

Sybil had mentioned a Nicholas and that he'd put two bottles into the spot under the stairs at Reider Castle. Perhaps that was how she'd come across the glass containers—the one that had been found by her side in the closet under the steps and the one she'd given him.

Dawson was tempted to reach to his waist and touch the bottle he kept in the leather pouch under his shirt. He'd decided the safest place for it was at his side at all times. He didn't trust anyone or anyplace else with the holy water. Of course, if the thugs decided to attack him again, they might discover it. Or break it—if they gave him another beating.

He winced. Even though he was mostly recovered from the assault from two weeks ago, he still had faint bruises that reminded him of the pain and trauma. He didn't relish getting caught and battered again. More than that, he didn't want to fall prey to the thugs because he wanted to uncover what had happened to his mum.

With every passing day, the pressure was growing to do something to solve the mysteries around her disappearance. And with every passing day, the pressure was growing to drink the holy water and be cured of his blindness.

That brief glimpse of life after so many years of seeing nothing hadn't been enough. It was as if the light had been turned on for a few seconds, long enough to remind him of all he was missing.

Sybil had given him the bottle. *Him.* So that he could see again. And to heal him from his war wounds. Although, since tasting the holy water, the sharp slivers of shrapnel hadn't bothered him to the same intensity as previously. Had the holy water worked on providing some relief?

So why was he having such a difficult time giving himself permission to drink it? Was it because he was worried it would put him into a coma and possibly kill him? Did he fear it might heal his bruises and broken ribs instead of his blindness? Or was he concerned the terrorists would see that he was healed and come after him?

Maybe he wanted to prove to himself that he could learn to

accept his blindness and make the best of his limitations. He was finally beginning to make peace with his condition. He was finally ready to accept himself. And he was finally attempting to be strong and independent.

It was also possible he wasn't yet ready to forgive himself for his mistakes that fateful day of his accident in Afghanistan. Maybe he never would be able to forgive himself. Maybe he deserved to be punished and to live his life in darkness for failing to protect those who'd been in his section and under his command, including Acey.

Besides, if he saved the holy water, he could give it to someone who needed it more than he did. If something ever happened to Acey or Baxter or even Chloe . . . he'd have a way to help them.

With a sigh, Dawson felt around on the sofa for the remote. As he connected with the device and turned down the volume, his thoughts flew back to the day Sybil had come to his flat with the bottle—how she'd thrown his TV remote out of his bedroom and into the kitchen and told him to get up and go find it.

He'd been so angry with her, but she'd been right to urge him to get up and start living. "I miss you, Sybs."

He pushed himself up from the sofa and shuffled the twelve steps it took to reach the kitchenette. He bumped against the corner of a cabinet and winced. Even though he was learning to get around better, it still wasn't easy. Of course, the slight improvement in his vision helped some. Maybe eventually he'd feel comfortable enough to phone for a ride and do his own shopping instead of relying on delivery services.

He reached for his coffee maker and the box of K-Cups beside it. As he fit one in, a knock resounded on the door—the friendly thumping that belonged to Acey.

"Finally." His heart gave an extra beat as he abandoned his efforts to make another cup of coffee and started toward the door.

Eagerly, he welcomed Chloe and Acey in, and for a short while, they chatted about ordinary things as if they were ordinary people having an ordinary day. When Dawson felt as though he would snap in half with the tension of all his questions, Acey casually made the suggestion that they ride up to Walsingham and have lunch at one of the quaint pubs while also giving Chloe an opportunity to visit a couple of the old buildings there and get snaps of unique architecture for her classes.

Once away from the town house, Acey and Chloe told him they'd rented a car specifically so they wouldn't have to worry about any bugs being planted inside, allowing them to converse freely during the twenty-minute drive to Walsingham. While it wasn't long enough for Dawson, he tried to digest everything that Chloe and Acey shared. The biggest source of information had been Lord Burlington—Harrison, as he'd asked to be called—during a clandestine meeting in a tunnel under one of Canterbury's many old churches.

While the meeting hadn't lasted long, Chloe had learned that both Harrison and Ellen had experienced trips into the past, as had Ellen's sister, Marian, and her father, Arthur.

The trips were dangerous, since they put a person into a coma for the duration of the time traveling. The only way to return to the present was to awaken the person with two doses of holy water—one dose to *heal* the body from the coma and another to *preserve* the body and keep it alive. Without the two doses, the person would die.

Harrison seemed to think Dawson's sighting of Sybil indicated she'd survived the time crossing and now lived in the past. Such a feat was apparently very tricky and not many could succeed, since when the body died in one era, it would also die in the other. Similar to waking up from a coma, two doses of holy water were required to make a time crossing permanent.

Because Dawson had seen his mum, Harrison speculated that she may have successfully traveled into the past too. But there was a chance her comatose body was being kept alive by the Hamin Sahaba so she could act as a courier for them, delivering holy water from the past to hiding places that still existed in the present.

Harrison believed the Nicholas Sybil had mentioned was the same Nicholas Worth whose family owned Reider Castle. Somehow Sybil had connected with him and had been at Reider Castle while Dawson had his overlap.

Harrison hadn't known anything about a Lady Wilkin. And none of them could safely do a genealogical internet search for her—not without alerting the Hamin, who were likely keeping tight tabs on all their online activities.

"Overlap." Dawson mulled over the word. It certainly described what had happened—as if his timeline had somehow shifted and lined up exactly with the past one. "It's all too coincidental, don't you think?"

Acey was driving and Chloe was beside him in the

passenger seat. From the direction of her voice, Dawson could tell she was half turned, partly facing him.

"I said the same thing to Harrison." She was as thrilled now as she'd been in Reider Castle, as if she'd landed upon the greatest discovery of her life. "But he's analyzed the physics behind time traveling and seems to think that an overlap is easier for those who share some kind of physical or emotional connection. Particles are drawn together more readily—sort of like the poles of two magnets that line up and move toward each other. That's why you could have the overlap with your family, but I couldn't."

"Can the overlaps happen more than once?" He couldn't begin to count the number of times he'd wanted to go back to Reider Castle and try again. But he hadn't been able to figure out an excuse, one that wouldn't put Isaac in danger from Hamin Sahaba—if that was the group who had attacked him.

"According to Harrison, the overlaps are difficult to facilitate since you have to be in the same vicinity and time as the person you're trying to connect with. And they also become more limited as a person's body becomes accustomed to the holy water."

"Then there's no guarantee that I could see Sybil or Mum if I went back to the underground lab?"

"No. They would have to be down there at the exact moment you are."

"But if I can overlap with Mum, I can get information about where the Hamin are holding her."

"That's what Harrison attempted in order to free his wife."

"And did it work?"

Chloe paused. "Both of them almost died."

"Don't think about doing it, man." Acey jumped into the conversation as he slowed the car to a stop. "If you fall into a coma, we don't have the two doses necessary to bring you out."

"I have one."

"Right. And that one is meant to heal you," Chloe insisted. "Harrison has concluded holy water has the capability of vibrating energy particles that are billions of times smaller than nuclei, and that the frequency and wavelength of the vibrations first heal what's broken in the body. Only after that will they rejuvenate a body so fully and completely that the speed of vibrations takes the person into a different realm altogether."

"So because I'm blind, the holy water won't send me to the past?"

"Not if it finds barriers in your system that need rejuvenating first."

"The holy water worked to transport Harrison only after he was healed?"

"Precisely."

"Then how was I able to have an overlap into the past? Wouldn't the residue have worked at healing me first?" Maybe it had. After all, his blindness had experienced a slight improvement, and he hadn't been in as much pain from the shrapnel.

"Harrison said the overlaps are different than the time traveling. The short experience is more like a vision, like the sighting of a ghost, because the body doesn't stay in the era but rather hovers between them."

"Fascinating." Dawson had never believed in ghosts, still

didn't. But if he hadn't known about the holy water before seeing Mum and Sybil, he probably would have suspected he was seeing spirits of some kind.

"Harrison has been studying records of sightings or overlaps," Chloe continued, "and he's concluded that people can have them many different ways."

Acey cut the engine, and silence descended, giving way to the noises outside. Dawson didn't need to see to know they'd arrived in Walsingham. Even though pilgrims no longer flocked to the Norfolk village the way they had in times past, it was still a popular destination for tourists.

People often reenacted the pilgrimage by starting at Slipper Chapel outside of Walsingham, where, historically, pilgrims took off their shoes—or slippers—and walked with bare feet the last mile to the Shrine of Our Lady.

Nothing was left of the original Shrine of Our Lady or the priory other than twin wells and a couple of stone arches. Even though Dawson intended to search both of the sites today, his gut told him that neither of those ruins would be secretive enough for a courier from the past to deliver holy water to the present.

Acey tapped his fingers against the steering wheel. "I don't understand how the holy water can be placed in a spot in the past and just show up in the present in that same place."

Chloe had bent over and seemed to be extricating her camera from its bag. "I didn't have long to confer with Harrison on that particular matter. But he seemed to indicate that the holy water itself has properties that defy time and space."

Out the window, a blur of pedestrians passed by the car, along with the hum of laughter and the chatter of tourists. The busy crowds would make it easy for the Hamin to blend in. "If Mum has been delivering water to the Hamin from Walsingham, then is she gathering it from the two original wells?"

Chloe straightened and pulled the camera strap over her head. "No, Harrison said the twin wells probably contained regular water, but that a third wellspring existed underneath the original priory and was more likely the source of the holy water."

"Would it still be there?" Thank heavens for Harrison and his wealth of information. They wouldn't have known anything if he hadn't been willing to explain all he'd already learned.

"Doubtful." Acey reached for his cane on the backseat floor beside Dawson. "King Henry the Eighth did a thorough task of eradicating every holy site when he went on his rampage of closing monasteries. It would have been filled in."

Dawson tried not to let disappointment settle inside. Of course there was no longer a source of the holy water in the area. If so, the Hamin wouldn't have beat him up looking for bottles that had been transported from the past. "What we need to discover today are any places that existed in the late thirteen hundreds and survived to the present. Those could be the hiding spots that Mum referenced. And if we can track those down, maybe we'll learn more about where they're keeping her."

Acey opened his door a crack. "We'll have to act like all the other tourists so the Hamin don't suspect we're looking for your mum."

"Don't you think they'll know that's why we've come?" Dawson had no doubt the Hamin had followed them to Walsingham. Or maybe someone in the group lived in town or nearby. Whatever the case, the Hamin would suspect they were searching for clues. Perhaps they were hoping Sybil was in the past and would start delivering holy water to him so that they could steal it.

As much as he wanted to forge ahead on his own, this was another time when his helplessness rose to taunt him. He couldn't search by himself . . . unless he drank the holy water and his sight returned.

His hand inadvertently went to the pouch under his garments. Should he just do it? Drink it so he could venture out on his own?

No. He couldn't at this moment. From everything he'd experienced, the holy water depleted a person's energy. After he'd tasted it at Reider Castle, he'd been so tired that he'd gone home and slept for hours. If the little amount could exhaust him, then drinking a whole bottle would put him out even longer.

For now, he was stuck relying on his friends and praying that he wasn't putting them all into the worst danger yet.

~ 6 ~

A CHILL CREPT UP DAWSON'S SPINE as he shuffled into St. Peter's Church in Great Walsingham. It was the same chill he'd felt before having the overlap with his mum and Sybil at Reider Castle.

That had to mean something.

"She's here," he whispered to Acey and Chloe, who'd stepped into the chapel next to him.

"Who?" Chloe whispered back, her breath hinting at the spiced ale they'd sipped during their lunch at one of the inns.

"Mum."

"Can you see her?"

"No, but I feel her presence."

"She's here right now?"

"I think so." He paused and concentrated, as if that could somehow make her materialize. Perhaps the holy water—or even God Himself—was somehow drawing him inexplicably together with his mum.

Other tourists mingled about the premises, and he couldn't risk saying more for fear of someone overhearing.

The interior of the stone building was cool but held a mustiness that all old buildings contained. Through his blurred vision, the nave stretched out ahead along with the shapes of the high arched ceiling supported by large pillars. Dark pews lined the chancel and contrasted with the whitewashed walls and large arched windows that were especially bright.

Over lunch, Chloe had advised Acey and Dawson on the most pertinent facts about the church—as well as useless details, like the fact that the pews were called "poppy head pews" because of their depiction of flowers, animals, saints, and other details of Norfolk life.

All he needed to know was that St. Peter's was one of the few remaining structures that had been in existence during the 1300s, retaining most of the original aspects. Chloe was certain it had been built between 1330 and 1340. The tower had been constructed in the 1300s too, and the belfry held the three original bells.

St. Mary's, which they'd visited first, had also been built in the 1300s, but they'd learned much of it had been destroyed by a fire in 1961. That meant most of the current structures wouldn't have existed in 1382.

Was St. Peter's a place his mum had hidden holy water for the Hamin?

Should he use Sybil's empty bottle of holy water—the one Isaac had given to him—and attempt an overlap? Doing so would be the best way to get the additional information he needed from Mum to find out the extent of her dealings with the Hamin. And yet, if the overlaps were difficult to create and wouldn't occur indefinitely, he had to be careful to use such overlaps strategically so his body didn't lose its ability to do them too soon.

Silently, he followed Acey and Chloe down the center aisle, counting on them to spot any niches or out-of-the-way spots. But the longer they surveyed the interior, the more convinced Dawson became that if his mum had used St. Peter's as a place to hide bottles of holy water, she would have done so in a more secretive part of the building. Perhaps in a side room. Or maybe an underground chamber.

"Does St. Peter's have a crypt?" he whispered as he stood beside Chloe near the altar.

"It's not mentioned anywhere in the regular literature. But I found a note in one of my older architecture books, indicating a way to it through the tower."

"Should we pop in and explore?"

Dawson, not giving his friends a chance to object, was already heading down the aisle to the tower. A moment later, he entered through an arched door into the circular interior with Acey and Chloe behind him. They observed the room and bells overhead until a lone older couple stepped outside. Then Acey made quick work of opening the half door in the tower wall.

Chloe crouched and peered inside. "A set of old wooden steps leads about twelve feet underground."

Dawson breathed in the damp air. The chill was back, and not from the coldness that emanated up from the dark passageway. Instead, it came from that feeling of being drawn—just like the magnet Chloe had mentioned earlier. Something, or perhaps even Someone, was leading him toward a new destiny, and he couldn't resist the pull.

"Let's go." He climbed through the door. Then using the

stone wall as a guide, he started down. Acey whispered that he'd stay back and stand watch. But Chloe's firm steps plodded behind Dawson, and he could faintly make out the beam from her torch as she held it up to light the way.

When his feet hit solid ground, he paused, letting his senses help him take stock of his surroundings. From what he could tell, he was in a chamber no bigger than a shed, and the scent of mildew and soil hung heavily in the air.

With Chloe bumping against him, he took a step forward, but he accidentally kicked a metal pail that clattered against a ladder and other tools. He caught a whiff of ammonia, maybe left in the pail?

Perhaps the place was nothing more than a maintenance room.

Chloe squeezed past him, knocking the pail too. The torchlight on her mobile swiveled from one wall to the next before returning to the wall straight ahead.

"There's another door," she whispered. "But there's a lock on it."

Subdued voices came from beyond the door.

Dawson cocked his head toward the sound. "I hear people on the other side."

Chloe held herself motionless as though listening. "I don't hear anything. Do you fancy yourself having an overlap?"

"I'm not sure." He listened for a few seconds longer but couldn't hear or feel anything. Whatever presence had been there was gone. "Let's see if we can get the lock open."

He started forward but tripped over something in his path.

Chloe's hand closed about his arm, steadying him and

keeping him from falling headlong into the door.

A curse pushed up his throat, and he had the urge to toss off her hold. The man he'd been just two weeks ago would have reacted that way. But he wanted to be different now, wanted to learn to accept his limitations without getting angry at himself.

Silently he counted to five, then he took a slower shuffling step forward, hoping Chloe understood that was his way of accepting her help.

Thankfully she didn't say anything. Instead, she acted as though he was the one helping her through the maze of supplies. When they reached the far wall, he fumbled in the blurriness until his fingers connected with the lock. A padlock.

He rattled it. "If you find me a hairpin or a paper clip, I can pick it open."

For several moments, she banged and battered around as she rummaged for something he could use. "A piece of wire fence?"

"Are there shears to cut off a section?"

More banging and battering. "Yes." After a few grunts and a sharp snip, she placed a tough four-centimeter piece of wire into his hand.

It was rusty, but it would work. "I need one more piece."

He bent it and wedged the first wire into the lock, using it as a tension wrench to tighten the core. Once Chloe had a second piece cut, he fidgeted with the end, bending it in a couple of places before inserting it. He jiggled the tip against the pins until one by one they clicked. In less than a minute, he tugged the lock open and removed it from the loop connecting it to the doorframe. Like the door at the top of the stairway, this was also just a half door.

"Good on you." Chloe reached past him and started to tug it open.

A strange chill slipped up his spine, and he shot out a hand and stopped her. In the same instant, he removed his Glock from the holster he had hidden under his shirt. He didn't know what they'd find on the other side, but his gut told him it wouldn't be safe. Part of him feared they'd encounter the Hamin, and he didn't want to be caught unaware. "Let me go first."

Chloe must have heard the steel in his command, because she released the door and backed up.

Using the techniques he'd perfected during the war, he cautiously widened the door and waited several seconds before slipping under. He tensed in expectation of a confrontation. Again he had the sensation that someone was nearby, but even as he stood still and used all his other senses to detect where the threat was coming from, he couldn't pinpoint it.

As he started forward, Chloe followed close on his heels. They appeared to be in a tunnel of some sort, made of stone, cracked and crumbled and aged with time. The ceiling was so low that he couldn't straighten and plodded along hunched over. Chloe's mobile light illuminated the way, but it was fuzzy and shrouded.

He paused after a dozen paces in. "Can you see the end of the passageway?"

"No." She positioned her torch on the dark hole ahead. "It seems to go on endlessly."

"Where does it lead?"

"I'm not sure. Maybe if I looked at a map of the town, I'd be able to locate a couple of places."

Underground tunnels weren't unusual in the UK. Some had survived from as far back as the Roman era. Others had been created during the medieval wars with the French as a means of protection. Pirates had also made use of tunnels when attempting to cart goods in and out of England to avoid paying heavy taxes. More tunnels had been built during the world wars of the twentieth century as well as during the Cold War as protection against an atomic bomb attack.

What had been the purpose of this tunnel? Had it been in use in 1382—the time that Sybil and his mum had probably crossed to?

"Do you see anything unusual?" he asked. "Any places where my mum might be hiding holy water for the Hamin?"

Chloe seemed to be rubbing her hand over the wall. "The architecture of this tunnel is clearly an ogival or pointed arch, tall and thin, which was typical of the Gothic period."

"So it's possible the passageway was built during the Middle Ages?"

"Right. I can also see the beginning of a ribbed vault." She paused. "With four parts instead of six, a standard design that could be more widely applied to columns or slender colonnettes."

"Can you repeat that now in English?"

She laughed lightly. "All I'm saying is that this was once an arched doorway of some kind that led into either another tunnel or an alcove."

He stuffed his Glock back into the holster, then let his fingers glide over the stone wall next to her. The change in texture told him he'd discovered the ancient doorway now filled in with a different stone. He smoothed his hand over the newer stone, searching for anything unusual. The stone was cold and damp and missing mortar in places. He traced the places the mortar had crumbled away, his mind envisioning what his eyes couldn't see. As he completed the path in the shape of an oval, he could almost picture the rock sliding out.

He wiggled it, and it moved. Was it possible he'd found a hiding place?

"Chloe, check this out."

He shifted the stone again. In the next instant, she was helping him remove it.

"How did you find this?" Her voice held a note of excitement.

He didn't want to explain that over the years since losing his eyesight, he'd learned to pay better attention to details that others missed. Instead, he shrugged and focused on getting the stone out.

As soon as it was free, he held the stone while Chloe pressed her face against the hole, her torchlight illuminating whatever was on the other side. "It is an alcove." She spoke almost reverently. "There's an altar."

"It has to be a hiding place for the holy water. Are there any bottles or ampullae?"

"Not that I can see."

"If you put your arm through the hole, can you reach the altar?"

She shifted and grunted. "It's a long stretch, but yes, I'm touching the altar."

Before he could voice his conclusions, the waft of a whisper passed by him along with a rush of damp air that was the same he'd smelled when he'd had his overlap in the dungeon at Reider Castle. And once again, he had the feeling they weren't alone. The energy, like earlier, had a sense of urgency . . . and desperation.

What if he'd been drawn to this place today so he could help his mum? What if he could facilitate an overlap and provide some assistance to her in a moment of dire need?

He dug in his pocket and tugged out Sybil's empty bottle.

"What is it?" Chloe whispered as she pulled her arm from the hole, took the stone from him, and began to wedge it back in place.

"Someone's here and needs help." He wet his pinky, dipped it into the bottle, and rubbed it around. Then, without a moment of hesitation, he stuck his finger into his mouth.

The same sensations he'd experienced the first time he had an overlap pulsed through him—the rush of air and the swirling dizziness, until a moment later his eyesight cleared, and he found himself looking at a woman a dozen paces away. A priest with a gray ring of hair surrounding a bald spot pushed up against her, one of his hands pinning her wrists together, his other forming a vise around her neck.

Dawson only had to glimpse the fear rounding her eyes to recognize she was in trouble.

His mind briefly registered the amazement that his vision was clear again. Then he reacted with an instinct he'd trained for during his years in the army. Stalking forward, he unsheathed the knife at his calf, while at the same time he drew in a fistful of the priest's robe and yanked him away from the woman.

Clearly not expecting Dawson's presence, the priest yelped and flailed his bony arms.

Dawson didn't wait to question him. With a grunt, he tossed the priest across the passageway. The man stumbled backward, hit the wall forcefully, then crumpled to the ground, unconscious.

The thrust hadn't been hard enough to kill, but it would knock him out for several minutes and allow the woman to flee.

He turned to her to find that she'd plastered herself to the wall and was watching him as though he was a ghost who had come out of the wall. He supposed in some ways he was. More likely, she was wondering if he intended to harm her too.

She was attired in a purple gown, one that was old-fashioned and long, similar in style to what Sybil and his mum had been wearing. Her hair, a light brown, fell in a single braid to her waist. Her eyes were a unique shade of blue-gray, one that was strangely alluring.

If he had to guess, he'd say she was in her early twenties. And she was exquisitely beautiful—delicate features, freckles dusting her nose, high cheekbones.

"Are you alright?" He didn't move, afraid she'd run away— or that his overlap would end—and he'd lose the connection with this woman before he could find out more about her.

"Yes." Her tussle—or perhaps now her fear of him—was

causing her to breathe hard so that her chest rose and fell rapidly, accentuating every swell and curve of her womanly form.

Had the priest been trying to take advantage of her? Dawson bit back an angry oath, despising men who used women. "You're safe now."

Her gaze shifted to his knife.

He slipped it back into his boot. "I promise I won't hurt you."

"I am in grave trouble." Her tone was soft-spoken but formal.

"If you tell me what you need, I'll try to help."

"Father James offered to assist me as well, and his intentions were less than honorable."

"I'm not like that." He'd never been the kind of man to force himself onto a woman or into a situation. He'd never needed to.

As if hearing his unspoken words, she examined him more carefully by the light of a nearby oil lamp resting on a ledge jutting from the wall, taking in first his face and then traveling down his T-shirt to his jeans, then his casual boots.

If this overlap was anything like the one he'd had with his mum and Sybil, it would be over before it had a chance to begin. He had to make arrangements to assist this woman while he still could.

But what could a man like him do?

If his mum was anywhere nearby, she'd surely be willing to help this woman. But as he peered beyond her to the long tunnel that led away from St. Peter's to some unknown destination, he drew in a breath of surprise.

The tunnel contained several more alcoves spaced evenly down the passageway. The closest one that he and Chloe had discovered held an altar with a simple wooden cross upon it.

Did the priests or monks use the alcoves as private places to worship or pray?

Farther down, another tunnel seemed to branch off. If the one they were in ran in a north-south direction, then the other intersected east-west. Where did they lead?

"I came to Our Lady, seeking safety and refuge from those who would ill use me." She was still studying him, as if trying to determine if he was friend or foe. "Alas, I fear I shall not find the miracle I beseech, and my stay at the priory will end in betrayal."

Her gaze lifted to his, and she peered deep into his eyes, so deeply he guessed she could see right into his soul to all the wrongs he'd ever done. He'd had a black heart for so many years, how could she see anything but his mistakes?

"I'm no saint, but I swear I won't hurt you." Could he really make that promise? He always seemed to hurt the people he cared about.

Her blue-gray eyes held his gaze a moment longer. She cocked her head, the slight upward tilt of her lips drawing his attention to her mouth. She had a pretty mouth, lips that seemed to be lush and expressive, likely a smile that was kind and beautiful.

"As you can see, I am too trusting." She didn't look again at the priest, but Dawson knew who she was referring to. Instead, she stooped and retrieved from the floor what appeared to be a cloak and a satchel.

Was she trying to escape from the priory? Had she asked the priest to help her through the secret tunnels to freedom? She didn't have far to go.

He glanced over his shoulder to find that the door he'd entered with Chloe was chained and locked. This woman would have no way of freeing herself, unless the priest had the key.

At the whispering of wind behind him, Dawson sensed his overlap was nearing an end, that in an instant he would be swept away and unable to help this woman get the key.

The best thing to do was arrange for another meeting. But how soon before he could attempt another overlap? And what if he couldn't manufacture one the next time he tried?

Maybe he could wait a few hours and try it. But he couldn't come back down in this passageway tonight. Not only would the church be closed for the evening, but if he returned, he would risk garnering too much attention from the Hamin.

No, he had to meet with this woman in a different place.

"The twin wells at the priory." He blurted the first thing that came to mind. "In the woods beyond, meet me there after sunset." Even though admission into the Walsingham Abbey grounds required payment and entrance through specific locations, the sprawling woodland was big enough that Acey and Chloe could surely help him get in without anyone noticing.

The young woman shook her head, her expression turning wary. "I cannot—"

"Do you know Lady Wilkin?" Maybe the connection to his

mum would reassure her of his trustworthiness.

"Lady Wilkin of Barsham. Of course—"

"I'm Dawson, her son . . ."

At a hard grip on his arm, the woman disappeared. For an instant, the walls of the present-day tunnels took shape, clearly enough that he could see the different shade of stone that now blocked the alcoves.

"Dawson, we have to go." The whisper behind him was urgent. Chloe.

The fuzziness settled slowly over his vision just as it had the last time he'd had an overlap, returning him to his life of partial blindness. He blinked rapidly several times, hoping the young woman from the past would take shape again. But his senses registered the changes that told him he was back in the present—the warmer temperature, the slightly lower ceiling, the faint light coming from the open door behind them.

"Hurry," Chloe whispered again, pulling him backward.

"I'm coming." He wasn't ready to go, didn't want to leave the beautiful woman behind. But it was an irrational feeling since she wasn't there anymore.

"Acey said a couple of Arab men just entered the church, and they don't look like tourists."

Dawson swayed against a crashing wave of exhaustion. If his overlap was anything like last time, he would need to sleep for a few hours before being able to function. Even so, if the Hamin were on their trail, he and Chloe needed to return to the tower room before the terrorists caught them snooping underneath in the old tunnels.

He let Chloe drag him along through the door into the

storage room. She stopped to press the padlock back in place before pushing him ahead of her toward the steps. Acey was halfway down and grabbed hold of him. Somehow, between Chloe and Acey, they managed to get him up and out of the tower room.

As they were making their way toward their rental, Acey stiffened but didn't change his limping pace. "They're heading into the tower now."

"They suspect that we're up to something." Chloe's hand trembled against Dawson's arm as she guided him.

A warning at the back of Dawson's mind told him he needed to put a stop to his investigating, that the danger was too real, and that he was bound to bring heartache to Acey and Chloe. But at the thought of his mum and Sybil and now the beautiful woman in the tunnel, he knew he was too far enmeshed in the past to do anything but let the rushing waters of time take him where they would.

~ 7 ~

THE MAN HAD DISAPPEARED before her very eyes. He had to have been an angel. Or maybe a saint.

Philippa Neville rushed the last of the distance through the underground passageway that led to the crypt of the priory. As much as she wanted to search for the visitor who'd called himself Dawson, she had to put as much distance as possible between herself and Father James.

Only seconds after Dawson vanished, Father James had started to stir. Even now, she feared he'd catch up to her and attempt to assault her again.

The attack had been unexpected after how polite and kind he'd been to her over the past few days. When she'd overheard him whispering about the network of tunnels underneath the priory, she hadn't been able to hide her interest, had believed she could trust him to help her locate a way to leave the priory so Uncle Hugo wouldn't be able to find her and insist she return to Thursford with him and marry Lord Godwin Kempe.

How wrong she'd been about Father James.

Why was she always such a poor judge of character? Was it because she tried to see the best in people and overlooked their flaws in the process?

With a shudder, she pulled her cloak tighter. Then she peeked through the half-open door of the crypt. From what she could tell, the underground chamber was as deserted now as it had been when they'd passed through a short while ago.

Deserted . . . save for spirits.

She'd heard that the old tunnels built in ancient times were haunted. But she'd never given such tales much credence. Until now.

Dawson had been so real, so fully present—certainly not the way she'd envisioned an angel or a saint. Providence Himself must have sent him to save her. After all, she'd been praying desperately for help. And he'd appeared when she'd needed him most.

Whoever he was and from whence he'd come, he'd been a blessing. And she would give much thanks to Providence during her prayer time later for the intervention.

She slipped into the long, dark chamber, then closed the door behind her. Was there a way to lock it? She fumbled to find something but came up empty.

With hastened steps, she started past the raised caskets of the saints of old who'd been buried in the crypt. The dampness of the room only added to the chill. She shouldn't have come alone, should have allowed Joanna to accompany her.

Philippa swallowed a sigh of frustration aimed at herself. Her cousin had tried to warn her. But she hadn't harkened . . .

She'd been anxious to plot a route of escape, one she and Joanna could use to take them out of the priory and away from Walsingham tonight or possibly on the morrow. She hadn't anticipated the chains and locked doors. Or having the priest betray her.

Her shoulders sagged as she neared the stairway that led to the prayer room above the crypt.

Ultimately, by coming to Our Lady, she'd been hoping Prior Thomas would give her sanctuary and permit her to reside in a guest chamber until she had the time to petition for a permanent state of widowhood that would allow her to serve the church. Joanna had been the one to suggest it, had heard of widows in the past who'd been allowed to retain their inheritance while pledging their lives to the Church, in a similar fashion to nuns.

Philippa had counted on her connections to the prestigious Willoughby and Neville families along with her large inheritances from both her father and late husband to bestow upon her some power.

The problem was that she didn't know how to leverage that power, had always depended upon Uncle Hugo to act in her best interest, had always gone along with his plans.

"No longer, Uncle. No longer." She pressed her lips firmly together as she climbed up the steep, narrow stairway. She had to find her own way henceforth, and that meant she had to stay out of her uncle's clutches until she could take the widow's vow and don a widow's veil in front of the bishop. If only Hugo Deighton wasn't such a determined man and so difficult to oppose.

At rapid steps from the opposite side of the crypt, she lengthened her pace. Reaching the top, she pushed through into the prayer room. Without windows, the chamber was lit by a lone sconce, and the shadows seemed to reach out to ensnare her.

"Lady?" came the breathless voice of Father James from the crypt stairway.

Philippa picked up her skirt and started to run. If the monk got his hands on her a second time, she doubted Providence would send Dawson for another rescue.

He'd claimed to be Lady Wilkin's son. Lady Cecilia Wilkin of Barsham. Although Philippa had only spoken with the middle-aged woman briefly a few times, Lady Cecilia had earned a reputation for her just and fair ways. Her husband was also known for his kindness. Surely if Dawson was anything like them, he was kind too.

But if he was the lady's son and a mortal being, how had he managed to come and go at will? Did he practice divination?

As Philippa reached the opposite door, her fingers fumbled with the handle. "Please God. Please." Her whispered prayer was fraught with desperation, a rife theme of late.

"Lady Philippa, wait." Father James entered the prayer room. "We had a misunderstanding, 'tis all."

Misunderstanding? How had the monk misunderstood her fighting against him and her adamant "release me at once"?

She jerked against the door, and panic welled up within her, the same way it had when she'd been in the tunnel. With a final scramble, she somehow managed to unlatch the door. She threw it open and stumbled into the cloister and the bright sunshine of the afternoon.

Several monks on their knees amongst the herb beds paused to stare. She didn't belong in this part of the priory. As a woman and a visitor, she was relegated to the guest chambers and the public area of the chapel.

She lowered her head and hurried down the open but covered passageway toward the side gate that led to the visitor's area. A glance over her shoulder told her that Father James had remained in the prayer room and was refraining from chasing her any farther. Of course, he wouldn't chance bringing attention to himself and his indecent interaction with her.

Philippa slowed her pace and tried to also slow her racing heart. But even as she passed through the gate and rounded the large central building to the front area of the walled complex, she couldn't ease the hard pattering. The Augustinian Priory of The Annunciation of the Blessed Virgin Mary had been her doorway to freedom—or so she'd hoped . . . because it contained the most special shrine in all of England—the Shrine of Our Lady.

The revered Our Lady was situated within the walls of the priory in a small chapel, and many who sought out the protection and healing of Providence there found it. Although in the past Philippa had visited the shrine as a pilgrim, this time she'd come for a different reason. This time she needed a miracle to escape her uncle's scheming.

But in the two days since she'd arrived, she hadn't experienced anything but uneasiness. Even though Prior Thomas had adamantly assured her he would help her gain an audience with the Bishop of Norwich, Henry le Despenser, he'd yet to make the arrangements. Part of her was beginning to suspect that the prior intended to delay until Uncle Hugo arrived, that he had no intention of aiding her.

As Philippa crossed the grassy yard, the lay staff worked quietly in the heat of summer—some pruning and shearing the grass and shrubs that grew in profusion, others painting the exterior of the wattle-and-daub outbuildings with white limewash, and a few engaged in assisting poor pilgrims who'd come to the priory for food.

She veered toward those poor pilgrims near the gate, catching sight of Joanna's wimple amongst those of the kitchen staff. Her own head covering had come loose during the altercation with Father James in the tunnel, and now she repositioned the opaque linen over her head and wrapped it around her neck, as was the custom, even for widows.

As Philippa reached the table, she nodded at the servant beside Joanna, who bowed her head and stepped away. Philippa took the place next to her cousin, picking up a wooden bowl and piece of bread and handing it to Joanna.

Joanna paused in ladling the soup from a cauldron, her brows raised in expectation. Taller by several inches, Joanna shared Philippa's same light-brown hair coloring and the pretty features that had once defined their mothers, who'd been twin sisters. While Philippa had light-blue eyes that were at times almost gray, Joanna's were a solid brown, always as warm and inviting as her heart.

A year older than Philippa's twenty-one years, Joanna had yet to marry. Not for want of a suitable man. She'd been in love for many months with Lance, a nobleman of equal rank and from a good family. But Uncle Hugo—Joanna's father—had been too busy scheming and making plans for Philippa, and he'd neglected his own daughter.

Finally Lance's kin had arranged for him to marry another woman. Their union had taken place earlier in the spring. To say Joanna had been devastated was an understatement. Over the past few months, her anger toward her father had only grown, so that she'd been the one to suggest they run away to frustrate her father's plans for Philippa.

Philippa could feel the attention of a monk standing at the opposite end of the table, offering a short blessing to each of the pilgrims who passed by with the bread and bowl of soup. Now was neither the time nor place to relay to her cousin the failed attempt to find an escape route.

Instead, Philippa bestowed a smile upon a poor woman with a fussing babe in her arms and a squirming toddler at her side. The woman didn't smile in return, the hunger in her eyes and the despair in her face too great to pretend otherwise.

"Would you allow me to hold your babe while you eat?" Philippa gentled her tone and added an extra slice of bread to the bowl.

The poor woman began to hand over her babe but then halted as the overseeing monk made a disgruntled sound at the back of his throat, then shook his head.

Philippa ignored him and held out her arms for the babe. She had every right to give away whatever she chose and comfort as many children as she wanted since her generous donations were funding the charity. In fact, she'd promised more money to the priory—even land—if Prior Thomas would aid her endeavor to connect with the bishop.

Prior Thomas had seemed pleased with her offer. But perhaps Uncle Hugo had bribed him with more and undermined her efforts. 'Twas entirely plausible. Her uncle was more devious than most men.

As she took the babe, she smiled again at the young mother. "What have you christened this child?"

"I haven't yet."

Philippa tugged the ragged blanket that served as swaddling away from the baby's face to reveal splotchy red skin and an angry, scrunched countenance. The infant was clearly as hungry as the mother, and Philippa offered the baby her finger for suckling. The simple comfort quieted the baby. Perhaps not for long, but it would give the mother a chance to eat.

With the meal in hand, the woman led her toddler to a bench positioned outside the gates of the priory. Philippa followed, cradling the baby and relishing the feel of the tiny bundle against her bosom.

Keen longing pierced her as it always did whenever she was around children. In the eight months she'd been married to Lord Neville, she'd failed to conceive. It had been her main duty, the primary reason Robert had married her, so he could finally have an heir for his vast wealth and estates.

But she, like his previous two wives, hadn't been able to provide what he'd desired. Some rumored the problem had been with Robert, that none of his mistresses had any children either.

Whatever the case, Philippa had beseeched Providence and offered many prayers to Saint Gerard that she would be fertile and give Robert his sons. But he'd died of wounds sustained last year during the revolt of the poorest villeins and working classes. He'd been in London when the masses had descended to wreak their destruction—marauding and murdering at will.

Although she hadn't been married long enough to develop

affection for him, she'd used the past year to honor him with a customary grieving period. She'd been grateful Uncle Hugo hadn't pushed her to remarry sooner.

She stroked the baby's cheek with her thumb as it continued to suck vigorously on her finger.

When Uncle recently suggested the time had come to marry again, she hadn't opposed him. Nary one bit. She simply hadn't expected Uncle to insist that she marry Lord Godwin Kempe. But the whole time she'd been grieving, Uncle had been plotting the arrangement.

When Godwin had visited last month, she'd known from the moment he came riding into Thursford why he was there. While she was soft-spoken and amiable most of the time, she'd had no choice but to tell Uncle she wouldn't marry Godwin, not now or anytime in the future.

To her dismay, Uncle hadn't taken her seriously, had belittled her concerns and told her he knew what was best for her.

"What is best for me? Hardly." Philippa released a huff of breath. Uncle had done what was best for *him*, and that meant orchestrating a deal with one of the king's young advisors, one Uncle could manipulate, one who would give him the privileges of court life, one with access to the king . . . all so Uncle could plot the king's demise with some of the other older nobility.

Not only did she refuse to play a role in her uncle's treasonous plans, but she also couldn't abide Godwin. He was but eighteen years, arrogant, and immature. She'd known him as a child growing up, and he'd been the same then as he was now: living for his own pleasures, gluttonous, and irresponsible.

'Twas not her place to be particular about a match. She hadn't spoken against Uncle's arrangement with Robert. Even if Robert hadn't been someone she enjoyed being with, he'd been a decent man, allowing her to run his home the way she saw best as well as giving her the freedom to continue her charity work. Overall, the union had brought the Neville fortune into alignment with the Willoughbys', making her the wealthiest widow in all of England. She dared not complain about that since it allowed her to be even more generous than before.

Nevertheless, this time she hadn't been able to submit to Uncle's choice for a spouse. He'd gone too far in matching her with Godwin. Even Joanna admitted as much.

"I am heartily glad we are able to provide such assistance," Joanna said as she scooped more soup into a bowl. "With as many people who are here in Walsingham, there are just as many needs."

"You are correct, my dear cousin." Philippa rocked back and forth on her heels, soothing the baby.

But for how much longer would they be able to stay?

She was praying the bishop truly would allow her to take the widow's vow and dedicate herself to the Church. In doing so, not only would she avoid a union with Godwin, but she would also be liberated from her uncle's control and become the sole executor of Robert's will.

The consecrated widows were allowed to live in their homes instead of entering a convent but were required to remain chaste and give of their time and wealth to the service of others. Apparently, many such widows remarried after a time, since the widow's vow wasn't seen as an irrevocable renunciation of marriage.

'Twas a good thing, or Philippa might not have agreed to the plan. She wasn't ready to forfeit marriage and children forever. But Joanna's suggestion to take the widow's vow had bought her more time. At least, she thought it had . . .

If only she could find someone to help her stay out of her uncle's clutches.

Philippa's mind flashed to the image of the tall, dark-haired stranger from the tunnel. He'd told her to meet him at the twin wells, that he wanted to help her. She'd sensed his sincerity and concern. She wasn't amiss this time, was she?

Whether he was mortal or otherworldly, he'd helped her once and would surely do so again. She had nothing to lose by taking a walk in the priory woodland at sunset and strolling past the twin wells. If he happened to be there and was willing to assist her, even in some small way, she would accept the offer.

In the meantime, she would continue to plead at heaven's gates for a miracle. If there was any place on earth where miracles occurred, it was here at Our Lady. If only the miracle would happen for her.

~ 8 ~

DAWSON AWOKE WITH A START. "What time is it?"

"Don't worry." Chloe's voice came from nearby. "It's not sunset yet."

Dawson knuckled his eyes, but everything was as blurry as always. Beneath him was the car seat, his head wedged awkwardly in the corner and his legs scrunched against the far door. "How long have I slept?"

"Several hours," came Acey's somber reply—from the front driver's side.

Dawson sat up, dizziness hitting him hard. He blinked through it to see the outlines of Chloe and Acey. Were his friends slightly more visible now? Had the ingestion of the molecules of holy water worked their healing on him just a little—like they had the last time?

He wiggled his fingers and toes. The shrapnel pain didn't seem quite as bad. But maybe he was only imagining it because he wanted to be healed so badly.

"How are you getting on?" Chloe asked.

"Right as rain." The words came out more sarcastically than he intended. He tried to peer out the side window, hoping to be able to see the sky for himself or even the fading of daylight. But the world remained mostly invisible and fuzzy, the same way it always had.

Disappointment pierced him. And longing. He wanted to see clearly again. More than anything.

After listening to Chloe relay Harrison's theories, he shouldn't have unconsciously allowed himself to hope the second overlap would restore even more of his sight.

"Where are the Hamin?" More than the sunset, he wished he could see where the Hamin were hiding and spying on them.

"I've located two," Acey replied. "Probably the same two fellows who followed us at St. Peter's."

After leaving the tower, Acey and Chloe had helped him into the back of their rental. He'd tried to stay awake, had managed to do so long enough to relay the plans for tonight, but then had promptly fallen asleep so deeply that he doubted anything could have roused him, even though he'd warned his friends they needed to wake him up even if they had to drag him into the River Stiffkey to do so.

Not that the river running through the middle of Walsingham was either cold or rushing at this time of year. But he didn't want to miss the opportunity to meet again with the beautiful noblewoman and felt an urgency to return to her that he couldn't explain to his friends.

"Chloe and me"—Acey hesitated—"we've been sorting out the different scenarios for getting into the woods without being followed."

Of course, Acey didn't think he should attempt an overlap in the priory woods, especially with a random stranger from the past. With as dangerous as the Hamin were, Acey didn't think the experience was worth the risk. Instead, he believed they needed to keep their focus on finding more information about Dawson's mom.

He hadn't come right out and said it, but Acey was also worried about exposing Chloe to additional danger.

"It's got to be you and me this time." Dawson combed a hand through his hair, smoothing the tousled waves down. "We'll all go into a crowded pub, make sure Chloe nabs a table in a central location where the Hamin wouldn't dare to go after her. Then the two of us will head over to the priory grounds."

"Right. My thinking exactly."

"And I was thinking that's rubbish." Chloe's voice held a note of irritation. "I've been there with Dawson for his other two overlaps, and I'm not staying back."

Dawson didn't blame Chloe for protesting their plans. If their roles had been reversed, he would have been interested in discovering more too. In fact, he was relieved Chloe had been with him on both of his overlaps. She'd remained calm and logical through all the strange events, hadn't questioned his sanity, and had kept him from questioning himself.

Chloe had explained how, during the overlap, he'd been nearly frozen to the spot, unblinking, unmoving—like he was in a trance. She hadn't noticed anything out of the ordinary in the tunnel—hadn't witnessed him save the young woman from the priest's attack, hadn't heard any of their conversation, hadn't experienced even the slightest change of temperature or scents.

How was it that he could literally stand in the same place

and yet be in two different eras at the same time? It was crazy. He was genuinely staggered. But now, after the second experience, he was all the more eager to overlap into the past again.

"Maybe we should wait," Acey said as though reading Dawson's thoughts. "It's been a long day."

If he failed to show up as he'd planned, he might never see her again. Yet even with Chloe and Acey to help him manufacture an overlap, he had no guarantees that he'd have another connection with her. It might not work. Or perhaps the timing would be off so he'd overlap when she wasn't there.

And what exactly did he intend to do for her if he went into the past and met her again? The short time together wouldn't give him the ability to accomplish anything useful.

If only he could stay with her longer. Then he might be able to assist her better. Not only that, but he'd be able to see his mum again. His mum. He'd actually get to talk to her, hug her, say that he loved her . . . and find out vital information about her disappearance that could bring about an end to the Hamin in the UK.

Maybe he'd also have the chance to tell Sybil how sorry he was for how he'd treated her. An apology would never make up for his rudeness and selfishness, but it was a start.

Yes, he wanted a longer stint in the past. But that kind of time crossing would take more holy water in addition to what he needed to facilitate his healing. From everything he could deduce, there was no source of the holy water in the present day—at least, not that anyone knew about. The sources were in the past. And the only way to get the water was to ask someone

JODY HEDLUND

in the past to leave it in a place that could still be accessed in the present.

Like in the tunnel beneath St. Peter's church . . .

Was there a way the woman he'd met could deliver holy water to him in the tunnel? Perhaps in the last alcove, the one that had the removable stone. If he timed his visit just right, he could be there when she placed the water on the altar.

Yes, that's what he'd do. If he could create an overlap with the noblewoman by the twin wells, he'd ask her to leave him holy water—enough so he could safely cross to the past and then back again.

"Hey, Dawson." Acey broke into his runaway thoughts. "Me and Chloe, we're here for you."

"I appreciate it—"

"But I have a bad feeling about this."

"It won't take long." He hated that he had to plead, hated that he needed to rely on them, hated that he had to push for his way.

Dawson sensed the two sharing a long look, as though feeling sorry for him. "Stop. I'm not keen for your pity." He fumbled for the door handle, his frustration quickly escalating into anger. He threw open the door and then stepped out.

He swayed and grabbed on to the car to keep from crumpling. An instant later, both Acey's and Chloe's doors opened, and Acey was at his side, grabbing his arm.

Dawson shook his friend's hand off. "Back off." The words tumbled out, filled with all the bitterness that had made a home inside him for so long.

Acey pulled away, no doubt bracing himself for a storm of fury.

Dawson drew in a breath, then tightened his grip against the car. He was doing it again. He was reacting the same way he had for the past eight years. He was letting his blindness and insecurities define him instead of accepting himself and all his weaknesses. He'd thought he was clearing out the mess, that he was doing better. But obviously he had quite a lot more work to do.

The busyness of the summer evening wafted around them—the clink of tableware at an outdoor restaurant nearby, the laughter and teasing of a passing group, the rumble of a lorry. At the scent of burgers and chips, his stomach gurgled.

"I'm sorry, Dawson," Acey finally said quietly.

"No, I'm sorry—"

"I have the feeling this is something you'd do even if you could see."

Dawson wasn't sure whether to be offended or not, so he didn't respond.

"If it's something you'd do with or without me, then I oughta stop treating you like an invalid and instead give you the respect you deserve."

"Yes, I'd do this with or without you . . . if I could."

Acey didn't respond for a beat. Perhaps he was exchanging more silent communication with Chloe. Whatever the case, Dawson pushed down his pride and waited.

"Time for supper?" Acey asked casually but with a hint of determination. "I hear King's Pub has terrific sandwiches."

King's Pub on High Street abutted the Walsingham Abbey grounds. In fact, if they exited out the back door, they would have only a short walk—albeit through private property belonging to the Abbey House, a mansion that was built in the 1700s over the ruins of the old priory.

Even if such a trek would involve trespassing through the private mansion grounds, they could stick to the woodland and circle around to where the twin wells were located, not far from the arched window remains of the priory.

"I'm hungry." Dawson released his tight hold of the vehicle. "How about you, Chloe?" He hoped she could hear his willingness to have her join in the next adventure. Even if it was dangerous, she didn't deserve to be left behind.

"I'm ravenous," she replied. "Let's go."

* ● ·

An hour later, Dawson crouched next to Acey and Chloe near the hedge that walled in the twin wells.

"Any sign of the Hamin?" he whispered.

"None yet," came Acey's wary whisper beside him.

The two Hamin who'd been trailing them all day had probably figured out by now that they'd gone in one door of the pub and out the other. No doubt they'd also realized their quarry had headed into the Walsingham Abbey grounds.

Thankfully, the area was huge and covered close to twenty acres.

"I've been here in the spring." Chloe's warm presence flanked Dawson's other side. "And it's gorgeous with all the snowdrops in bloom. Just gorgeous."

Dawson tried to focus on any usual sensations that would alert him to the presence of someone from the past. He'd decided to wait to attempt the overlap until he felt something—the swirling or whispering he'd encountered previously. But during the fifteen or more minutes they'd been skulking around in the growing darkness, he hadn't sensed anyone or anything.

Maybe she wasn't coming. Or maybe he was naïve to think he could arrange for this kind of connection.

"In the spring, the whole town is overrun," she continued, "with people on holiday from all over the UK. With it being such a busy place, I can completely understand why the Hamin would be able to move about unnoticed."

Dawson tried to picture the flowers, woodland, and grounds the way he remembered them from the time he'd visited ages ago. The twin wells were two wide holes in the ground surrounded by cement perimeters and covered with black iron grills. An old stone bathing pool—also covered with a metal grate—lay only feet away from the wells, and a reconstructed Norman doorway stood just beyond, its low arch of stone covered in ivy and moss.

The "Well Garden," as it was now known, wasn't too far from the priory ruins. He hoped it was a place the young woman could easily access. If only he'd thought to ask her name.

Perhaps this attempt at an overlap would amount to nothing. And perhaps all he was doing was putting Acey, Chloe, and himself into unnecessary danger with the Hamin.

He couldn't hold back a sigh.

"Any feelings of a presence yet?" Chloe whispered, apparently sensing his frustration—or hearing his sigh.

"Not a thing."

Acey leaned against his cane, his leg probably sore after the long day of walking. The strain in his tone reminded Dawson of all that could go wrong in an instant. "Maybe we oughta go."

"Guess so." Dawson pushed up.

Immediately, a whisper swirled in the air around him. If he hadn't already heard it now twice, he might not have recognized it, might have mistaken it for the breeze rustling in the leaves. But his pulse picked up speed with the certainty that it was her.

He lifted the empty bottle that he'd used for the other overlaps, wet his finger, and delved in as deeply as he could reach, trying to scrape at the bottom where he hadn't yet wiped away the residue.

"She's here?" Chloe jumped up beside him.

"Yes. I think it's her." He hoped it was her and rubbed against the jar hard, needing as much as possible so he could communicate for as long as possible.

He could feel Acey rise on his opposite side.

Dawson took one last swipe of the bottle, then stuck his finger into his mouth.

A tingling rushed along his nerve endings, moving from his arms to his hands and then from his legs to his feet. The whispering was closer, and the scent of woodsmoke lingered in the night air. Gone were the neat hedges cut to perfection and the manicured lawn. Instead, tangles of shrubs and tall grass interspersed with wildflowers grew among the trees.

"There he is," came the soft but sophisticated voice of the woman.

He pivoted to find the outline of a woman in the trees behind him. Even though she was shadowed and wore a head covering and a cloak, there was no hiding her beauty, grace, and poise.

He ducked under a limb, old twigs and leaves crackling beneath his feet. A jolt of energy coursed through him along with a strange sense of desire, the kind of desire he hadn't experienced in a long time.

He quickly closed the distance. Within the thickness of the shrubs, there was also another woman. He couldn't make out her features clearly, but he could tell she was slightly taller and more willowy.

"You are here." The first woman reached out and grazed his arm, as though she needed to reassure herself that he was real.

"I don't have long," he whispered, unable to keep himself from touching her arm in return, needing to prove he wasn't imagining things either.

"Likewise, I do not have much time before my uncle arrives here at the priory and forces me to return with him. Mere days, if that. I must be away soon."

"I'll take you to my mum's—Lady Cecilia's—home. But before I can do so, I need you to provide me with holy water."

"Yes, I shall try." She peered up at him, her eyes wide and guileless.

"The water must come from a spring in the crypt."

"I have not heard of such a spring."

"You have to find it for me—if possible, at least three tablespoons."

She nodded agreeably.

"Once you have it, place it in the last alcove in the tunnel where I first saw you. In the middle of the altar. Do it tomorrow at high noon."

"Ask him why," came whispered instructions from the other woman.

"It'll allow me to stay with you longer and lead you out of the priory. Without it, I'll keep disappearing." He didn't know what she understood about the powers of the holy water. He couldn't go into detail at the moment and hoped his brief explanation would suffice.

At the barking of a dog, she glanced in the direction of the priory, as if she was afraid that someone might be searching for her. The priest from earlier, perhaps?

He followed her gaze. An enormous stone cathedral-like building stood where only ruins existed in the present day. It was all he could do not to let his mouth drop open. He wasn't a student of history or architecture like Chloe, but the magnitude of the old priory chapel was beyond awesome. Even in the dark, he could distinguish the tall spires rising to the heavens. He could see the stars, the planets, and the endless expanse of the universe—something he'd taken for granted in the days before his blindness but never would again.

He couldn't use up his time in the past with admiring everything he could finally see again. He had to focus on her and making the next set of plans. "If all goes well, I'll meet you here in the woods again tomorrow night just after sunset."

She turned her face up to him, the dusting of freckles captivating him. Or maybe it was the way her lips pressed together almost seductively. Or was it her eyes, the shy way she regarded him through her lashes?

Whatever it was—maybe a combination of everything—her beauty was overwhelming. "I don't know your name." He was surprised at the breathless quality of his voice, as if he was already smitten by her. Was that even possible with a woman he'd only just met?

"Philippa." Her response was tentative.

"She is Lady Neville to you," came the terse whisper of the other woman.

"Philippa." He tested her name, needing to show the other woman he wasn't easily intimidated. "Will you be safe until tomorrow evening?"

She hesitated. "I hope so."

He wanted to know everything—why her uncle had so much power, why she was running from him. But he'd have to wait to ask questions until he saw her next time—if there was a next time. "If your uncle comes, find a place to hide until he's gone."

"He will not rest until he sees me wedded to the man of his choosing."

Wedded?

"Get down." A strong hand clamped powerfully on Dawson's shoulder and dragged him down. The world turned suddenly black, the starlight gone.

He didn't want the connection with Philippa to end, didn't want to lose sight of her, wished he could go on admiring her pretty face. But she was gone, and darkness crowded in to take her place, along with a strange feeling of loss so that all he wanted was to find a way to see her again.

He shoved against Acey, but his friend pinned him to the ground, this time harder. "Hold still. Those same two men are nearby looking for us."

Dawson twisted a hand free.

Acey yanked him down again. "Fine if you want to get yourself killed. Or even me. But think about Chloe. Please."

The harsh words halted Dawson's struggle. Once again, he was being a selfish idiot. Even in this moment, he was thinking more about himself and the woman who'd captured his attention than his friends or even the search for his mum.

He flattened himself to the ground next to Acey and remained immobile, even as his thoughts raced a million miles per hour. He'd set in motion the plans to help Philippa. But he couldn't forget his true mission—to free his mum from the Hamin and, in doing so, put an end to the terrorist threats once and for all.

~ 9 ~

DAWSON RECLINED ON THE SOFA in his mum's town house and cradled his bottle of holy water out of sight of any hidden cameras. The droning from a podcast over a Bluetooth speaker hopefully was masking their conversation.

"You sure about this?" Acey whispered.

Dawson nodded. It was time—actually, past time. At well past ten o'clock at night, he had to take it now or risk being unable to wake up by noon tomorrow so he could return to the tunnel under the tower at St. Peter's Church in Great Walsingham.

Of course, Acey and Chloe had offered to retrieve the holy water if he wasn't awake by then. But he refused to put them into a situation where they'd draw more suspicion from the Hamin. He'd put himself at further risk, but not them—if at all possible.

As it was, they'd managed to sneak out of the Walsingham grounds, back to the car, and returned to Fakenham without any altercations. During the short ride, even though he'd been exhausted, they'd conversed about his overlap and the plans he'd made with Philippa about going back into the past for a longer duration and all the reasons why he wanted to do so.

JODY HEDLUND

Although Acey and Chloe agreed he should drink Sybil's bottle of holy water, they didn't think he needed to cross time to solve the mystery of his mum's disappearance. They believed he could do so without having to take such a risk.

And it was a huge risk. Chloe had reminded him that the possibility of his surviving the crossing was slim, that he'd likely end up dead or maybe even trapped in the past forever.

If his mum and Sybil were alive in 1382, maybe it wouldn't be such a bad thing to go there to live with them. Yet, if there was a chance his mum was still alive in the present day, then he wanted to return and help with her rescue.

Whatever the case, Chloe and Acey were staying the night at his town house, and as they'd entered, they'd made sure to state loudly enough for anyone listening that Chloe wanted to take more snaps tomorrow in Walsingham.

Dawson had insisted on giving up his room and crashing on the sofa. Now, he was ready to drink the holy water and discover if it could work a miracle on him the way it had for Harrison.

With his head upon the armrest of the sofa, his eyelids were heavy. He needed to ingest the liquid before he fell asleep. But he also had to make sure his friends were on board with the new plans. "So, you'll wake me in the morning before it gets too late?"

"Got that right." Chloe responded with the same enthusiasm she'd had from the start of their quest.

Through his tired haze, he could only distinguish the dark form where Acey sat in a chair nearby. Maybe when he woke up tomorrow, he'd be able to look at their faces and really see them, their expressions, the emotions in their eyes, all the many things he wasn't able to discern.

But even if he never regained his full sight, he would keep living on his own and move toward greater independence. He'd begun the journey toward appreciating the blessings that he had in his life, and it was a journey he had to continue no matter what might happen with his eyesight.

"Good, then." He tried to keep his tone casual so the Hamin wouldn't hear the echo of excitement growing inside him.

Before he could find a last-ditch excuse not to drink the holy water, he turned his head toward the wall—away from view of any hidden cameras. He popped off the cork he'd already loosened, then tipped the bottle to his lips, letting the liquid pour down his throat.

In the next instant, he passed out.

● ● ●

"There is no spring in the crypt." Joanna poked her head behind another raised casket.

Philippa brushed a cobweb out of her face and held up the oil lantern to give her a better view of the stone walls, stone containers, and stone ledges around the underground chamber that held a treasury of ancient artifacts and relics.

"Do you think there's another crypt someplace else to which Dawson was referring?" Joanna asked.

Philippa whispered a silent prayer. 'Twould seem that they needed Divine intervention again, this time in locating the obscure spring of holy water.

At the creak of a board above their heads, Philippa froze. Was someone else awake at this late hour?

After their meeting with Dawson near the wells, she'd wanted to wait for a short while, lest he decided to appear again. But eventually the silence told her Dawson had returned from whence he'd come.

She still didn't know what to think of his appearances. Joanna had insisted on accompanying her to the wells. And Philippa had relented, hoping Joanna could confirm what she was seeing.

Thankfully, Joanna had not only seen the young man but had also heard him speak. And now her cousin was speaking of Dawson as if he was indeed a real person they'd interacted with—a real person who'd vanished before their eyes.

Even if Philippa couldn't comprehend him after the second visitation any more than after the first, she was choosing to believe he was part of the miracle she'd sought when she'd come to Our Lady in Walsingham.

If Providence was using Dawson to direct her, then she couldn't ignore the instructions, no matter how bizarre they might appear. After all, Lady Richeldis, the founder of Our Lady, had experienced strange visions and instructions as well on the same plot of land. The brave woman had likely been uncertain, perhaps even scared, the same way Philippa and Joanna were. But she'd persevered, following the plans given to her in the visions, down to the size of the chapel she was to build.

Philippa bent and swept her hand over the stone floor

under the last casket, hoping to feel some moisture, a puddle, anything that could be contrived as a spring. But as with the others, she felt nothing but the dust of the decades that had passed since the last body had been laid to rest inside the crypt.

At the creak of additional boards overhead, she paused again. Someone was most definitely awake in the priory at the late hour. And that someone seemed to have entered the room above the crypt—the dark prayer room.

She rose and stared at the ceiling, as if somehow Providence might give her the ability to see through the boards and learn who was there. Was it one of the monks coming to pray? Or someone like Father James who had more sinister ideas?

As the steps crossed toward the door leading down into the crypt, Philippa motioned at Joanna and nodded toward the corner of the crypt farthest away from the stairs. Joanna wasted no time in joining her there, and together they crouched behind the largest of the coffins—the one that apparently held the body of Lady Richeldis herself.

At the squeak of the door opening at the top of the steps, Joanna rapidly snuffed the oil lamp and placed it under the casket to keep the smoke from rising and giving them away.

"Find her at once," came the quiet but steely voice that belonged to Prior Thomas.

"I cannot be certain she went into the tunnels, only that she inquired about them." The second voice was that of Father James.

"Show Lord Deighton's men where you believe she might have gone."

Her uncle's men were here?

Philippa drew in a sharp breath, and in the next instant, Joanna pinched her arm in a warning to remain quiet.

If a contingent had arrived tonight, that meant she'd run out of time to save herself from becoming ensnared in her uncle's schemes.

Footfalls started down the stone stairway. At least three pairs. The clink of weapons against chain mail informed her of all she needed to know. Uncle Hugo's men were indeed searching the premises of the priory for her.

They'd likely timed their arrival to coincide with the fall of darkness, hoping to take her unaware and giving her scant opportunity to escape. The plan would have worked any other time, save that tonight she'd gone straight to the crypt after her encounter with Dawson.

As the low light of a lantern grew brighter—likely one Father James carried—she crouched lower against the coffin, pressing against Joanna, needing her cousin's fortitude. Joanna held herself motionless, and Philippa tried to do the same.

The door on the opposite side of the crypt opened, and a moment later, the footsteps faded away as Father James guided Uncle's men to the tunnel where he'd taken her earlier today.

How long would they explore the underground passageways before realizing she hadn't made her escape through one of them? That she couldn't possibly open the locks? How long before they came back through the crypt and glimpsed the hems of their dresses or their slippers beneath the raised coffins?

"We have to get out of here." Philippa pressed against the cold stone wall at her back, wishing for the solidness to seep into her and lend her its strength.

"If we go anywhere, we shall encounter more of my father's men." Joanna spoke with such surety that Philippa didn't doubt her.

"Then what shall we do?"

"We must climb into the coffins and hide there." Joanna was already rising and pushing against the stone lid in an attempt to move it.

Philippa recoiled in horror, not only at the prospect of getting into a container with a dead person but also at the irreverence of disturbing these saints who'd been laid to rest in this holy place. "I shall do no such thing."

"You must or you will find yourself married to Godwin ere the night is over."

Philippa flattened herself farther against the wall, neither option viable. As she fought against her rising panic, her fingers brushed against an indent. She traced it to discover a half door. It was likely a storage chamber . . . but it would provide a better hiding place than the coffins.

"I think I found a closet." She glided a hand over the door more rapidly, searching for a handle and praying it wasn't locked. Her fingers connected with another deeper indent. A handle.

She tugged on it, and the door opened soundlessly.

Joanna wasted no time in crossing and kneeling beside her. Although the darkness of the crypt was complete now that the men were no longer close, Joanna forged into the unknown anyway, bumping into something.

Philippa hesitated only a moment before climbing through

the doorway after her cousin. She pulled the half door shut, giving it an extra tug to secure it all the way. She hadn't noticed the door earlier when they'd been looking for the spring. It must have blended well into the whitewashed wall, or perhaps one of the coffins had obscured it from notice.

The question was whether Father James knew about the closet. If so, he'd instruct Uncle's men to search it when they came back through the crypt after they finished scouring the tunnels and alcoves.

Even here, she and Joanna would have to find a way to conceal themselves, just in case their pursuers located the half door.

Ahead in the blackness, Joanna continued to make a racket. "There are crates filled with ampullae, the kind sold to pilgrims."

Philippa inched forward until she made contact with Joanna. "Does that mean they hold holy water?" If so, she could leave at least three of them in the alcove Dawson had mentioned.

Joanna seemed to be shaking a container. "No, from what I can tell, they are empty and have never been used."

Philippa skimmed her hand over the crate before she reached inside and connected with a tiny bottle. It was smooth but coated in a thick layer of dust and cobwebs.

She traced a fancy *W*, likely representing Walsingham. She turned the ampulla over and felt the pattern of a flower. The bell shape along with the six petals had to be a snowdrop that grew in profusion in early spring.

Why would the empty ampullae be stored in this particular

closet . . . unless there was a wellspring nearby that the monks had once used to fill the containers? Was it the hidden well Dawson had indicated was located under the priory?

"The wellspring must be here in the closet." Joanna thumped and thudded as she continued to search through the darkness.

"You are making enough noise to wake the dead." Philippa sat back on her heels. "Perhaps we should wait to commence a search until after we know Father James and Uncle's men have passed back through."

"And if he searches this closet?" Something crashed against the floor—likely one of the ampullae. "We have to hide—" She halted abruptly.

"What?"

"I have located another half door." Joanna's voice contained a note of excitement.

Philippa suspected her cousin had offered to accompany her to Our Lady because she longed for adventure. Of course, Joanna was a kind soul and wanted to help her. But Joanna had always been restless, as though waiting for her life to truly begin.

"Make haste," Joanna said as she scraped open the door. "We must keep going."

Philippa followed the sound of Joanna's voice, crawling through a maze of crates and canisters until she reached the far end of the closet and bumped into Joanna's feet. Her cousin had halted halfway through the next door.

"Is it safe?" Philippa asked.

"I have reached another set of stairs."

"Perhaps we should wait." At least until they had light to guide their way. There was no telling what might loom ahead.

Joanna moved forward. "We shall be safer here than in the closet."

Philippa wasn't so sure. But she ducked into the new hiding place—which was damper and colder with an earthy scent. And as she closed the door and started down the steps after Joanna, the darkness felt heavier.

After about a dozen steps, she reached the bottom to find that Joanna was crouched on the floor. "This has to be it. The wellspring."

Philippa lowered herself and reached out a hand to find an iron grate covering a large hole. "I agree. It must be the wellspring." What else could it be?

How had Dawson known it existed here? She supposed if he had the ability to appear and disappear at will, he had other capabilities she couldn't begin to comprehend—like the ability to whisk her away to safety. All the more reason to do his bidding and place holy water in the alcove.

She tugged at the grate. "Can we draw water out?"

Joanna's fingers brushed against hers as she also hefted the covering. "Of course there is a way to draw the water. We must discover it."

Philippa joined her cousin in exploring for a latch or anything else that might give them a clue about how to access the water. The thick bars were rusty and rough against her fingers, but she could find no evidence of a lock or latch.

How much water did the wellspring contain? If the monks had poured water from this spring into the ampullae, perhaps the water source had long past dried up. Perhaps that was why the above closet was filled with dusty, empty ampullae that hadn't been touched in decades, maybe even since the time of Lady Richeldis.

"Here." Joanna ceased her searching. "The slats here slide open." A soft clank was followed by a scraping. "'Tis an opening wide enough for someone to place a hand through."

Philippa envisioned the monks from hundreds of years ago descending the stairs, ampullae in hand, quietly and reverently kneeling before the wellspring, perhaps using a ladle to spoon water into the containers, praying over each one before sealing them and taking them to the chapel to the sick and diseased pilgrims who needed miracles. 'Twas a beautiful picture. One she would have liked to witness.

Joanna seemed to be stretching her arm through the opening. "'Tis dry."

Disappointment wafted through Philippa. Did that mean she wouldn't be able to supply Dawson and receive his help in return?

"Wait." Joanna's tone changed, the excitement returning as she stretched farther. "I have located a puddle about the width of my hand."

"'Tis something, then."

Joanna brushed against Philippa as she sat back up. "'Tis not much, but let us hope 'twill suffice for Dawson."

"Yes, let us hope indeed."

~ *10* ~

DAWSON'S DREAMS WERE FILLED with images of Philippa. He was lying beside her, both of their heads on the same pillow, morning light spilling across her face. He was counting her faint freckles, caressing his fingers down her bare arm, and waiting for her to rouse so he could watch her sensual lips turn up into a smile meant just for him.

Then in the next instant, he found himself watching her from a distance as she stood with another man before the priest from the tunnel, and she was reciting wedding vows.

"No." He wanted to shout at her not to marry the bloke, but he couldn't get his voice to work. All he could do was murmur.

"No." He tried again, but she kept reciting the vows.

"Dawson?" A hand shook his shoulder.

Was it Philippa? Could he reach her in time to keep her from having to marry the man her uncle had arranged for her? A man she was going to great lengths to escape.

"We've waited long enough," came a whisper near him. "We have to go. It's what he'd want."

At another shake, Dawson attempted to open his eyes. But everything about his body felt heavy, like he was still halfway in

111

a deep sleep. He was too tired to wake up, wanted to stay asleep and keep dreaming about Philippa.

"I'll go alone," a woman was saying in a hushed tone. "You stay here with him."

"No. You can't go by yourself."

"I'll be in and out within two shakes."

Dawson tried to make sense of the whispered conversation above the loud strains of country music playing in the background.

Chloe and Acey were with him. But where?

He slid his fingers over the faux leather fabric of a sofa. He was lying on the sofa in his mum's town house in Fakenham. His friends had come up to visit yesterday. They'd gone with him to Walsingham. And they'd stayed the night . . . because he'd finally taken the holy water.

With a jolt, he opened his eyes. The brightness of the room told him the night had passed and that it was well into the day.

Had the holy water healed him?

He blinked, the brightness all he could see.

A sense of panic pulsed through him. What if it hadn't worked? Perhaps the holy water didn't heal all ailments, especially in certain instances. He couldn't imagine it would give Acey a new leg in place of the one that had been amputated. Maybe his situation was like that, and he wouldn't regain eyesight that had already been lost.

Swallowing hard, he closed his eyes to the haze of darkness and blurriness that had become familiar over the past eight years. He breathed in and then out, releasing the tension. If he wasn't healed, he'd be okay. He'd already resolved last night to continue his journey toward a healthy mindset whether or not his vision was restored.

"Hey, Dawson?" Acey whispered above him. "You awake?"

"Yes." His voice came out hoarse.

"Well?" Chloe's whisper radiated with anticipation.

Slowly Dawson pried open one eye. A face appeared above him, but it was out of focus. He opened his other eye, and the world seemed to tilt on its axis—the room, the walls, the couch. He quickly closed his eyes and fought against the dizziness.

His heart began to beat hard against his chest. Something had changed in his vision. Was it possible he could see . . .?

Hardly daring to believe it was true, this time he lifted his lids only halfway.

Acey's face filled his vision. Red, unruly hair, a bushy beard, scruffy sideburns, and worried brown eyes creased at the corners with crow's feet. His face was fuller, paler, and most definitely older. "When's the last time you shaved?"

At Dawson's soft question, Acey's eyes widened and turned glassy. He pressed a fist to his mouth, but not before Dawson witnessed the tremble of his lips.

A strange vise gripped Dawson's chest, and tears stung the backs of his eyes . . . eyes that worked.

"I'll be gobsmacked." The whisper came from Chloe, who was sitting on the edge of the sofa, by his feet. Her eyes were also wide and filled with wonder. Dawson had gotten a glimpse of her that day in Reider Castle, and now he took her in again: her shoulder-length blond hair, rounded face, short nose, and small mouth that hung open.

The heat in his chest and eyes swelled. He could see. Holy Mary and Joseph. He shifted his arm and braced himself for shooting pain.

Nothing happened.

A tear trickled down Acey's cheek even as he swiped at it.

Dawson couldn't hold back a tear of his own and wiped it away just as quickly.

"This is tremendous." Acey shook his head and rubbed at his eyes as if to wake himself up from dreaming.

Dawson sat up and looked around his mum's town house, seeing her fingerprints everywhere—the bright-blue chair next to the TV that matched the blue of the sofa, the white throw pillows with splashes of blue, the glass coffee table with gold edging and legs, the collage of paintings on the wall above the sofa with more of the bright blue.

The place was cluttered now with his discarded clothing, balled-up socks, and takeaway boxes. But he couldn't get enough. He started to stand, but Acey's heavily tattooed arm darted out and held him in place.

Dawson met his friend's gaze, something he hadn't been able to do in years. In spite of the wonder, Acey's eyes also held a warning, one that reminded Dawson the Hamin might be watching their every move through hidden cameras. At the very least they were attempting to listen to their conversation.

If the Hamin learned he'd been healed, they'd stop at nothing to capture him, and no doubt they'd beat him—even torture him—until he revealed the details of all that had transpired over the past few weeks since Sybil's death.

The truth was, he was in more danger now than ever. And

by association with him, Acey and Chloe would be in trouble too.

What should he do?

He plopped back against the sofa. His mind spun with all the options, and only one stood out among the many. He would have to keep his healing a secret for now, at least until he gathered the information he needed to bring the Hamin down. And the only way he could gather that information was to meet with his mum and find out all she knew.

All the more reason to travel to the past.

He wanted nothing more than to glance over at the clock on the wall above the TV, but he closed his eyes to avoid the temptation. "What time is it?"

"Half past eleven." Chloe's answer was normal, absent of the worry he'd heard there only a moment ago when he'd been awakening. She was playing this dangerous game too. "Are you ready to head back to Walsingham and indulge me again today with more exploration?"

He released what he hoped sounded like an exasperated sigh. "Fine, as long as you plan to treat for coffee."

She rose. "Absolutely. Let's crack on with it then, yeah?"

Less than five minutes later, they were on their way. As soon as they were speeding down Fakenham Road, Dawson finally allowed himself to take in the scenery, drinking it in like a starving man. The bright blue of the sky, the few wispy clouds, the vibrant-green hedges alongside the roads, the farm fields beyond, the colorful cars passing by.

Acey darted glances at him in the rear view mirror all the while Chloe kept up her steady discourse of various types of architecture that she hoped to photograph so she could use them as she taught her students. They made no mention of the healing or holy water just in case the Hamin had bugged the rental car overnight.

The sights were almost overwhelming to Dawson, and he had to close his eyes on several occasions to give himself a break from the sensory overload. When they finally entered Little Walsingham, it was already past noon. Even so, Dawson knew they had to find a public place where they could make plans to work out the details of his time crossing without the risk of the Hamin hearing them.

Although he was anxious to get the holy water out of the hiding place before the Hamin discovered it first, he suggested they get sandwiches and eat them in a park well away from any listening devices.

As they settled in the shade, Dawson had to work hard to keep from gaping at everything around him—especially the joy on the faces of the children as they played with abandonment on the swings and slides and other equipment.

Acey offered some protest again to Dawson's plan to cross to the past, but when he finally silently acquiesced, Dawson knew his friend had come to the same conclusion—the only way any of them would ever be truly safe was if Dawson was able to get the intel on the Hamin. Then when he returned, they would be able to work with government agents to track the terrorists down and lock them away.

The trouble was, he would fall into a coma once he drank more holy water. And a coma would most definitely draw the attention of the Hamin. To avoid that, Dawson suggested they stage an accident that would incapacitate him for a few days. They agreed the accident couldn't be anything too serious that would permanently injure him. But at the same time, they needed his injuries to be believable enough to require hospitalization.

Of course, the nearest hospital was in Norwich, about thirty miles to the east of Walsingham. They couldn't know for certain what would happen to his body in the past if his present-day body was transported by ambulance to Norwich. But they speculated the crossover would happen wherever he drank the water. That meant he needed to find a safe place within Walsingham to make the crossing, a place in the past where he could remain undisturbed until the effects of the holy water wore off and he was strong enough to function. He'd have to cause the accident and drink the water in that exact spot.

They finally decided the grounds outside St. Peter's Church were probably the best place, particularly a woodland in the north corner of the grounds that was adjacent to Mill Lane.

"Three days," Acey said as he finished the last bite of his sub.

"One week." Dawson crumpled his wrapper and wished he could toss it into the rubbish bin nearby. But that was definitely not something a partially blind person would do.

"One week in a coma is too long and will draw suspicion."

"Three days is way too short." Already part of his first day would be spent sleeping off the effects of the time crossing. Then he'd have to find Philippa and help her escape before heading to Barsham, where Philippa had indicated his mum lived. Barsham was only a few miles from Walsingham, but they'd likely have to walk the distance. "What if something goes wrong?"

"That's what I'm afraid of." Acey stood and helped Chloe to her feet before taking hold of Dawson's arm.

Dawson wanted to jump up and prove he could get around by himself, but he resisted the urge and allowed Acey to assist him.

"Five days?" Chloe offered. "That should be enough time to get the information you need, but hopefully won't alert the Hamin that you drank holy water."

Dawson started toward the car, making sure to measure his steps as he'd always done. "I have a feeling no matter how long it is or what we do, we'll draw their suspicion."

Acey ambled beside him. "We'll do our part here to keep you safe. You just do yours there."

Dawson nodded. He'd learned long ago that usually the best-laid plans never worked out the way a person wanted. But he prayed this time the mighty hand of God would guide him and that he'd be able to accomplish everything he needed in the past and somehow beat the odds and be able to return to the present.

~ 11 ~

AT A DISTANT SOUND, Philippa picked up her pace. The bells for the divine office of sext had already rung, calling the monks to prayer. She was late in making it to the alcove Dawson had indicated. And now she hoped she wouldn't fail in her quest altogether.

She and Joanna had spent the night in the chamber with the ancient wellspring. The voices and footsteps of the men searching for them had passed by on multiple occasions. Each time they'd waited motionless. But no one had discovered the half door behind the coffin that led to the supply closet.

They hadn't dared to light a candle or lamp but had instead tried to make the best of their situation.

Only after the footsteps had retreated upstairs and grown silent overhead had they ventured back into the supply closet. Even then, they'd hastened, taken only three of the ampullae and corks, then returned to the wellspring. They'd worked together to carefully scoop out a spoonful into each, using several funnels and small spoons, which they guessed had once been used to measure out and pour the holy water into the ampullae.

She didn't know if the water was truly holy water. Neither

she nor Joanna had any ailments and thus no reason to test the water's miraculous power. Even if they had, she wouldn't have wanted to use rare water on herself, not when only a scant amount remained. She just prayed it would help Dawson.

Though such a petition was selfish in nature, she'd beseeched Providence anyway because she and Joanna needed Dawson's assistance now more than ever. Without it, she didn't know how they would escape from the priory. Guards were likely positioned at every exit, including those at the end of the tunnels. In addition, they were probably still searching hither and yon in town and the surrounding countryside.

Regardless of how difficult an escape would be, she had to try, couldn't give up yet. After another glance over her shoulder, she raced as fast as she could manage, picking up her skirt so she could lengthen her stride.

She'd had no choice but to relight the oil lantern from the flame already burning in the sconce at the top of the stairway leading to the priory. The light was risky, but without it she would have gotten lost amongst the network of tunnels. As it was, she hoped she was in the right one leading to the spot where she'd first seen Dawson.

Both times she'd interacted with him had been hasty, and she hadn't given much heed to his physical attributes. Other than to note he was darkly handsome, she couldn't even recall what color his eyes were.

The truth was, a man's character mattered much more than comeliness. And she longed for a man who felt the same way about her—that her inner qualities were of more importance than the outward.

However, most men made no secret that they lusted after her for both her beauty and wealth. She was a prize to be gained, a jewel to display, a possession to be used.

While Robert hadn't misused her, he'd never shown her any tenderness or passion. She'd endured his visits to her chamber in the dark of night. His time spent in her bed had been infrequent and never lasted long. If only the enduring had produced a baby . . .

Godwin, likewise, lacked tenderness. Lust he had in plenty, and during his last visit, he'd cornered her in a passageway and attempted to steal a kiss from her. He'd had overmuch to drink and had been clumsy, thus allowing her to sidle away. But the incident had been less than pleasant, and she dreaded a lifetime of such encounters.

She sighed. Perhaps she expected overmuch, had set her standards too high. Had she been wrong to reject Godwin? What if he would eventually mature?

No. She had to wait, had to choose a man with better character. And she couldn't in good conscience have a union that might facilitate the demise of young King Richard.

Therewith, she wouldn't have control over her own life unless she broke away from her uncle. And breaking away was proving to be more difficult than she'd anticipated.

Was Dawson the way to freedom? Or was she exchanging one man's control for another's?

A low arched door loomed ahead. It looked like the same one Father James had indicated would take her out of the priory. He hadn't told her where the exit led, and she wasn't proficient enough with directions to speculate.

As she came upon the alcove off to the side, she slowed her steps. Was this the spot?

She held up the lantern and examined the altar and cross. She'd been too shaken after Father James had turned upon her to pay close attention to the details of her surroundings. But from what she could assess, this was correct.

Stepping through the arched doorway, she found herself in a nook that was no more than three square feet. She bowed her head and lifted a silent petition to Providence that He would take the water, just as He'd done many times throughout Scripture, and use it to perform a miracle. The Savior Himself had turned water into wine, had walked on water, and had healed with water. Water was indeed special. She prayed it would be so yet again.

Carefully she removed the three ampullae from the bag she'd made with her veil. She arranged them in the center of the altar in front before signing the cross above them.

As she turned and peeked out of the alcove into the tunnel, she waited, hoping she could feel Dawson's presence in the similar fashion that she had yesterday right before he'd appeared in the garden. It was almost as if she'd sensed him nearby, possibly heard him.

Holding her breath, she waited. What she really wanted was another visit, even if short. Somehow, even in the brief interludes with him, she sensed a kindness and concern toward her, though she was naught but a stranger. At least, she hoped she'd sensed that . . .

After a moment of hearing and feeling nothing, she moved out into the passageway. She couldn't waste any more time, had to return to the closet before the monks finished their midday prayers. She cast a last glance at the ampullae on the altar but then stopped and drew in a sharp breath.

The ampullae were no longer there.

She searched the area, the floor, the walls, the small bench to no avail. The containers had vanished into air, just as Dawson had.

Her heart did a strange flip. Did their disappearance mean Dawson had them? She could only pray it was so.

• ● •

Dawson leaned against the rental car, his muscles tensing with every passing moment in the afternoon sunshine.

Ten minutes had elapsed. Ten minutes was long enough, wasn't it? They'd decided it would look too suspicious if they all three went in again. In fact, they'd debated sending in Chloe by herself but had realized it would take her too long to pick the lock on her own, so this time Acey had gone with her.

The Hamin were nowhere in sight, which hopefully meant they'd believed Chloe's excuse about the need for more snaps.

Even so, Dawson kept expecting them to pull into the car park of St. Peter's. He wasn't sure what he'd do if they showed up and tried to interfere. He had the feeling he'd end up revealing his healing.

As he waited, he'd hoped to feel the whispering sensation that told him someone from the past was nearby. He wanted to feel Philippa's presence, and after his intimate dreams of her last night, he longed to see her again. But he had none of the sensations he'd experienced previously. In fact, a part of him questioned whether he'd really seen her at all or if he'd simply imagined it.

Another minute ticked by and then two before the tower door opened and Chloe stepped out followed by Acey. Dawson pretended to stare straight ahead and not notice them, but he was acutely aware of every detail—the gentle way Acey guided her at the small of her back, the pulsing of the vein in his neck that showed his worry, the steady pace of his walk that was a testament to how hard he'd worked to recover from his injury and get used to his prosthesis.

Had they found any holy water? Or had they been too late? Perhaps the Hamin had figured out their plans and had already gone down into the tunnel and gotten to the holy water first.

As the two neared him, Dawson caught the glint of sunlight on a windshield of a car slowly winding its way into the car park. Was it the Hamin? The driver looked decidedly Arabian.

If the Hamin were just coming now, that had to mean they hadn't been at the site during the past thirty minutes to interfere with any transfers of the holy water.

As much as he wanted to turn and size up the thugs who had been trailing him for the past weeks—perhaps were even the two who'd beaten him up—he stared straight ahead like a partially blind person would do. He had a performance to enact, and he needed to do it well to convince anyone who was watching and listening that he was still a bitter and troubled man.

"Ready to head to the next place?" Acey passed him by, and

as he did so, he slipped something into Dawson's hand—a small container that was no bigger than a travel-size shampoo or lotion bottle.

Acey swung open the driver's door, but before he could get inside, Dawson shoved his friend so he stumbled away from the car.

"Hey, man, what was that for?" Acey's question was loaded with indignation.

Dawson scowled. "I'm sick of being left behind."

"I told you we were just popping in for a few minutes for Chloe."

"And you thought I'd slow you down. As usual."

"That's not it." Acey raised his hands as if that could magically calm the situation. "I swear."

"Admit it. After only one day of sightseeing, you're already tired of me tagging along."

Acey expelled an exasperated sigh and shook his head.

"We didn't mean to make you feel left out, Dawson." Chloe jumped into the conversation, her words coming out in a rush, as if rehearsed.

"You never mean to." Dawson inched his way into the open driver's door of the rental. "But the truth is, I can handle myself just fine."

"We know that." Chloe's tone was too cheerful. She was a terrible actress, and he had to put an end to the performance now before she gave away their act.

Shaking his head with as much disgust as he could muster, he ducked down into the car. "If you know that," he mimicked, "then you won't mind if I drive to the next location."

"Drive?" Acey sounded genuinely panicked. Either he was afraid Chloe's bad acting would ruin their cover too, or he'd missed his calling to become a movie star.

Dawson fumbled with the keys, and in the next instant, he turned over the ignition.

"You can't drive." Acey stumbled toward him.

"Watch me." Dawson didn't bother to close the door and jerked the gear lever into Drive. In the same motion, he rammed his foot against the gas pedal. The car jerked forward, the tires peeling against the gravel.

He pretended to lose control of the wheel, all the while guiding the car toward the trees at the northeast end with his knee while uncorking the ampulla with his hands. He couldn't lose his hold on it until after the accident, needed Acey and Chloe to find it right away and hide all traces before the Hamin started investigating.

Behind him, Acey and Chloe shouted after him, "Stop! Hit the brake!"

As the trees loomed closer, he didn't slow down. Instead, he lifted the ancient container and prepared to drink it, hoping his body concealed his motion from the newcomers.

His timing had to be just right. As the car careened toward the nearest tree, he finally tipped the liquid into his mouth and propelled himself from the open door.

He hit the ground, and as he did, the world went black.

- 12 -

"WE MUST VENTURE TO THE WELLS." Philippa strained to break free from Joanna's hold. The bells were ringing for compline. That meant sunset had come and gone, and the monks were assembling for their last prayers before retiring to their pallets.

"We cannot leave right now." Joanna slipped around Philippa as though to block her way. "The moment we step outside, we shall be spotted, then our efforts to escape will most certainly come to naught."

Philippa stared through the blackness in the direction of the door, despair weighing on her more heavily with each passing second. She was hungry, thirsty, and tired. And now instead of being in the woodland by the twin wells the way she'd arranged with Dawson, she was stuck in a hidden room underneath the crypt.

"We will have to make an attempt to leave eventually." She straightened her shoulders, refusing to let the circumstances crush her. She would continue to practice gratitude, as was her habit. And she would cling to the hope that they could find a way to meet with Dawson. After all, Providence had worked a miracle in passing along the ampullae. He could surely orchestrate another miracle.

"We shall wait until the middle of the night." Joanna spoke decisively. "Then we shall traverse the tunnels and discover another way out of the priory."

"If one tunnel exit is locked, surely all of them will be."

"We cannot know for certain unless we check."

Philippa wasn't sure if her cousin's plan would amount to anything. But Joanna was right about the peril of sneaking around the priory aboveground. Someone would most certainly notice them no matter how careful they were.

Staying underground and escaping by way of the tunnels would be the better alternative. If they could manage the feat, then they'd look for Dawson. They would benefit from his aid in getting away from Walsingham undetected and helping them to find another place to take refuge.

She lowered herself to the bottom step. "I have not said it oft enough. You are a good friend, Joanna."

The shuffling of steps and swish of linen told her Joanna had taken a seat on one of the steps too. "You have been like a sister to me."

"Likewise. Though we have experienced losses, I am grateful we have been able to spend more time together. I shall cherish the memories." The long walks together through the parks surrounding Thursford Castle, the days embroidering in the sunny parlor between their bedchambers, the early morns distributing leftover food to the poor, the hours praying in the chapel. They'd had many whispered conversations, sharing friendship, encouragement, tears, and hopes for a better future.

"I shall miss you," Joanna whispered as though they were already parting ways.

"We shall yet have the chance to make more memories together."

Joanna released a soft, unladylike snort. "You always see the brighter side of every situation."

"And you always see the practical side." Philippa smiled. "We have made a good team."

"Just like our mothers."

"They were so happy together, were they not?" Philippa's mother had died first, during a third attempt at giving birth. Philippa had been only ten at the time, but she'd witnessed the way the loss had affected her father, turning him morose and silent and distant. When he'd died of a chest seizure two years later, Philippa had felt as though she'd lost him long before that.

After the death of her father, she'd gone to live with her uncle and her mother's twin sister at Thursford, along with Joanna and her four siblings. After being an only child for so long, Philippa had thrived amongst the busy chaos of her new home. And her aunt had doted on her too . . . until the dear woman had a freak riding accident and died of injuries sustained after being thrown from her horse.

Not long after, Uncle had started making plans for Philippa to marry Robert Neville.

"I never expected to be on the run from Father," Joanna whispered, her voice raw, revealing the hurt deep inside at having been betrayed by a man she'd believed had her best interest at heart.

"And I never expected to be on the run from him either. He was always a good man." Philippa didn't need to say more.

They both knew that the man had lost his moral compass the day his wife had passed away. It was as if she'd been the steady presence of good in his life that kept him from giving way to evil. "I have faith he may yet see the error of his ways."

"I have no faith in him at all." Joanna's tone was bitter. The lack of faith and the bitterness weren't unexpected, not after he'd failed to form a match for Joanna with the man she'd loved.

"Do you think our mothers were happy in their marriages?" Philippa had always believed her mother had made a heart match with her father. But as a young girl, what had she known about love compared to what she knew now?

"I like to think my mother was happy," Joanna said through a yawn. "But I cannot see how she ever cared about a man like my father."

"He seemed to treat her kindly."

"Kindness is not enough. When I get married, I shall do so for love or not at all."

Joanna had made such declarations in the past, especially when they'd both been younger. But now that she was nigh to twenty and two, was such a dream possible? "I admire your expectations and your determination, Cousin. I truly do. But I cannot help but wonder if at times you aim too high."

"Perhaps you aim too low."

"Perhaps."

"When you are away from my father's control, then you will no longer have to settle for a loveless marriage and instead will be free to give your heart to a man of your own choosing, a man who adores you body, soul, and spirit."

Philippa couldn't keep from smiling at Joanna's passion. "If such a man exists, I would like to meet him."

"I pray that you will."

A part of Philippa's heart yearned to experience that kind of love with a man. But she'd already learned life didn't turn out the way they wished. In her case, if she could avoid a union with Lord Godwin Kempe, she would be satisfied with that.

•　•　•

Dawson's head pounded with a force that propelled him to his knees. In the next instant, he retched into the grass. He heaved several times until his stomach was empty.

As he sat back on his heels, the darkness of night hedged him in so completely he felt disoriented. Where was he? And what had happened to him?

He blinked rapidly to the sight of a tree a foot away. Faint starlight—or moonlight—filtered past the leaves overhead to reveal not only the one tree but also an entire woodland spreading out all around. The distinct scraping trill of crickets filled the balmy night, as did the scent of damp soil and grass.

Everything came together to inform him that he was someplace he'd never been before. In fact, his senses were on overdrive with all the new sounds and smells and textures, all so different that he had no doubt he'd made it to the past.

He waited for the dizziness to assault him, the rushing, the whispering that had happened during his past overlaps. But this time, he felt a calm he'd never before known along with vitality and strength.

His mind replayed the last few moments he remembered. The fake fight he'd staged with Acey and Chloe, the car accident he'd initiated, then drinking the holy water and diving out of the moving vehicle.

He stood and felt dampness along his scalp. He reached up a hand and winced at a cut near his hairline. He'd been injured during the crossover, had hit his head, maybe even suffered a concussion. But from what he could tell, the gash wasn't too deep, was even starting to dry.

Dry?

A sudden panic seized him. How long had he been out? The darkness meant that sunset had already passed. But how late was he in meeting Philippa by the twin wells where he'd instructed her to go?

He tapped at his digital watch, but the bright light was gone. He guessed his modern devices wouldn't assist him in the past, that he might as well dispose of them before drawing too many questions.

Quickly he shed his watch, phone, wallet, and spare change, stuffing them in the hole at the base of a tree and covering the spot with brush. As he removed his Glock and tested it, nothing on the gun moved, not the trigger, not the magazine release, not even the slide.

He tucked the gun away with the rest of his possessions, keeping only the knife sheathed in his boot along with a smaller pocketknife in his jacket.

Then he made his way to the edge of the woodland and peered out, easily finding St. Peter's in the same place that it stood in the present day. From what he could tell by the faint moonlight, the church was fuller, with wings on either side of the building.

He guessed sunset had passed hours ago. If Philippa had shown up by the wells, she was likely no longer there, had probably retired for the night.

Should he wait for the morning and seek her out then? What if he walked up to the priory doors and asked for her? He could make up a story about how she was needed at his mum's home, that he'd come to escort her there.

But waiting would mean wasting precious time. After all, he only had five days before Acey gave him the first of the two doses of holy water to wake him up. Already he'd slept longer than he'd anticipated.

Could he break into the priory using the tunnel that started at St. Peter's?

Through the dark shadows, he studied the old church, seeing nothing out of the ordinary. All appeared quiet and deserted.

Even so, he crept cautiously across the open churchyard past the gravestones, until he reached the building. There he flattened himself against the wall and moved along the perimeter toward the tower. As he rounded the structure and caught sight of a man leaning against the tower door, he pulled back abruptly.

He waited several seconds, then peeked again, taking note of the man's strange clothing, including a feltlike cap with flaps covering his ears, a long shirt made of chain mail, loose leggings, pointed leather ankle boots. And naturally, he wore a weapons belt containing a sheathed sword strapped around his middle.

His head was tilted back, and his eyes were closed—at least from what Dawson could assess. Clearly the man wasn't expecting a threat from outside the chapel. That meant one thing: He was standing watch for anyone trying to leave the tunnel . . . perhaps Philippa and her lady friend?

Philippa had indicated that she might not be safe at the priory much longer before her uncle came after her to take her home and make her marry the man of his choosing. What if her uncle had already arrived and this guard was one of his men? It was also possible the guard worked for the priory.

Either way, his presence probably meant Philippa was hiding and men were still hunting for her. If they'd found her, they would have no need to post this guard . . . and possibly others like him at various exits in hopes of capturing her as she tried to sneak out.

Dawson's speculations might be wrong. The parish of St. Peter's Church might always post a guard at the tower door of a church that was on the outskirts of town and deserted. What did he know about the Middle Ages and the customs?

Whatever the case, he had to find a way to disable the guard. This entrance was likely the best one to use for getting into the priory. And if Philippa had gone into hiding, then it was possible she was down in the tunnels someplace. After all, she'd placed the ampullae into the alcove earlier in the day, which had to mean she'd had access to the tunnel. That also meant she'd had access to the wellspring.

If he could locate the wellspring, perhaps he'd have a chance at finding her. He was good with picking up on clues. That's one of the reasons why he'd excelled during his intel days in the army. And even though the tunnels would be dark and he wouldn't have a light, he'd still be able to navigate, thanks to the recent years of learning to do so with his blindness.

He paused. Had he really just found a way to be grateful for the past eight years of not seeing? He wanted to scoff that he'd experienced nothing but misery during that time. But maybe he needed to start considering the ways the hardship had benefitted him.

After assessing the situation more carefully, he crept back around the building to approach the guard from the other direction—a shorter route and hopefully less noticeable. He was within two feet when the bloke opened his eyes and shifted, having heard or sensed another presence.

Before the fellow could react, Dawson lunged and slammed the man's head back against the stone tower hard enough to daze him. With two more well-placed hits, he knocked the man unconscious.

He blindfolded the man with a scrap of linen. After a quick search around the tower room and the storage closet underneath, Dawson located a bell rope and bound the fellow with it, but not before divesting him of the chain mail and weapons belt.

Even though Dawson didn't know how to use a sword, he donned the mail shirt and weapon anyway. It couldn't hurt him, would perhaps help him to blend in better to the time period. Once in costume, he descended into the storage room to find the door was locked from inside the tunnel.

He was able to wedge the door open enough to slip his

hand through. With some finagling, he maneuvered the ancient padlock around so he could access it. Then using the pin from his pocketknife, he poked and jiggled at the keyhole, guessing that the interior mechanism wasn't as complicated as a modern padlock. A moment later, he was rewarded with the click of the lock opening.

Once the door was free of the chain, he cautiously entered the tunnel. Damp darkness surrounded him, but he made his way by feeling along the wall, making use of the internal sense of direction he'd developed over the years. He followed the tunnel toward the priory, bypassing crossroads that led in other directions, perhaps to other churches.

The trek was a little less than a mile, and he imagined Philippa as she'd made the trip earlier in the day to place the holy water there for him. Where would she be now? Should he try checking the crypt?

Once the tunnel began to widen and the ceiling lengthened so that he no longer had to crouch, he guessed he was nearing the priory. It wasn't until he came upon a larger room that contained caskets that he knew he'd finally reached the priory crypt. As he crept through the chamber, he felt an internal tug, as though his body was drawing him forward. Did that mean she was nearby? That, somehow, they shared a connection that had formed during the overlaps?

"Philippa?" he whispered. "It's me, Dawson." He felt his way from casket to casket, letting his fingers do the seeing for him. But as with every other room, he could find nothing to show him where she was hiding—if she was still hiding. He couldn't rule out the possibility that she'd already slipped past the guards on duty and was now free.

As the wall guided him to the far end, he paused. If the wellspring was under the crypt, then perhaps a secret passageway led there. But where would the door to such a passageway be hidden?

He skimmed his hands along the final wall, this time searching for a door—likely a half door, since that's what the others had been so far. As his fingers passed over a slight depression in the stone, he halted and followed the line.

"Finally," he whispered, moving downward until he found another indent, slightly bigger. He pried at it until it swung open. As he crawled inside, the tugging in his gut grew stronger. He had to be getting closer to her.

~ 13 ~

SOMEONE WAS IN THE STORAGE chamber above.

Philippa pressed herself against the wall at the bottom of the steps beside Joanna, wishing she could be brave like her cousin. But her hands trembled within the folds of her cloak.

So far none of the other searchers had located the door to the storage room behind the raised caskets. She guessed they'd been too focused on checking inside the caskets to notice the secret door.

But this new person had not only found the door but was crawling through the storage chamber.

"Philippa?" a man called softly.

Something inside her seemed to leap in recognition. Was it Dawson? She started to move, but Joanna grabbed her arm and pinched her through her sleeve.

"'Tis Dawson," Philippa whispered.

Joanna's hold wavered. "How can you be certain?"

Philippa used the moment of indecision to break free.

"Wait." Joanna's whisper lacked conviction.

Philippa started up the steps, using the wall to guide her through the darkness. Her heart beat a strange rhythm, one of anticipation and eagerness. He'd come for her. He was seeking her out. What other man had ever done something like that for her?

She reached the landing at the same moment that she heard the door open. "Dawson? Is it really you?"

"Yes," he whispered in return. "How are you?"

"I had begun to fear I would never leave the priory." Without any light, she couldn't see him, but she felt him push through on his hands and knees. A moment later he rose, and one of his hands glided up her arm, as though he was reassuring himself of her presence. In the next instant, he gently grasped her other arm.

"I was hoping to find you here."

She had a sudden need to lift her fingers to his face and let them explore the contours so she could test whether he was mortal or apparition. She still wasn't sure. "Are you here to stay this time?"

"I have five days."

"'Tis not long, but I thank you for using your brief visit to aid me and my cousin."

"Then the other woman is with you?"

"Yes, Joanna."

He paused as though he was scanning the darkness behind her. Was he looking for Joanna or the wellspring?

"Are you both ready to go?" he asked.

"Most certainly. Shall I light a lantern?"

"It will be safer without."

Joanna started up the steps. "And how will you find your way in the dark without any light?"

Dawson's hold on Philippa's arm wavered, as though he

wasn't sure what to tell them.

Philippa hesitated too. Should she use more caution like Joanna? Or perhaps this man deserved her faith and trust until he proved unworthy of it.

She squeezed his hand.

The contact seemed to give him permission to speak freely. "I spent the past eight years mostly blind. The holy water has recently restored my sight."

Chills prickled Philippa's skin.

Joanna, thankfully, didn't scoff at the statement.

"You are indeed blessed." Philippa pressed his hand again, a strange sense of awe wafting through her, the same she'd felt when the holy water had disappeared from the prayer alcove. The hand of Providence was at work. Of that she had no doubt.

Dawson released his grip on her arm but then clasped her hand within his, settling his fingers as though he had no intention of letting go.

Her heart skipped an odd beat. And she was suddenly attuned to the warmth and pressure of his skin against hers.

"I can guide us safely back to the tunnel entrance without a light." He tugged her forward. For a moment, all she could feel was the strength of his grasp, the muscles in his hand, the determination in his every move. The connection was strangely intimate, one that made her aware of how closely he stood.

"Ready?" His question held concern, as though he truly did care whether she was ready for this new but dangerous adventure they were about to embark upon.

"Yes." She'd sensed his kindness during their previous brief interactions, but this time she felt the full force of it and was slightly overwhelmed by it, by him.

He exited through the half door into the storage chamber, the movement forcing him to release her hand. She crouched low and made her way to the other side. As she straightened, she could feel him waiting.

His fingers skimmed her arm before clasping her hand. She sensed he meant nothing by it except to guide her through the dark. But the contact and gentleness of his touch was new, different, almost exhilarating.

As he led her forward through the storage chamber and crypt then into the tunnels, she made no effort to extricate her hand, had no desire to. He maneuvered expertly in the darkness, whispering instructions to "watch your step," "duck here," or "we're turning."

Joanna stayed close, her hand upon Philippa's shoulder, and they traveled swiftly—although Philippa suspected Dawson had slowed his pace for their sake. The tunnel gradually grew lighter as they neared the end, revealing Dawson ahead of her, his shoulders hunched to keep from bumping the tunnel ceiling.

"We're here." He paused at the doorway she'd seen earlier, the one that had been previously chained and locked but was now open. Had Dawson done this?

Still holding her hand, he pushed through the exit with such confidence that she had no doubt he'd been the one to figure out a way past the lock and chain. As they moved into what appeared to be another storage chamber, she could only watch him with growing admiration.

When they reached a set of stairs, he stopped and listened. Then he squeezed her hand and whispered, "Wait here. I want to make sure the guard is still tied up."

She nodded, unable to form words to express her appreciation for all he'd done and was still doing.

He hastened up the steps and disappeared.

Joanna sidled close. "You like him."

"I barely know him."

"You are smitten. 'Tis easy to tell, even in the dark."

Was she? She'd never been smitten with a man before, not the same way Joanna had been with Lance. "If I am, 'tis only because he is a good man."

"Take care, Philippa. You are accustomed to men using you and need not give your heart to the first one who shows you an ounce of kindness."

Dawson ducked back through the opening above, and Philippa reached for her cousin's hand and pressed it in warning, having no wish for him to overhear their conversation.

She wasn't giving her heart away. Most certainly not. But she didn't have to deny herself the pleasure of the feelings he was evoking within her, did she? Feelings that she'd always wanted to have for a man but never had. It wouldn't hurt to enjoy his company. After all, he'd indicated he would only be visiting for five days and after that would be gone again.

He started back toward them. "We're good to go."

With faint light falling upon him, she allowed herself to admire him. He was tall with a strong frame, broad shoulders, slender torso, and powerful aura. His hair was as dark as a rook and cut short. He lacked a full beard like most noblemen, but he had a distinct layer of scruff on his chin and cheeks.

As he reached her, he held out a hand, this time giving her a choice. Now that they had some light, he was making sure she knew that he wouldn't hold her hand if she didn't want him to.

The choice was all too easy. She willingly returned her hand to his. As his fingers wrapped around hers again, warm pleasure spilled through her middle. She liked his touch. She could own freely to it, and she liked it enough that she wanted more.

Such a desire felt brazen, and she chastised herself as she followed him up the stairs into the closet. She'd heard the stories of the decadence and debauchery at court, where noblemen and women engaged in illicit affairs. She'd always been relieved that she was away from the scandals, that she could maintain the piety of a chaste life without taint or temptation. She wouldn't change now.

As they entered the tower room, they passed by a guard tied to the center post, his hands and feet bound. His eyes were also covered, which was an intelligent idea, one that would prevent the man from witnessing who had bound him, keeping Dawson's identity a secret, at least until they were away from Walsingham. Hopefully by then, they would be somewhere safe.

Would she ever find that place? She'd thought the priory would be a refuge. But she'd only found herself trapped once again.

Once outside, he didn't release her hand, and now that they were out in the open with the moonlight shining upon them, she could feel Joanna watching her, likely staring directly at her hand within Dawson's.

"Where are we going?" Joanna asked as pointedly as always.

"To Lady Wilkin in Barsham."

"You claim she is your mother."

"Yes."

"I was not aware she had borne a son."

Dawson had narrowed his gaze upon the surrounding open area to the south where the River Stiffkey could guide them to Barsham. "If she's home, she'll welcome me."

"If?" Joanna spoke the word tersely.

"She was recently visiting my sister in Canterbury. And I can't guarantee that she'll be back yet."

Philippa cast Joanna a silent plea, one she hoped communicated the need to be more gracious to this man who'd risked his safety to help free them.

Joanna conveniently ignored her and pretended to adjust her wimple.

Dawson drew Philippa with him as he started around the church building toward the woods in the opposite direction of the river. He apparently believed they'd be safer going a more roundabout way to Barsham.

He moved swiftly and silently, and she allowed him to lead her, her thoughts focused entirely upon him and the way her hand felt in his. Only after they were ensconced in the woodland did he stop. This time he released her hand and took a step back, glancing between Joanna and her.

The shadows of the woodland prevented her from having a clear view of his features, but she sensed something was bothering him. "What is it?" She had a strange need to clasp his hand again but refrained.

"Your head coverings." He reached for her veil but then let his hand fall away. "If someone glances our direction, they may spot the white."

"Should we remove them?"

"It would be safer and draw less notice."

"Very well." She tucked her finger into the first pin and pulled it loose, but while fishing for the next pin, she fumbled to hold on to everything, and her veil slipped into her face.

Dawson held out a hand. "Would you like me to hold the pins?"

She paused.

Beside her, Joanna did too.

Usually Philippa relied upon a maidservant or Joanna for help with her hair. Never had a man offered to aid in the task. But he seemed sincere. And his expression was filled with only kindness. Even so, his offer was most unusual.

"I can assist you, Philippa." Joanna was efficiently taking off her own wimple.

"I don't mind." Dawson reached up for the pin Philippa was loosening, leaning into a shaft of moonlight that revealed his features more clearly than she'd seen them yet—well-defined cheekbones that tapered to a rounded chin, a fine nose that drew attention to an even finer mouth. And his eyes . . . they were a mesmerizing shade of green, surrounded by dark lashes and brows that somehow had the power to make her breathless and weak.

He was more than handsome. He was simply divine. And a new and strange flutter wove through her insides. Light. Airy. Weightless.

With their fingers brushing together against the pin, he stalled.

His attention dropped to her face, the moonlight illuminating her in the same measure it was him. Could he see interest? How captivated she was by his appearance?

Slowly he made a visual circuit from her cheeks and nose to her mouth and chin, then up to her forehead before dropping to her eyes.

As their gazes collided, the flutters began again, but faster.

She was definitely experiencing a strong physical attraction to him. But how could she feel something for this man she'd just met when she'd never felt anything for her husband during the months they'd been together?

Dawson's eyes darkened, the green deepening with wanting—or at least she believed it to be so. Except that in the next instant, he quickly withdrew his hand from the pin and cleared his throat.

She finished twisting the pin free, and as soon as she did, he divested her of it, careful not to touch her this time.

"My thanks," she whispered.

He didn't respond save to leave his palm open with the pins, awaiting the others.

Joanna had ceased her efforts and was staring back and forth between them, her brows rising ever higher.

Philippa removed the next pin. She was sure to hear an earful from her cousin later, but for now, she felt helpless to do anything but let this current of attraction take her where it would.

- 14 -

DAWSON SWALLOWED HARD, trying to push down the desire that had arisen swiftly and intensely. He shouldn't have allowed himself to take in Philippa's beauty, but when she'd studied him with such open curiosity and admiration, he'd been helpless to resist doing the same.

The trouble was, her beauty was addictive. One look wasn't enough. Now that he'd taken in her sweet-natured face, that dusting of freckles, and the light gray-blue eyes, he only wanted more.

After living for so many years without being able to see a beautiful woman, he found it difficult to ignore the voice inside telling him that he deserved to stare at her as long as he wanted. That he had a right to admire every detail of her, every nuance of her emotions, every tiny move of her lips, every shade of light that changed in her eyes.

But he focused instead on his palm and the pins he was holding so he wouldn't look back in her eyes and see the interest there, interest she wasn't making any effort to hide.

It wouldn't be fair for him to encourage her. Nothing could come of such interest when he was leaving in five days. Besides, now wasn't the time or place to get carried away by his desires—not when she was vulnerable and not when he needed to concentrate on escaping from Walsingham and traveling to Barsham before the light of dawn made hiding more difficult.

She tentatively placed another pin in his palm, this one encrusted with a pattern of emerald leaves.

"It's pretty." He examined it, the moonlight making it glint.

"'Twas once my mother's." The hint of sadness told him she'd lost her mother.

"Has she been gone long?"

"Nigh eleven years." For several moments, while she finished unpinning her head covering, she explained Joanna's relation as cousin, that their mothers had been twin sisters and had already passed away.

"Your father?" He couldn't keep from staring as she finally took the head covering away, revealing her light-brown hair coiled up with even more pins.

"My father is also deceased."

"Which is why your uncle is in charge?" As a young woman in the 1300s, she would most likely have very few rights.

"He has been attempting to regain control ever since my husband died."

Husband? Philippa had been married?

"But I am resisting Uncle's efforts, as you are well aware."

What kind of man had she married? Had he been a good husband? Had she loved him? The questions crowded his mind so that he didn't know where to even start asking them.

"As a widow, I have rights." Philippa glanced at Joanna.

Her cousin nodded curtly as though to encourage Philippa to remain strong.

"You're too young to be a widow." The words were out before he could censure them. She'd lost her husband, and all he could say was that she was too young? He was an insensitive cad. "I'm sorry for your loss. I can only imagine how difficult his death was."

She paused in folding the linen cloth and began fingering it and creasing it without looking up at him. "I wish his death had been difficult." Her words were soft, almost inaudible. "But I regret that we did not share a fondness for each other."

Joanna expelled an exasperated sigh. "What Philippa means is that Lord Neville, her late husband, was cold and distant."

"He was still a good man," Philippa chided.

So she hadn't loved her late husband? The thought should have made him sad for her. But instead he was relieved. But why? Because she wasn't grieving? Why did he care whether Philippa might or might not have had feelings for her late husband? Her previous and present relationships had no bearing on him.

"And you?" she asked shyly. "Have you a wife and children?"

"No." His response was too rapid, but the longer he was around this beautiful woman, the more he felt like a bumbling adolescent. "After the injury that caused my blindness, I wasn't doing well . . . wasn't stable enough to be in a relationship . . ." That was putting it mildly. The truth was, he'd felt sorry for himself and let his self-pity take him down a path toward destruction.

If he could turn back the clock, he would take the road Acey had, one of making the best of his limitations. His mum had been pushing him that direction, and all he'd done was resist her efforts at making him independent. Finally, she'd moved back to Fakenham. Sure, she'd probably needed to for her work. But deep inside, he'd known she'd done it for him, to cut him loose and force him to stop relying on her for so much.

Of course, she'd been right to do it. But at the time, he'd felt helpless and alone and resentful, not unlike how he'd felt after his dad had abandoned their family years earlier. Then, after Mum had gone missing, he'd blamed himself. Maybe if he'd made more efforts to become independent and hadn't been so demanding, she wouldn't have moved and put herself in danger.

"You have never been wed?" Joanna asked with a thread of disbelief in her tone.

"Is that a crime?" He supposed most men in the Middle Ages were married by the time they were twenty-nine.

"No, 'tis not a crime." Philippa answered him seriously while shooting Joanna another look of censure.

Joanna just shrugged. "Now that we have established that neither of you are currently married, you may both continue being enraptured of one another."

"Joanna!" Philippa hissed.

Enraptured? Was that what he was feeling for Philippa? He wanted to deny it, but what was the point? It had been so long since he'd interacted with a woman that he was rusty at it. No doubt his clumsiness would push her away more than draw her in.

"We may as well be forthright." Joanna took Philippa's

head covering and tucked them both into a satchel she wore slung over her shoulder and across her body. "There is no sense in pretending you are not fascinated with Dawson."

Philippa grew more rigid, and mortification rolled off her in waves.

Although he was accustomed to bluntness from his sister and mom, he didn't want Philippa feeling uncomfortable because of him. He had to find a way to alleviate her embarrassment. He held the pins out to her and offered a smile at the same time. "I won't deny I'm fascinated with you. What man wouldn't be?"

"You and every man in England," Joanna said with certainty, retrieving the pins from him before Philippa could and slipping them into her satchel too.

"You exaggerate, Cousin. And if there is aught truth in what you say, 'tis only because I am coveted for my wealth."

He'd presumed she was wealthy, probably titled. Why else would her uncle be so interested in her match if not for what he stood to gain?

Joanna picked at dust or cobwebs that clung to Philippa's garments. "Even if you were a pauper, any man would still have you if he could."

Philippa shook her head.

But Joanna spoke again before Philippa could. "The king himself would take you as his mistress if he were but a few years older."

"Hush now." Philippa's tone was softly scolding, and she fidgeted with her braid, clearly not seeing or understanding just how appealing she was. But her unawareness added to her charm.

She wouldn't seriously consider becoming the king's mistress if that was a possibility, would she? No doubt the king already had a match arranged for him to a princess somewhere. Yet marriage wouldn't keep the king from commanding a woman into his bed. The prospect of that happening to this beautiful and gentle woman was too awful to consider.

He knew they needed to get moving and make use of the darkness of the night for as long as it lasted. But for a reason he didn't understand, he wanted to reassure her. "You deserve much more than becoming a mistress to the king or being forced into a marriage by your uncle. You should have a man who will love and cherish you above his own life."

Philippa dipped her head, her lips curving delicately into the beginning of a smile. If the light had been sufficient, he guessed he would have been able to see pink in her cheeks. The very sight of her demure innocence sent a shaft of heat through him, so unlike any desire he'd ever felt before that he had an almost visceral need to reach for her and . . . and what?

He took a step back, trying to diminish the sharpness of his longing. Joanna wasn't exaggerating. Any man would have her if he could.

"Why don't you want to marry the man your uncle has chosen for you?" The question was out before he could stifle his curiosity.

She lifted her chin, the action somehow showing an inner strength. "I refuse to be a part of my uncle's plotting of treason against the king."

He'd expected her to tell him that she wasn't attracted to the man or he was cruel or she didn't like something about his character. But treason added a new level of seriousness to her dilemma.

"Tell me more." He started forward finally.

While they hiked through the woodland, she kept to his heels with Joanna bringing up the rear. The two explained the political situation as best they could, making him wish he'd paid better attention during history classes when they studied King Richard II. But all the old kings had blended together in his mind, too many Edwards, Richards, and Henrys to keep them all straight.

But now, with Philippa's future at stake, he wanted to understand the situation. As the two women shared, he learned that Lord Hugo Deighton was not only Philippa's uncle but was Joanna's father and had aligned himself with a group of older noblemen who didn't like King Richard or the young men he'd surrounded himself with. Apparently the older noblemen wanted a more mature king to lead their country and had their sights set on Henry Bolingbroke, who was also of royalty.

The marriage of Philippa to Lord Godwin Kempe, one of Richard's young advisors, would provide her uncle a way to infiltrate and exert more influence upon the king. Ultimately, her uncle hoped to depose the king and put someone else on the throne.

As they walked, Dawson was tempted to reach for her hand again. But after the candid conversation about Philippa's attractiveness, he supposed both women would see right through his efforts at *helping* to what it really was—desire for her. Plain and simple.

Not that he didn't want to help her. The longer he was with her and the more he heard about her uncle's ambitions, the more he wanted to find a solution for her troubles.

"What will your kin say at our appearance?" Philippa asked as he veered toward the south—at least, from what he could tell by the position of the stars.

"I admit, I've been away from my mum for four years." He paused at the edge of a grassy field, one that hadn't been planted in the spring but instead was overgrown with weeds and flowers.

Joanna stopped beside him and eyed him warily. "Then you do not know what kind of reception we shall receive?"

"She'll receive me." In spite of the strained relationship he'd had with his mum during her last days, she'd never stopped loving him. She made that abundantly clear when she visited him on the weekends.

Even after the passing of the years, she wouldn't turn him—or these women—away. He was certain of it. But how long would they be able to stay with her? Probably not indefinitely. Taking refuge with her was only a temporary solution to a bigger problem.

"She will be heartily glad to see her son." Philippa's tone held a note of censure aimed at Joanna.

He slid a sideways glance at Philippa, who'd positioned herself on his other side. Her eyes were wide with a trust he wasn't sure he deserved. For too many years, he'd done nothing but let the people in his life down. What if he let her down too?

He shifted his gaze to the field ahead. The night had grown

silent, as if the nocturnal creatures had settled down to sleep. He estimated a couple of hours remained before dawn.

Could they reach Barsham before then? They were taking a long way around to avoid the roads and thoroughfares. But maybe he'd been worried about drawing attention for nothing. The nightlife for people in the Middle Ages was different than in modern times where the pubs and clubs kept partygoers out until all hours.

Whatever the case, they had to keep going and get as far from Walsingham as they could before someone discovered the guard tied up at St. Peter's. It wouldn't take long after that for a search party to be on their trail, likely well-trained knights on horseback who knew how to track and would stop at nothing to get Philippa back, especially since she was so valuable to her uncle.

It was up to him to keep her safe. That was his mission, and he couldn't get distracted by anything else, including her.

~ 15 ~

PHILIPPA HAD NEVER MET A MAN quite like Dawson. He interacted with her as though he valued what she had to say, as if her future was important, and as if he truly cared that she had some input into it.

From behind, she mostly had a view of his back. He held himself with confidence and purpose beneath the chain mail hauberk. His stride was equally confident and purposeful. But he wasn't domineering or arrogant. He oft stopped to consult with Joanna and her almost as if they were equals.

As he led the way through an open meadow, he glanced from side to side, constantly assessing everything around them as well as in the distance. He was clearly a sharp man who didn't miss many details. Losing his eyesight must have been devastating.

She wanted to question him more about it, but she didn't want to probe too personally too soon. She also wished to ask him about himself, about his relationship with his mother and sister, where he'd been living recently. But again, the questions seemed too forward.

At the forefront of all unknowns about this man was his connection to the holy water. He'd obviously retrieved the ampullae she'd left for him in the alcove in the tunnel. But how had he been able to get the containers without her seeing him? Did he have the special powers of a saint or angel that allowed him to come and go to places at will without being seen?

"So, your father lives in Thursford?" He directed his words to Joanna, who was a much better conversationalist and had been answering all of Dawson's queries before Philippa could manage to think of an answer.

"He has a home there as well as one in London."

"And Philippa's late husband's home?"

"He possessed a castle near Norwich as well as several other manor homes throughout England."

"Why can't she live in those homes anymore?"

"First she must gain her independence. To that end, we have sent a petition to the bishop to allow Philippa to take the widow's vow."

"And what's that?"

"'Tis a custom for widows pledging themselves in service to the church similar to the process of becoming a nun."

"You want to become a nun?" He tossed this question to her directly this time, his dark brows rising as though this piece of news was unexpected.

As with every occasion he spoke to her, she felt both shy and warm at the same time. "I shall do so temporarily."

"And what will you do once you're done being a temporary nun?"

"I shall then have the freedom to choose my own husband."

"Then you do want to get remarried someday, just not now?"

"If Uncle chooses a better match, I would not oppose it."

Joanna released a snort. "Philippa wants to have children more than she wants a husband. In fact, if she could have babies without marrying a man, she would."

At her cousin's bold words, mortification spilled through Philippa, and she focused on the long grass crunching beneath her steps. "'Tis not true."

Dawson was quiet for several strides. "It's perfectly alright to wait for the right man. Someone handsome and charming and interesting."

"Someone like you?" Joanna asked with false innocence.

"No one would want me. I'm dark, moody, and boring." He held aside the thorny bramble so they could pass through.

Philippa sidled past, grateful for his consideration. "You have nary such traits."

"I do, more so than I'd like."

Ahead, the moonlight gleamed on the surface of a winding stream, likely a tributary of River Stiffkey.

The distance from Walsingham to Barsham was over a league—more the way Dawson was leading them. Since they'd been traveling for an hour or longer, she guessed they were at least halfway.

Low clouds were forming overhead, humid and laden with rain, likely rolling in from the coast of the North Sea, which was less than a half day's ride. They were already losing the light of the moon and stars to guide their way and would soon be plunged into darkness, at least until dawn broke.

Dawson seemed to be listening intently, cocking his head first one way, then another, his brow wrinkling with his concentration. Joanna didn't pester him, waited patiently, obviously beginning to trust him too.

"I believe we'll soon have trackers on our trail," he finally offered.

"How can you tell?" Joanna asked.

"The distant bark of dogs."

Joanna paused and tilted her head to listen. Philippa tried to pick up on the sound, too, but couldn't hear anything. A part of her should have been worried. But strangely, with Dawson, she felt as though she might actually prevail against her uncle.

"What shall we do?" Joanna stared into the distance the way they'd come, anxiety now crinkling her brow.

Dawson studied the tributary and then began making his way down the steep grassy bank into the water below. When he reached the edge, he plunged in up to his thighs. "We will have to travel in the water and hope to throw them off our trail."

Joanna wasted no time in hoisting her gown and sliding down the bank. She didn't bother to test the water and instead hopped in beside Dawson, splashing and not caring that she was getting wet.

Philippa gripped fistfuls of her skirt and edged a slippered foot down the bank, feeling the dirt cascade beneath her. She was the first to admit she was neither adventurous nor daring, but she forced herself toward the stream.

As she reached the rushing water, she dipped one foot in but then drew back, wishing she were braver like Joanna.

Perhaps if she simply jumped in, she'd fare better.

"Make haste, Cousin." Joanna held out a hand to assist her. "We can tarry no longer."

Before she could take Joanna's aid, Dawson was in front of her. Without asking permission, he lifted her into his arms and then positioned her so that she was cradled against his chest.

At the realization that he intended to carry her, her pulse came to a halt. "No, my lord. You cannot possibly convey me like this."

"I don't mind." He slogged forward, and the movement threw her off-balance and forced her to wrap her arms around his neck. After a few minutes of traversing tensely, she finally expelled a full breath and loosened her grasp.

"It's not so horrible now, is it?" His voice rumbled close to her ear.

Her gown was dragging in the water, growing heavier, adding to her weight. "I cannot be an imposition any longer. I beg you to put me down."

"You're not imposing. I promise, if my arms get tired, I'll let you know."

"You are too kind."

He was silent for several sloshing steps. "I can't remember the last time anyone thought I was kind."

"'Tis easy to see you are kind. I noticed it from the moment I first saw you." Each stride he took jostled her against him, against every hard sinew of his chest and arms, against muscles she'd never known existed in a man.

"I haven't been a kind man in recent years. I allowed my difficulties to become my master instead of mastering the difficulties."

"Perhaps we are all at fault for giving way to the pressures of our difficulties from time to time."

He drew her weight more fully against him.

He was so near that her senses could hardly take him all in, although they were endeavoring to do so to the fullest—the graze of his breath against her cheek, the spicy, woodsy scent of his skin, and the rise and fall of his chest.

With her late husband Robert, she'd only ever felt suffocated by his breath and crushed by the weight of his body.

But here in the dark, in the middle of a stream, while racing for her life, she was attuned to Dawson. And she loved every nuance of this connection to him. None of it felt suffocating or crushing. Instead, she felt safe and cherished.

"My thanks," she whispered.

"For what?"

"You are a gallant and winsome man."

"You think more highly of me than you should." His voice hinted at humor. "Has it occurred to you that I like helping you because you're so sweet?"

She loved his compliments. His words from earlier replayed in her mind. *I won't deny I'm fascinated with you. What man wouldn't be?*

She was accustomed to attention and praise. But Dawson was more sincere, genuine, and real than any other man she'd met. Or maybe she was simply more attracted to him than she'd been to anyone else.

Perhaps Joanna was correct in desiring to marry for love or not at all. If this connection with Dawson was a taste of what a love relationship could be like, then maybe she ought to seek more from her next marriage than merely a man she could tolerate. Maybe her expectations *were* too low, as Joanna had accused her. Did she need to aim for love after all?

She would have no choice in the matter if her uncle captured her. And even if he didn't find her today, how would she evade his grasp in the long term? Besides, the more people she involved in her plight, the more peril she was bringing upon them.

"I do not wish to jeopardize you for helping me, but I fear that is exactly what I am doing."

"I'm not worried." He glanced over his shoulder at Joanna splashing along after them.

"I also fear bringing peril to Lord and Lady Wilkin. If they shelter me, they will garner my uncle's wrath."

As he shifted forward again, his face was even closer to hers, his breathing becoming more labored with his efforts. "Whatever the danger, we'll face it together. And I'm confident that with my mum's help, we'll find a solution to keep you safe."

"I pray you are right."

He paused. This time she could hear the distant barking above the rustling of the stream. Her uncle's men were drawing closer.

~ 16 ~

A BURST OF ADRENALINE SURGED THROUGH DAWSON. At some point during their escape, they'd been noticed. Maybe a caretaker or a priest at St. Peter's had seen them leaving the tower. Or perhaps another guard had spotted them from a distance.

From the sound of the barking dog, Dawson guessed he had about a ten-minute lead. It wasn't much time, and with the women, he couldn't go faster. Although the stream would mask their scent, the pursuers would eventually spot them in the water.

His best option was to locate a place to hide Joanna and Philippa and then do his best to lead the trackers astray.

He peered through the predawn, searching the banks and even the landscape above the stream.

"We can hide there!" Joanna said from behind him, obviously realizing, as he had, that they wouldn't be able to outrun their pursuers. "Over on the opposite side."

With clouds having moved in to cover the sky over the past hour, he felt as if his blindness had returned. His other senses were already working overtime to aid him. And now, as he crossed to the bank, he skimmed his free hand along the terrain and let his fingers do the exploring,

A moment later, he discovered what Joanna had spotted: a patch of heavy brush.

From what he could observe, it was thick enough to hide behind. In full daylight, it probably wouldn't provide sufficient cover. But here, in the darkness—even if their pursuers had torchlight—the women would hopefully remain hidden.

Joanna was already scrambling out of the water and crawling behind the brush. He released his hold of Philippa and began to lower her. She clutched his neck for a fraction longer than she needed to before unwinding her arms. As her feet found solid ground, her body pressed against his, her breath bathing his neck. For an eternal, delectable second, he relished the contact.

She wavered too, as though she was loath to leave him. But in the next instant she backed away, moving into the shrub with her cousin.

He assessed the area again before peeking behind the brush. Shadows stretched over them, concealing them well enough. "Stay here until you no longer hear the men searching, then head out."

"Are you not hiding with us?" Philippa's question was rushed and full of worry.

"No, I'll backtrack and go to Barsham a different way."

Both women were silent a beat. "You intend to distract them?" Philippa was the first to ask.

"I can move fast and stay ahead of them." Once upon a time he'd been in excellent shape. But he hadn't kept fit the way he should have over recent years. Now he wished he hadn't resisted Sybil's efforts to get him to join her CrossFit or kickboxing classes.

Even so, he'd do his best to keep the trackers on his trail. "Go directly to Barsham. Ask for Cecilia. Tell her you're my friends."

"If she is absent?" Joanna asked.

"Tell anyone at home that Dawson, her son, has sent you and that he'll soon follow." He started to move away, but Philippa clutched his hand.

Her fingers were warm, her grasp strong. "Godspeed, Dawson. I shall be praying for you." She was clearly a pious and sincere woman, good-hearted in every way. She deserved her freedom.

He hadn't had time to doubt what he'd done by coming to the past. He'd been too busy since the moment he'd awoken. But if he'd had any doubts at the back of his mind, they were gone. In fact, he was relieved that he was here to help her.

He squeezed her hand in return, then turned and made his way back up the stream. When he'd gone far enough to keep the trackers away from the women, he climbed up the bank and began to run. He wouldn't be able to outpace anyone who was on horseback—even if he'd been in perfect shape. Eventually, he'd have to find a way to elude them. But for now, all he cared about was leading them far from the stream so Philippa and Joanna could sneak away and make it to Barsham before the trackers realized he no longer had the women with him.

As he raced in a westerly direction, he had to rely again upon the innate sense of direction that had developed over the years of blindness. Was this another occasion where God was using his hardship to his benefit?

His mum had always liked to quote the Scripture verse: "*And we know that all things work together for good to them that love God.*" After his injury, he'd hated when she'd spoken the words, believed the verse was nothing more than a platitude, a trite greeting-card or wall-hanging saying that glossed over the pain.

But what if he'd been wrong? If God operated outside of time and space, then He could literally do anything at any point. What if God was more brilliant than anyone could comprehend and was able to interweave *all* things, including the tiniest details from the past, present, and future?

The terrain beneath his feet was level, indicating that he was still on farmland. From what he could tell, the flat, arable fields of Norfolk had been farms in the past just as they were in the present. It boggled his mind that he was experiencing life hundreds of years ago in a different era but that, essentially, the land around him was unchanged.

After running for what felt like an hour, he could hear the barking of the dog not far behind him. On the one hand, he was relieved that Lord Deighton's men had picked up on his trail and were tracking him—and hopefully not the women. But on the other hand, he wouldn't be able to go much longer, not with his breath coming in gasps and his muscles spasming with the need for oxygen.

Not only was his body weak but the sky was also beginning to lighten. That meant his pursuers would soon be able to see him from a distance.

He had to find a hiding place.

Some of the fields were in the process of being harvested with large mounds of cut grain. Probably meadow hay. Maybe he could find a pile to hide under. Hadn't there been an early Saxon king who'd escaped by hiding in a hay bale? Or maybe it had been an oak tree? Or a marsh?

Whatever it was that had helped the kings and warriors of old escape from their enemies, Dawson had to make use of their strategy now.

He veered toward a new field, letting the scent of freshly cut grass guide him. A light mist had begun to fall. He could only pray that it would help wash away his scent and footprints so his pursuers would lose his trail.

With the landscape beginning to take form as dawn neared, he picked up his pace, scanning the surrounding fields for cut hay. At the same time, his mind scrambled to find another solution, another place to hide if he couldn't find hay. Perhaps he could climb a tree or duck into a barn.

As the mist turned into a gentle rain, he suspected God was answering Philippa's prayers for him. A few moments later, when the gentle rain turned into a heavier downpour, he offered his own prayers—of gratitude. The tracking would become more difficult now.

Even so, he continued to search for a hay mound and was finally rewarded as the darkness gave way to an overcast sky of dawn. He stumbled to a halt in a half-harvested hayfield with rows of cut hay left to cure in the sun—except that it wouldn't be able to cure today.

As he made his way to an out-of-the-way stretch, he

collapsed to his knees, gasping for every lungful. He let himself rest only a moment before tunneling into the long grass, careful not to leave any evidence behind that he was there. When he was sufficiently covered, he held himself as still as possible.

He doubted the laborers would come out to the fields in the rain, so he allowed himself to rest for a couple of hours, falling in and out of sleep. When a sufficient amount of time had elapsed, he crawled out and took stock of his surroundings. The rain had stopped, but the fields were drenched and muddy. The slight breeze told him it might not be long before the wind picked up and perhaps pushed the rain clouds to the sea.

It was time for him to move along. First he stopped at a large puddle and rinsed the bits of hay off his body. And although he was wet and bedraggled and felt out of place in the heavy chain mail, he was presentable enough.

He hiked south until he reached a main thoroughfare—the road he guessed connected Walsingham to Fakenham and Barsham. At the morning hour, it wasn't busy, only a cart ahead and a few people walking toward Walsingham—perhaps pilgrims on the way to the shrine.

He considered trying to find the stream and the hiding place where he'd left Philippa and Joanna. But he was counting on them being long gone from there by now. As tempting as it was to search for them, he knew the best thing was to act normal, to pretend to be just an average man from the Middle Ages.

After all, Lord Deighton and his men didn't know what he looked like. If they were still out scouring the countryside, they wouldn't have any reason to suspect he'd been the one to assist Philippa and Joanna.

Even so, he continued forward cautiously.

The closer he drew to Barsham, the more people he met on the road, until finally he glimpsed the thatched roofs and wattle-and-daub-timbered homes clustered tightly together. The village was busy in spite of the wet morning, with the tradesmen already at work, if the clinking and hammering and chopping were an indication.

As he stood on the outskirts and took in the scene, a fresh sense of wonder rendered him speechless. Here he was smack dab in the middle of the year 1382. And it was real. The curls of smoke rising from holes in the thatched roofs and joining with the low clouds. The narrow street with a pair of oxen yoked together, struggling to pull a cart through the mud. Raised garden beds behind the homes.

A few women clustered at a well, their garments long and shapeless and plain—at least in comparison to what Philippa and Joanna had been wearing, clearly showing a difference in their social status.

One man stood outside a cottage in front of a pole lathe, a stack of wood beside him, his fingers moving in practiced rhythm with a piece of oak he was carving. From the shape of several other pieces nearby, Dawson guessed they were the backs and sides of a cabinet.

In a grassy embankment off the side of the road, a boy was guiding a herd of sheep. Attired in a loose tunic and leggings, the lad watched him curiously, probably wondering what he was doing in their peaceful village on this rainy morning.

Dawson nodded at the boy. "Can you tell me where Lord and Lady Wilkin live?" It felt odd to refer to his mother as a titled lady with a new last name. But he guessed she'd had to get married to survive. How else could a single woman find a way to support herself? He had only to think of the difficulty Philippa was having to know the laws didn't show any favoritism toward women.

The boy pointed to a wagon path that led to the north. "There, yonder."

"Many thanks." Before the boy or any of the other villagers could stop him to question why he was there, he started down the single-lane road. Littered with puddles, some in deep ruts, the path wound through a sparsely wooded area. As he rounded a bend, the land cleared before him.

He paused and took in the wild beauty of the sight, the low clouds rolling over the hills and brushing against the castle towers, the flags flapping in the breeze, and the damp grass growing a lush green. Amidst it all, an imposing castle stood on a hillside, with a thick square keep at the center surrounded by inner and outer walls with embattlements all along the perimeter.

After only seeing the remains of castles weathered by time and wars during modern times, he hadn't been prepared for the grandeur of what they looked like in the Middle Ages. It was truly magnificent.

He aimed for the bridge that spanned a moat and led to a gatehouse with a crenellated tower. His thoughts had been filled with Philippa all morning, and he hadn't been able to stop worrying about Joanna and her. But now his mind shifted to his mum. He hoped she was back from Canterbury and that he wouldn't miss the opportunity to see her.

When he reached the bridge, he peered beyond the gatehouse toward the keep, hoping for a glimpse of Philippa or his mum. But the gates were closed, and no one was in sight.

"Halt!" came a command from the tower. A soldier stood at one of the open arched windows, armed with a bow, the arrow aimed at Dawson.

Dawson didn't have to be told twice. He froze and kept his gaze trained on the weapon and the man, ready to dive off the bridge at the first sign of hostility. It was no wonder the women had been hesitant to show up here at his mum's home. He could only pray they'd had a more welcoming reception—if they'd made it.

"Who are you?" the guard called. "And what is your business?"

"I am Dawson Huxham. I'm here to see my mother, Lady Cecilia."

The guard lowered his bow and arrow, studying Dawson as though attempting to find a family resemblance.

"If she's here, she will verify that I'm her son."

Without answering, the man lifted a horn and gave two short blasts. In the next instant, the portcullis began to rise, the chains clanking and squealing. When the inner and outer gates had both been lifted, Dawson hesitated only a moment before continuing across the bridge.

Although he'd been putting himself into danger since the moment he stepped into the past, this time his heart began to race at triple the speed and his mouth went dry. Maybe it was the daylight or that he was exposed out in the open. Whatever it was, his mind flashed back to Afghanistan and triggered an explosion, one that ricocheted through his limbs.

His pace slowed with the need to stop, crouch, and cover himself. Shouts seemed to rise around him. Screams. Blood. Blinding pain. Blackness.

Panic began to claw at his chest. What was he doing here?

"Dawson?" A faint call broke through the haze of battle.

He shook his head. As his vision cleared, he focused on the path beyond the gatehouse that led up to the keep and a woman running toward him, her gown and head covering flapping in the breeze.

Drawing in a breath, he crossed the bridge and passed through the first gatehouse. Even though the skies were still gray, he pushed back the ghosts of that day in the war. Instead, he focused on the woman.

His mum. Even in a long gown and with her hair covered in a white linen cloth, he recognized her face. Though she'd aged since he'd last set eyes upon her before leaving for the war, she was still a beautiful woman with slender features and the same athletic figure.

As she drew nearer, he could see the tears coursing down her cheeks.

What did she think of him here? And why the tears? Uncertainty weighed his steps.

But she only hastened her pace. A moment later she launched against him, throwing her arms around him and hugging him fiercely with the same love and acceptance as always. "Oh, Dawson." She spoke his name in a half sob.

He wrapped her into an embrace, his throat aching, eyes stinging.

How was it possible he was getting to see and hold his mum again, after having her funeral, after accepting that she was dead? It was surreal.

But he was here, having located her after less than twenty-four hours in the past. Now, thankfully, he would have plenty of time to talk to her, plenty of time to sort out what had happened to her, and plenty of time to learn where the Hamin were holding her.

His mum extended him to arm's length and examined him from his head to his toes, tears still dampening her cheeks. "I was shocked when Lady Neville and Lady Deighton informed me of your assistance."

"Then Philippa and Joanna made it safely?"

"Yes, several hours ago. I knew you had sent them when Lady Philippa told me that you were recovered from your blindness."

"Yes." He managed the one word before his voice lodged in his throat, unable to squeeze past the lump there. He'd been healed. The realization still blew his mind.

"I spoke of your blindness to no one except my husband." She lifted a hand to his cheek, then to his hair, smoothing it back the way she always had. "You drank the bottle Sybil left for you?"

He nodded, taking in the determination, strength, and savvy that had always characterized her face, so much like Sybil's.

But the anxiety in his mum's eyes—that was different.

"The Hamin discovered your healing and sent you back?"

"No." He cleared his throat, trying to swallow the swell of emotion. "I was careful, Mum. Acey and Chloe helped me, and I've come back for five days. That's all."

The worry didn't go away.

"Philippa provided me with the two doses necessary to return. Acey and Chloe have it—"

"We shall pray the Hamin do not interfere."

How were his friends doing? Were they even now sitting at his bedside at a hospital in Norwich? Had they been able to fool the Hamin with the staged accident? Or were the Hamin even now plotting how to capture Acey, Chloe, and him?

"Dawson?" Another woman's voice came from the pathway leading to the keep. The sweet and gentle voice of Philippa.

He stepped back at the same time his mum broke the connection. His gaze shot to Philippa as though it had a will of its own. Yes, he was eager to see her again, but only because he wanted to reassure himself that she was okay.

She wasn't running, but she was rushing down the path toward him. She'd changed clothing, was attired in a dry gown. Like the previous one, it sculpted her curves, showing off her lithe and graceful form. Her head was devoid of a covering, and her light-brown hair hung in one long, thick braid. Her cheeks were flushed and her eyes bright.

She was more beautiful than he remembered, and his body began to thrum with strange need. More people trailed behind her, among them Joanna, who had also changed clothing.

As Philippa neared, he took several steps forward to meet her and was unprepared when she pressed against him and wrapped her arms around him. "I have been so worried all morn," she murmured.

He needed no encouragement or prodding to hug her in return.

Tension seemed to ease from her body, as though she'd been waiting anxiously for his appearance and could now relax. She held him only briefly before she released him.

He couldn't keep his hands from lingering on her back and then shifting to her arms.

"You are unharmed?" She peeked up at him through her lashes, her cheeks flushing now with additional embarrassment, likely because of her outward display.

"I'm perfectly fine." His assurance came out soft, almost intimate.

Her lips lifted into a small smile that drew his attention to her mouth. "Your mother has been most gracious to us since our arrival."

He didn't want to stop looking at this ravishing woman, but if he didn't foster his self-control now, it was liable to flame out of control the next time. He pried his hands loose from Philippa and nodded at his mum. "Thank you for giving them refuge."

His mum was studying Philippa intently, as though the young woman was part of an important case that she was bent on solving. In the next moment, she quirked a brow at him, questioning what was going on. Did she think he had a thing for Philippa?

He quickly shook his head. "Philippa needed my help. That's all."

His mum's brow only rose higher. "Yes, Lady Philippa explained how you came to her aid in the crypt and helped her escape from the priory through the tunnel leading to St. Peter's."

"She's attempting to flee from her uncle."

"So you traveled to the past to help her?" Mum tilted her head in that way that dared him to defy her. As much as her directness had always intimidated him, he relished experiencing it now after all this time.

More people were gathering around them. From their fancy and colorful attire, he guessed they were members of the household and not servants. It was strange to see so many people dressed in such heavy layers of clothing in the summer. And wearing hats or head coverings.

For a moment, he felt as if he were back at an annual medieval festival with costumed performers, tournaments, and historical reenactments set against the backdrop of a massive stone castle.

Except this was all too real with the haze of smoke, the dampness of soil, the waft of horseflesh and manure. The strange stillness of the air was devoid of the loudspeaker voices, the blaring of music, and the cheering of crowds.

How had his mum adjusted to living in such a foreign time and place? Hopefully she wouldn't need to much longer.

"I came to help you." He met his mum's gaze directly. "And to help Philippa."

Philippa made a move as though to touch him but then clutched her hands together in front of her. "If not for Dawson, I would be languishing as a prisoner at the priory. I am most grateful for his aid, and I intend to reward him as soon as I am able."

"Of course, my lady." Mum bowed her head toward Philippa, clearly deferring to her as a person of higher social rank.

This time he was the one who reached for Philippa, grazing her arm. "I didn't help you for a reward, Philippa. I don't care about that."

Her gaze dropped to his hand upon her. Her lips opened just slightly, and she inhaled a short breath, as though she was affected by the contact, even one so simple.

Again, his mum seemed to be watching their interaction. He didn't want her to get the wrong idea about Philippa and him. Yes, they had a connection through the holy water, and there was an undeniable attraction. But that was all.

He lifted his hand away from her. He had to be careful, couldn't touch her again, even innocently. As beautiful as she was and as much as he might like her, he was returning to the present and would never see her again after this week.

Mum made all the introductions to her husband's family who'd come out to greet him—mostly women and children, since her husband and his sons were gone for the day. It wasn't until they reached the keep and he parted ways with Philippa and Joanna that he stopped his mum on the stone steps that led inside.

He had to do this now before anything interfered. He let the words rush out. "I'm sorry."

She halted beside him.

Yes, he'd come to help his mum escape the Hamin. And

he'd come to free Philippa from her uncle's control. But ultimately, if he was truly honest with himself, he'd wanted to see his mum again to apologize.

He needed to make amends with her just like he did with Sybil. "I'm sorry for treating you so horribly after my accident, especially the last year or two. I was an absolute terror, and I regret not appreciating you more."

His mum reached up and smoothed his hair back again.

Oh, how he'd missed the way she'd always been able to soothe him. She'd helped him through the loss of his dad, made him realize he hadn't done anything wrong, even though he'd blamed himself for Dad's leaving. She'd helped him during his long recovery after he'd been released from the hospital. And once again, she'd tried to make him understand he wasn't to blame for Acey's injury or the privates in his section who'd lost their lives. In fact, she'd reminded him so often of all the other heroic things he'd accomplished during the war, that she was the reason he still wore his dog tags.

He owed her his life. Even if he did still carry the burden of all that had happened, if not for her, he wouldn't have survived those first terrible years of blindness. "I shouldn't have gotten angry when you moved. I understand now why you did it."

"I've already forgiven you, Dawson."

"If I'd tried harder to become more independent, maybe you wouldn't have felt the need to break away from me and move to Fakenham. Maybe then you wouldn't have been captured—"

"You're not to blame for my disappearance."

He swallowed hard against the guilt that had plagued him

since the day he'd gotten the news she was gone.

She pressed both hands to his cheeks, framing his face and forcing him to look at her. "Even if I hadn't moved, I was already in terrible danger."

With all he'd recently learned about the Hamin and holy water, he knew she was right. She'd been in peril long before she'd moved to Fakenham. But that didn't change the fact that he'd treated her abysmally after she'd moved. "I should have done everything you told me, should have been kinder—"

She cut him off with a finger to his lips. "I have forgiven you. Now it's time for you to forgive yourself." Her eyes were glassy with tears. And love.

How was she able to keep loving him in spite of his mistakes? "I love you, Mum." He'd waited for years to tell her that again.

Her tears spilled over and ran down her cheeks. "I love you too, Dawson."

As she smiled at him through her tears, he lifted a silent prayer of gratefulness that he'd had this chance to see and speak to her again. Now he prayed he'd have the opportunity to do the same with Sybil.

- 17 -

"SO YOU DON'T KNOW WHERE the Hamin are located?" Dawson perched on the edge of the cushioned chair.

Mum sat in a chair beside him in her chamber. A low fire crackled in the hearth, taking the chill out of the damp day and helping to dry him after he'd washed up in the guest room assigned to him. His mum had called it a bath, but it had felt more like wading in a kiddy pool. At least a manservant had been available to help wash his hair, getting out the filth of both the hay pile and the stream.

Since his other clothes had needed laundering, he was borrowing an outfit from Mum's husband—strange tight pants made of wool, with coarse stockings laced to the hem of each pantleg. A vest—called a doublet—went over a long shirt and had to be laced up the front too. Even the collar had to be attached by a lacing needle.

The clothing colors were brighter than he'd imagined them to be in the Middle Ages. He wasn't sure why he'd expected mostly browns and grays. Maybe because that's always what he'd seen in the movies. But his doublet was royal blue and the shirt underneath a dark red. His mother even wore a bright-yellow gown decorated with fancy embroidery and tiny pearls.

"When the Hamin kidnapped me," Mum said quietly, "I was blindfolded the whole time."

They were alone in the room and had been for an hour or more. They'd already talked extensively about the events that had led him to the past as well as all that had happened with Sybil. From everything his mum had relayed about his sister, she'd had a rough beginning to her time in 1382, but she'd survived and was happily married to Lord Nicholas Worth and living in Canterbury at Reider Castle.

He wanted to visit Sybil before he returned to the present, but he didn't have the time for such a trip. Mum and her husband had just returned, and the 165-plus miles to Canterbury were not easy to traverse in the Middle Ages due to poor roads, bandits, and the lack of transportation. His mum and her husband and his retinue of guards had traveled by horseback. But Dawson didn't know how to ride a horse and had no desire to learn. Going by sea was easier and less time-consuming but still would take more time than he had.

In addition, his mum had shared how going anywhere was dangerous at the moment because of the plague—the deadly Black Plague he'd studied in history classes. Apparently, pockets of outbreaks were occurring, the most recent one in Kent. His mum and her husband hadn't known about the plague until they'd arrived. Thankfully, the worst of the outbreak had passed, so they hadn't been at high risk. Even so, her husband had used extra care to limit their contact with people there as well as on their return trip.

Dawson swiped up a handful of the honey-crusted nuts from the spread a servant had delivered. The silver tray sat upon the pedestal table between Mum and him. He'd already eaten most of the food and was still hungry. But more than food, he was eager for details so he could stage a rescue when he returned to the present, perhaps even similar to the one Sybil and Harrison had staged to save Ellen Burlington. "You must have picked up on some clues for where the Hamin are keeping you—sounds, scents, textures, anything."

"*Were* keeping."

"What?" He shoveled in the nuts and began chewing. But suddenly something in his mum's expression brought all his hopes crashing to a halt.

"I died in the present, Dawson."

He tried to swallow the mouthful of nuts, but they stuck in his throat. He'd known it was likely she'd died. Even so, the disappointment was too thick, too overwhelming.

He pushed up from his chair and paced to the opposite side of the room. The large, canopied bed occupied the center of the chamber. A wardrobe and dressing table took up another area of the room. As with her town house in Fakenham, her touch was everywhere in the decorative pillows on the bed, the bright rugs on the floor, several colorful hangings on the wall.

This was her home now. Forever. She would never be able to come back to the present.

"I thought you knew I was gone. And I am sorry to have to share such news with you." She'd risen from her chair and stood facing him.

His breath was hot in his lungs, and he clenched his fists, wishing he could punch something. He'd been holding out hope that he could find her and that they'd have each other, that he'd have family again. And he wasn't ready to let go of that possibility.

"But you must know, my death was truly for the best. I lasted for a year in my coma as a courier for the Hamin. And every week I worried that if I failed to deliver the holy water as they had instructed, they would carry through with their threats to bring harm to you and Sybil."

"What threats?"

"They threatened to hurt both of you if I refused to cooperate."

He could understand her worry, especially now, after having been attacked and beaten himself. He'd been so vulnerable and weak. And even though Sybil could defend herself well enough, he doubted she would have been able to fight her way free of the Hamin if they'd captured her.

"It's a wonder the Hamin didn't go after Sybil sooner," he said, "especially after her involvement with Harrison Burlington."

"I imagine the Hamin watched the two of you carefully for many months following my death to see if you experienced healing or anything else unusual. Perhaps they concluded that my body died in the past as well as the present and was unable to transport any more holy water."

His mind traveled back to all the times he'd felt as though he was being watched or spied upon. He'd chalked it up to paranoia. But it was possible he'd sensed the Hamin keeping close tabs on him.

He let the tension ease from his fists even if the tightness still gripped his chest. "At least Sybil is safe from the Hamin here."

"But you and Acey and Chloe are in terrible danger." Mum held herself regally, more poised and graceful than he remembered. While so much about her was still the same, he supposed it was inevitable that she would change and adjust to her new life. "If they discover the connection you have to the past and the holy water, they will surely kidnap one of you and make you their new courier."

"How many couriers do they currently have kidnapped and hidden away?" He couldn't save his mother, but perhaps he could save others.

"I have been ever on the lookout for another courier that they have sent to the past. But I had not heard of anything unusual . . . until I gained news of Arthur Creighton's visit—a name that was familiar to me from the present. 'Tis why I initially set out for Canterbury, so I might investigate his presence. 'Twas happenstance that I learned of Sybil's arrival."

"So it's possible the Hamin haven't sent anyone else back?"

"My guess is they did not save an ampulla of the holy water to do so."

Which meant that Acey and Chloe were in more danger than he'd realized. If the Hamin learned of the extra vials of holy water the two had, maybe they'd kidnap both Acey and Chloe to become couriers. And then he'd have no way to return to the present, no way to protect his friends, and no way to stop the Hamin.

He shook off the morbid thought. "What exactly did the Hamin do with the ampullae you provided for them?" She'd already explained that she'd left the bottles in the alcoves in the tunnels underneath Walsingham, just as he'd suspected. There were several places, and she'd been instructed to alternate among them. She'd delivered one bottle weekly, nearly draining dry the wellspring under the crypt. Mum had been surprised that Philippa and Joanna had been able to gather enough to give him.

"The Hamin Sahaba are led by the Arabian royalty and have sold each bottle for millions of dollars—sometimes billions—to the highest bidders on the black market."

"And here I thought those sheiks were growing wealthier because of increased oil production."

"Well, that too. But they have known about the powers of the holy water for decades. They discovered instructions regarding the water in ancient scroll fragments found in the Dead Sea area, fragments that contained references to the Tree of Life from the Garden of Eden and the preservation of so-called life-giving seeds that once belonged to the tree."

Dawson returned to his chair as his mum explained the theories behind the holy water, particularly the belief that it was related to the Tree of Life and the seeds. Legends—as preserved in the Dead Sea Fragments—detailed how the seeds had been placed in unspecified locations of the world for safekeeping. The water sources that had contact with the seeds apparently gained healing qualities, and it had become evident to the Hamin that Canterbury and Walsingham had been areas where the seeds had been taken.

Mum had worked in Canterbury for years, following the activity of the Hamin as they searched for clues about the holy water. When the Hamin had started to focus more of their energy and time in Walsingham, she'd moved to Fakenham to continue her investigation. She'd been caught by them while excavating under the old crypt, and that had been the end of her life as she'd known it.

During her recent visit with Sybil, she'd learned more about all that had transpired over the past four years, including the events that had led to Arthur Creighton, along with his daughter Marian, crossing into the past. Mum hadn't been able to visit with either as apparently Marian had recently had a child and her husband had been unwilling to accept any visitors for fear of putting his wife and newborn in peril of the plague. No one knew what had become of Arthur, but rumors circulated that he'd been taken to the Continent and put into hiding until the accusations about his being a witch faded away.

"So the holy water is available in Canterbury?" Dawson sat back and stretched his legs out in front of him, finally starting to feel warm and dry.

His mum now reclined in her chair too. "A wellspring was uncovered last year, one that is now being carefully guarded but that has already caused much conflict."

Before he could question her further, a knock sounded upon the door.

"You may enter," his mum called.

The door opened and a maidservant stepped inside with a bowed head, the white of her head covering all he could see. "Lady Neville requests the presence of Lord Huxham for a stroll in the gardens."

At just the mention of Philippa's name, Dawson's pulse raced forward. After their greeting outside the gatehouse, he hadn't seen her again. His mind had returned to her a few times, but mostly he'd been consumed with discovering all he could about his mum and the Hamin. He still didn't have enough intel to track down their headquarters on his return to the present day. He needed his mum to give him even more details about everything she remembered from the time she'd spent as their prisoner—although most of it had been in a coma.

A slant of sunshine now slipped past the crack in the closed shutters. The rain of the early morning had passed. As much as his body betrayed him with the desire to be with Philippa, he had to listen to the warning bells inside telling him to keep his distance since she was a temptation he wasn't sure he could resist.

"She awaits you in the gardens, my lord." The servant didn't move, clearly expecting a response.

Dawson found it strange the servants were addressing him as their lord when he had no special status. Perhaps they assumed he was of the nobility because of his mum. "Tell her I'm not able to—"

His mum cleared her throat and stood. "You may inform Lady Neville that my son and I are finished with our conversation for now, and that he gladly accepts her invitation."

The servant bobbed her head before she backed out and closed the door.

As soon as they were alone, he leaned forward and whispered, "I can't go on a walk with Philippa."

"You cannot refuse a woman like her. She is likely the

wealthiest woman in the country and subsequently one of the most powerful."

He'd already guessed as much. Even so, he didn't want to fan the embers that had sparked and were smoldering between them. He had the feeling they were all too easy to stoke and couldn't take any risks. "I think it's for the best if I don't spend time with her."

"For whom? You or her?"

"For both of us."

"And why is that?"

He fidgeted with the loose lace in his doublet. How could he answer without embarrassing himself and revealing his attraction to the beautiful woman?

"'Tis clear you harbor fondness for her." His mum spoke matter-of-factly.

Were her proper words the medieval way of saying he had the hots for Philippa? And was it really that obvious to everyone that he desired her?

"Look, Mum—"

"'Tis clear she harbors fondness for you as well."

"It doesn't matter. Nothing can come of any fondness or attraction. I'll be leaving the past in four days."

His mum only looked at him, as though she didn't quite believe him.

"Harrison Burlington made it back to the present and so did his wife."

"Anything can happen in four days, Dawson." Her tone had an ominous ring to it.

"I'll be fine."

"You must know how her presence here will impact my husband and me." She spoke the words kindly, but there was an edge to her tone.

"She fears she'll bring her uncle's wrath upon anyone who shelters her."

"She is correct. She will."

He stood abruptly. He didn't want to drag his mum and her husband into a conflict with Lord Deighton, but a strange need to protect Philippa swelled within him. "You won't betray her and turn her over to her uncle, will you?"

"And what will you do if I say yes? Hide and run forever with her?"

"If that's what it takes to keep her safe, yes." The words came out with a force he didn't understand, only he wouldn't let anyone—not even his mum—bring harm to Philippa.

They faced off, staring at each other as they had whenever they'd clashed when he'd been a teenager. After a moment, her lips curved into the semblance of a smile. "You already feel more than fondness for her. She has cast her spell, and you have succumbed to it."

He shrugged, unwilling to say more. Instead, he set his mouth firmly.

Mum's smile widened. "Have no fear, Dawson. My husband and I are of the same mind. Neither of us like Lord Deighton. He is too ambitious and conniving. He should not be allowed to use Lady Neville in his scheming any longer."

"You'll agree more when you hear of his plans to use her to undermine the king."

"I have no doubt I will." His mum's eyes danced with

humor. Was she laughing inside at having manipulated him into admitting how much he already liked Philippa, an admission he hadn't wanted to make even to himself? But now that it was out in the open, he couldn't take it back.

He sighed. Mum always did have a way of getting him to admit to any crime—great or small. "I see your interrogation skills are still in full form."

"Yes."

"I still don't intend to take a walk with her."

"Why not?"

"I don't want to lead her on or trifle with her feelings."

"Then be careful."

Was it really that simple? He opened his mouth to protest further.

Mum cut him off with a stern look. "If you slight her, she likely will not summon you again. Not because she is spiteful but because she will honor your decision."

"What decision?"

It was her turn to sigh. "You really are ignorant of the ways of women."

"I haven't exactly had the occasion to date in recent years."

"'Twas a decision of your own making, Dawson, and not because you could not have a relationship."

A bitter rebuttal was on the tip of his tongue—one about how women hadn't been knocking down his door to date him. But he bit it back. He hadn't come to the past to argue with his mum. He'd come with the hope of repairing their relationship. And the truth was, he could have dated. There had been women who'd accepted him with his blindness. The problem was that he hadn't accepted himself.

"Go and enjoy the company of Lady Neville." His mum waved at the door. "Who knows? Maybe you will fall in love with her and decide to stay here in the past."

"That won't happen, Mum."

"Falling in love or staying?"

"Neither."

"We never can predict the course our lives will take."

Her words sent a tremor through him. He had no intention of falling in love with a woman from a different time period. That was out of the question. Not even with a woman as appealing as Philippa.

And yet . . . could he entertain the idea of pursuing Philippa if he remained in the past with his mum?

He gave himself a mental slap. No, he couldn't stay. With the jeopardy Acey and Chloe faced with the Hamin, Dawson needed to get back and take out the terrorists more than ever. Besides, he didn't have control over the decision. Acey and Chloe intended to bring him out of his coma, and he would have no easy way to inform them not to.

The fact was, he had to go home. And there was no changing that.

His mum began to steer him toward the door. "If nothing else, you must go to Lady Neville for my sake. She is an honored and important guest in my home, and I would not offend her in any way."

When Mum pushed him out into the hallway, he didn't resist even though he knew he should.

~ 18 ~

"HE IS NOT COMING." Philippa forced herself not to glance in the direction of the keep, regardless of the overwhelming longing to twist around on the stone bench and watch for Dawson's approach. But she couldn't appear eager, not even when she was practically going mad with the need to see him again.

"He will be here." Joanna stood under a nearby apple tree, the blossoms having given way to the beginning of fruit. As willowy and tall and pretty as she was, the blossoms only made her all the fairer, as though she were a woodland nymph standing guard.

"The request was too forward of me." Philippa felt the heat color her cheeks again as it had since she'd given way to Joanna's coercing to send for Dawson.

"He has made it clear he intends to depart in five—now four—days. If you hope to discover if he is a heart match for you, then you cannot afford to squander a single moment. You must take advantage of every second of every day while he is here."

A soft laugh bubbled up, and Philippa couldn't hold it back.

"What exactly is humorous about the situation?" Joanna spoke sternly.

Philippa tried to wipe away her smile, but her lips quirked with one anyway. "You are a romantic."

"And you are much too practical for your own good."

"I am here, am I not?"

"Yes—" Joanna halted abruptly, then dropped her voice to a whisper. "He draws nigh."

Philippa stiffened and a bevy of honeybees seemed to start buzzing inside her stomach. "What should I do?"

"Make him come to you."

Although Philippa was inclined to stand up and warmly greet Dawson's approach, she didn't move. The sunshine suddenly felt too warm upon her bare head—another of Joanna's suggestions, to leave off her head covering.

Why was she listening to her cousin's counsel? Joanna wasn't exactly the model of courtly love since she'd lost the one love of her life. Although to be fair, the loss wasn't because of Joanna's lack of trying.

"When he offers his hand to help you up, do not release it, so that he will hold it during the walk."

"Really?"

"Yes. Now hush."

A moment later, his steps neared. "Hi, Joanna."

"My lord." Joanna gave him a brief curtsey.

Philippa couldn't make herself pretend indifference the way Joanna had suggested. Instead, she shifted on the bench so she was half facing Dawson. Though he'd greeted Joanna, his attention was squarely fixed upon her.

Those incredible green eyes were upon her and her alone. Dark, churning, and filled with something she didn't understand but that made her want to press against him as she had when she'd greeted him upon his arrival at the castle.

She hadn't meant to do it, had simply reacted in her relief at seeing him. But the moment her body had connected with his, undeniable longing had shaken her, so much so she hadn't wanted to release him.

She'd gained her first look at him in daylight and discovered he was more handsome than she'd been able to ascertain in the darkness of the previous occasions. In fact, she'd been almost speechless at the sight of him. He'd looked especially rugged and hard. Even tired and dirty, he'd held an appeal that had done strange things to her insides.

The longing had taken siege of her heart so that when she'd returned to the chambers she was sharing with Joanna, she hadn't been able to keep from spilling her feelings—that she liked Dawson more than she'd ever liked any other man, that she was attracted to him in a way she'd never felt before, that she wanted to spend more time with him.

Joanna had listened to her passionate declaration and then had begun issuing orders to the servants for brushes, ribbons, and even perfume. The servants had spent the past hour fashioning Philippa's hair and doing their best to groom her to perfection. Then Joanna had sent one of the servants to beseech Dawson to take a walk in the gardens.

Now, as he halted but a foot away, his gaze swept over her starting with her hair, curled and entwined with ribbons, then moving to her neck and to the low neckline of the gown she'd borrowed from Lady Cecilia. The wide expanse of open skin was unadorned since she didn't have access to her jewelry. His sights continued following the swell of her chest to her narrow waist before returning to her face.

"You're beautiful." He spoke the words so reverently and with so much awe that she couldn't hold back a smile.

"Thank you, my lord." She started to rise, but Joanna shot her a glare that pinned her in place.

For another long moment, Dawson seemed to be taking in her face, her smile, even the freckles that she'd wished away more times than she could count. As though finally realizing he was staring, he cleared his throat. "Would you care to take a walk?" He offered the suggestion as though it was his idea.

From the corner of her eye, she could see Joanna making the motion of holding out a hand. Joanna did it several times. Was her cousin telling her to wait for Dawson to extend his hand or instructing her to hold her own hand out?

Seeing her attention directed toward Joanna, Dawson glanced under the apple tree. Joanna froze and pretended to inspect an apple the size of a button as if it held intense interest.

Philippa ducked her head to hide her humor, then began to rise.

In the next instant, she felt Dawson's touch against her arm, assisting her to her feet. And as always, his touch left her breathless.

When he dropped his hand, Joanna made another motion, this one a grasp, almost a lunge. Her cousin gestured twice, before Dawson shot her another look. Joanna froze with her hand outstretched and acted as though she was swatting away a bug.

Philippa didn't understand what her cousin was communicating this time. Instead of trying to make sense of the commands, she started forward down the garden path directly ahead, the one that led through the roses.

Dawson fell into step beside her, crossing his hands behind his back, giving her no opportunity to accidentally stumble and reach for his hand—another of Joanna's suggestions earlier when she'd been advising her how to behave during the walk.

For a few more steps, Philippa tried to recall any further counsel, but at the stiffness in Dawson's demeanor and the reserve in the way he held himself, she had the feeling he was uncomfortable. She had to stop thinking about herself and instead needed to put him at ease.

"How fares your reunion with your mother?" She offered the question, genuinely interested and wanting him to know it.

"I'd hoped that we could have a permanent reunion." His voice held a note of sadness. "But I'm afraid it won't be."

She didn't understand whence he'd come or whither he was going. He hadn't offered an explanation yet, and she wasn't sure how to broach the topic. She and Joanna had already allowed that the holy water had the capability to bring him to them, almost as if the holy water gave a person the capability to travel to various places. They couldn't comprehend how it happened, but they couldn't doubt that it did.

"So you had hoped you might transport her with you back to wherever you came from?"

He cast her a sidelong glance. "Wherever I came from?"

"Yes, clearly the holy water brought you to me. And I suspect you will use the holy water in the other ampulla I gave you when the time nears for you to depart."

He halted so abruptly that she was already a pace ahead of him before she stopped and turned to find his eyes wide and filled with surprise. "Where do you think I'm from?"

She studied him a moment. "Are you from heaven? An angel?"

"No." He scoffed. "Most definitely not an angel."

"A saint from the past?"

He scoffed again. "Do I look like a saint?"

She didn't really know what a saint looked like. But from his answer, she could safely assume he didn't categorize himself as one. "Then you are mortal? Perhaps from another country?"

"I'm English."

"But . . ." He was different. Not like any Englishman she'd ever known.

"But I'm not of your time."

"Then you are visiting from the past or the future?" She posed the idea almost in jesting, but Dawson didn't reject her question this time.

Instead, he glanced at Joanna, following behind them as a chaperone but maintaining a substantial distance. He then met her gaze directly. "Please don't think I'm crazy if I tell you I'm from over six hundred years in the future."

His eyes radiated with so much sincerity, how could she not believe him? It was odd to think she was receiving a visit from someone from a future time. Those sorts of things only happened to important people, didn't they?

"You think I'm mad, don't you?" he whispered.

"No," she said softly, not sure why they were whispering. "I am simply trying to understand why Providence chose me to receive your visitation, as I am but an ordinary woman—"

"Believe me"—he leaned in and finally clasped one of her hands—"you're the most extraordinary woman I've ever met."

At the ring of passion in his whisper and the sincerity of his compliment, warmth cascaded through her face, and she quickly ducked her head to hide the effect he had upon her. She focused on his hand grasping hers. Seeing where her attention had landed, he began to pull away.

Before he could do so, she captured his hand and let her fingers slip through his. The caress was light, but he became suddenly motionless, as though she'd bound him with chains. Had she overstepped herself by touching him so intimately? Was she being too brazen?

Her heart hammered hard. She'd been with Robert, had some experience with a man, albeit very limited. She wasn't a young, naïve girl anymore, and if she wanted to hold Dawson's hand, why shouldn't she? Why shouldn't she express her interest? In fact, she would caress him again.

With a trembling breath she brushed the pad of her thumb over the back of his hand.

He still didn't move, didn't seem to be breathing.

When she peeked up at him, his green eyes were dark—like a forest under a midnight sky. She couldn't fathom what his look meant. But she wanted more of it, more of him.

She intertwined her fingers more securely against his.

He didn't grasp her or caress her in return, but neither did he pull away.

She started forward once more, tugging him along. As he settled into step beside her, he relaxed his hand within hers, seeming to give himself permission to have this moment with her.

"Will you tell me about where you live and what 'tis like?" she asked, although tentatively. "I do not wish to pry, but I should surely like to hear about the future. It cannot be so very different than now, can it?"

Dawson released a short laugh. "It's drastically different. So different, I don't even know where to start in describing it to you."

"I give you leave to try."

As they passed the blooming roses of all shades, he stared ahead, his mind clearly hundreds of years away from her. Why should she embark on fostering a heart match with a man who would disappear before her very eyes in a few days, never to be seen again? Was she being a fool? Or was it possible to convince him to stay?

"I don't know exactly how to start explaining what life is like in the twenty-first century."

"If 'tis too troublesome, you need not speak of it."

He hesitated a moment. "We have a thing called technology, and it's revolutionized the way people live." For a short while, he described some of the *technology*—modes of communicating long distances, methods of traveling in metal wagons, mechanisms that could do the laundry or wash the dishes in place of a person. He described the place he lived and how it had modern aqueducts that brought water into the home along with automatic lighting that didn't require a fire or candle or oil lantern.

It was all so fantastical that she could hardly imagine it. And yet she believed him regardless. He described it all so assuredly and with overmuch detail to be fabricating anything.

As he paused after telling her about a shop where everyone went to purchase all manner of food items, she stopped ambling and lowered herself to another stone bench, this one beside a bed of flowering forget-me-nots. She didn't release his hand and instead gave a gentle pull.

He took her cue and sat beside her, letting their hands rest in the space between them.

"Do you find fulfillment in your life there?" she asked.

A shadow passed across his countenance. "I admit, I haven't really lived fully during the past years."

She waited, sensing he needed to unburden himself.

He remained quiet for so long, she began to think he would say no more. But then he sighed sadly. "When my life went dark because of my blindness, I let that darkness spread to all areas of my life. I realized too late that just because I couldn't see, didn't mean I couldn't live."

"At times, we all become blind and need Providence to open our eyes."

He shrugged, clearly unconvinced.

"Perhaps you have needed someone in your life to help reveal the beauty."

"I'm not sure I would've been able to see it, even with help. My mum and sister tried. And I'm a stubborn man."

She squeezed his hand. "Then 'tis good for you that I do not give up so easily and will make it my mission while you are here to teach you to see the beauty of life."

"I do see it now." He peered around, the green of his eyes lightening as he took in the gardens.

"Yes, but next time your life grows dark, will you be able to continue to see it?"

A small smile played at his lips, a smile she would like to see much more oft and more fully. "Okay. How do you do it?" His voice held a note of playfulness that she liked just as well. "How do you stay so positive?"

Her own smile pushed for release. "'Tis a secret I only share with people I like."

"And do you like me?" He cast her a brief sideways glance.

Though his tone was nonchalant, the look was enough to send her pulse racing. She wasn't exactly sure how to respond. Should she keep the moment light? Playful? Or should she be truthful and sincere?

She had the sense that their connection was tentative, that he was holding himself back, that if she pushed him overmuch, he would pull away altogether. Rather than admitting she favored him a great deal, that she felt things for him that she'd never felt with any other man, she released his hand and stood.

She'd witnessed the art of playing coy and had practiced it enough to know how it was done. She walked across the stone path to a cluster of forget-me-nots, bent, and plucked one. As she straightened, she angled herself so he could watch her. Then she brought the delicate bloom to her nose, closed her eyes, and drew in a breath of the fragrance.

His gaze was on her as intensely as she'd anticipated, and it sent shivers of pleasure through her.

She brushed the petal against her lips. Then she turned to

face him while holding out the forget-me-not. "I also only give flowers to those I favor."

He focused on the flower for a long moment, unmoving. Then he stood and crossed to her. As he took it, he brushed his fingers against hers, almost intimately, almost purposefully, as if he was now the one playing coy with her. Then he brought the flower to his lips and pressed a kiss of his own there, his eyes capturing hers as he did so. He seemed to lock her up, bind her, and make her breathless all in one motion.

She couldn't make herself look away, guessed he could see right through her coyness to the desire he was awakening inside her.

"No doubt you have given many men flowers." He lowered the bloom, gently fingering it. And yet something intense, even demanding, imbued his statement.

She lost her ability to think, to play any more games. All she could do was answer him with the truth. "You are the only one to whom I have ever given a flower."

"Then I will cherish it."

"'Tis a forget-me-not. You must keep it so you will never forget me, no matter where you are, this century or another."

He caressed it again. "I won't forget you, Philippa. Ever." His voice was low. "You can rest assured of that."

"Nor I you."

He tucked the bloom carefully into his pocket. Then he cleared his throat. Was he intending to call an end to the walk? He couldn't. And she wouldn't let him.

"Now that I have established you are favorable," she rushed to say, "I shall share my secrets with you."

An imperceptible tension eased from his shoulders. "Are you sure I'm favorable enough for such an honor?"

He was sharp and witty. And she liked that about him immensely. "You are favorable enough, my lord. But perhaps I shall still put you to the test."

"I'm terrible at tests."

"I guarantee you will succeed at the lessons I shall give you."

"Is this more of your endless optimism, or are your lessons too easy?"

"'Tis never difficult to experience the beauty around us." She held out her hand. When he hesitated, she reached for him, giving him no choice but to lock his fingers with hers.

As they resumed walking along the path, she smiled at the beauty of the garden and then up at the sky, letting the sunshine touch her face, not caring that it would only darken her freckles. "The first thing we must always do to experience beauty is slow down and pay attention to details. Too oft we move hastily or let the busyness of life distract us."

She expected another clever comment, but he was silent. So she continued. "I put aside the concerns of my life for a short while, then I simply bask in the beauty of the moment and all that it contains."

She cracked open one eye to peek sideways at him. He'd closed his eyes and lifted his face to the sun too. Though he wasn't smiling, peace radiated from his countenance.

She breathed in deeply of the summer air, her attention catching upon a nest in a low branch of another apple tree. The tiny chirps coming from within beckoned her. "The first thing we shall enjoy is this." She tugged him toward the nest.

"Baby birds?" He didn't resist, although his voice held doubt.

"Yes. We shall savor every detail."

Most men she knew wouldn't show interest in flowers, nests, or anything else in the gardens. But somehow, with Dawson, she sensed he was different, that he'd understand, that he'd let her teach him how to see the beauty that existed all around.

She didn't know how long she would have with this incredible man. But for this afternoon, she wanted to take her own advice, slow down, and relish every moment of their time together.

- _19_ -

SHE WAS A SAINT. In the early morning light, Dawson stood beside Philippa, the crowd of paupers outside the gatehouse receiving the leftover food from the feast of the previous night.

A cart was laden with the platters and trenchers they'd gathered from the kitchen, and they worked together, with Joanna and one of the kitchen servants, to evenly distribute the food.

Philippa loaded a half-eaten trencher with several pieces of meat and handed it to a stooped-shouldered older man whose clothing was so thin and worn it wasn't even worthy of being made into rags.

He took the offering, and his rheumy eyes filled with adoration. "Thank you, my lady."

She gave him a smile, just as she had to all the others. Her smile and kind words seemed to bless each person almost as much as the food did.

No doubt about it. She was an amazing woman.

Dawson had spent most of yesterday with her, walking in the gardens, losing track of time as she showed him how to stop and simply enjoy the smallest of moments—the chirping from a nest of baby birds, the taste of a ripe strawberry, the rustling music of the wind in the leaves. She lived thoroughly and experienced everything richly, and he'd enjoyed spending the afternoon with her.

During the feast last night, he'd found himself seated by her side. Once more, he'd relished her companionship. She was interesting and smart and conversed well about many things.

Whenever he'd stepped away from her, the other men used his absence as an opportunity to approach her, giving him an insightful picture of how many men coveted her—likely for her beauty as well as her wealth.

It was also growing clearer why her uncle intended to use her as a bargaining tool to better himself and his political aspirations. He could have any man he chose for Philippa. Joanna had been right—every man was eager to have her.

But would they treasure her the way she deserved? Especially if they sought her for selfish reasons?

Philippa hadn't seemed to notice the attention, was as oblivious as always of the way she exuded beauty and sweetness. She only needed to smile or speak, and men fell all over themselves at her feet in adoration.

He'd stayed with her last night until the final stragglers left the great hall. And as they'd parted ways, she'd requested that he join her early in the morning for his second lesson in learning to experience the beauty of life. He hadn't been able to deny her, although a part of him knew he needed to.

And now, he was glad he'd come. The air was crisp, and a low mist clung to the hills and woodland beyond with the morning light casting an ethereal glow over it all. The low rays of sunshine illuminated Philippa too, making her look angelic.

Though she wore a head covering, a few tendrils of hair floated near her cheeks, which were flushed from her exertion. And her pleasure. It was obvious she found great pleasure in serving others.

As they'd walked down the path toward the gatehouse a short while ago, she'd informed him that her second lesson was that beauty could be experienced by sacrificing oneself to serve others.

He hadn't believed her at first. But the longer he'd worked beside her in handing out the food, the deeper his contentment had grown.

As the servant in the cart handed Philippa the last of the scraps, she passed them on to a young boy. She crouched in front of him, spoke to him for several moments, then rose and laid a hand on his head before he scampered away.

Some of the paupers were sitting in the grass eating. Others had taken their share and were walking along the wagon path back to the village.

Philippa wiped her hands upon a towel while turning her smile upon Dawson. "What do you think of your second lesson?"

"I'm learning that it really is more blessed to give than to receive."

By the brightening of her eyes, it seemed his answer pleased her. "I have learned that as well."

Would his life have been different if he'd applied her lessons on experiencing beauty? If he'd stopped to appreciate the small things? Or if he'd served others instead of thinking only about himself?

It was naïve to believe such platitudes could solve all problems, but a part of him wished he'd been able to put her principles into practice during his years of blindness to determine if they would have made a difference in his life.

Joanna and the servant began to haul the cart through the gatehouse. Dawson wasn't ready to go back, wanted to linger in the early morning with Philippa and discover more about her. "What made you so wise?"

Philippa lifted a hand and grazed the pin with the leaf pattern that was tucked into her head covering. "My mother was a lovely woman. I would not be who I am if not for how diligently she poured her life into me."

His mum had done the same to him. As a single parent, she'd sacrificed much for Sybil and him over the years. She'd loved them more than enough to make up for their dad's absence. And now here in the past, hopefully, she was finally getting to slow down and enjoy life.

He didn't have much time with her, needed to make the most of what they did have left. And instead, he was spending every moment with Philippa, was drawn to her like a wilted bloom craving sunlight.

As they ambled behind the cart, he silently chastised himself. He hadn't come to the past to be with Philippa. He'd come to be with his mum, and he couldn't squander the time he had with her.

• • •

Dawson parried a blow from Lord Wilkin before the older man

stepped back and nodded. "Good. You are a quick learner."

Dawson sheathed his sword—the one he'd pilfered from the tower guard at St. Peter's—then wiped a sleeve across his brow, the afternoon having grown warm. "Thank you. You've been a good teacher."

As lord of Barsham Castle, the nearby village, and the many farms in the area, his mother's husband, John, was a respected and wealthy nobleman. Middle-aged, he held himself with a distinguished air, with silver threading his dark-brown hair and trim beard. His face was ruddy, even more so now after the past hour of sword drills.

When Dawson had revealed his lack of sword-fighting skills, John had suggested the lessons. Even though Dawson hadn't discussed what John knew about Mum's previous life and her traveling to the Middle Ages, John's lack of questions, his easy acceptance of Dawson's inability to do some of the most basic medieval tasks, and his patience in teaching him spoke loudly enough. John knew Mum had crossed time and that now Dawson had too.

Apparently, John's first wife had died a couple of years before Mum's arrival to Walsingham. When he'd met Mum at the priory during one of his weekly visits to Our Lady Chapel, he'd been smitten with her. Upon learning that she'd come to Walsingham without money or means to care for herself and was working in the priory kitchen and being mistreated, he'd offered her work in the kitchen at Barsham, where she wouldn't have to worry about such abuses.

From what John left unsaid, Mum's early days hadn't been easy. And Dawson was grateful to the nobleman for giving her refuge and protecting her. Eventually, he'd fallen in love with Mum and asked her to marry him. Though initially their union had caused a scandal, Mum had convinced John to perpetuate the story that she was of noble birth but had run away from her family for private reasons. The excuse had helped. But more than that, as people had gotten to know her, they'd respected her for her intelligence, generosity, and spiritedness.

A servant handed Dawson a mug, and as he guzzled the liquid, he tried not to grimace at the warm, weak ale that was both bland and bitter. He took his fill, then handed the mug back to the servant with a nod of thanks before turning to face his mother's husband. "I'm ready for another round if you are."

John cast a glance to where the ladies were sitting on blankets in the shade of the keep, chatting and watching the sword drills. "I do believe Lady Philippa would like to claim your time for her own."

Dawson had purposefully avoided looking at Philippa. He'd known if he did, he'd only get distracted and fumble around with his sword like an idiot. Even so, he'd felt her presence and interest.

Who could avoid noticing her whenever she was near?

Certainly John's sons hadn't missed the opportunity to be around Philippa and stare at her whenever they could. Even now, they practiced their sword drills in the open bailey with the armed men who lived at Barsham Castle, showing off their skill and attempting to gain her favor.

He didn't count himself among such men, and even now, he didn't want to become a lapdog she summoned whenever she needed to occupy herself.

John took a last swig from his mug. "Lady Philippa cannot take her eyes from you."

Dawson shot his gaze to her. She was watching him with a sidelong look while speaking with his mum. At his glance, she dropped her attention to the chain of flowers she was braiding in her lap.

He still carried the flower she'd given him yesterday in the gardens. He'd told her he wouldn't forget her. And that was one promise he'd easily be able to keep.

"I've already spent too much time with her, John." Even though the women were far enough away that they couldn't hear the conversation, Dawson lowered his voice. "And as much as we might enjoy each other's company, you can't forget I'm leaving."

"You can stay." John paused in wiping his forehead again. "I hope you know you are welcome here in my home, that I would do anything for Cecilia."

"I appreciate that." Dawson had spent the whole morning with his mum after returning from distributing food to the poor. He'd assured himself that she truly was happy with her new life and that she loved John.

He'd also pressed his mum for more information on the Hamin. She didn't know exactly where the Hamin had kept her, but she'd picked up enough clues to narrow it down to a couple of places. One was a bunker below a mosque. She'd guessed it was the mosque in King's Lynn since that was within easy distance of Walsingham but not close enough to draw attention. And it was close to the sea, which provided an easy escape route should anything go wrong with their operations.

She'd also suspected another pocket of the Hamin operated out of a fishing cottage near Heacham. The scent of the lavender from nearby Norfolk Lavender had been easy to distinguish. But she hadn't known which house the Hamin were using—perhaps one under the guise of fishing.

"Even if I had a way to stay—which I don't—I feel called to return to where I'm from so I can help put an end to the group who abducted and badly used Mum. I need to stop them before they hurt someone else." Like Acey or Chloe.

"I understand, and I respect that." John nodded toward Philippa. "But you might also have the power to keep another group from abducting and badly using Philippa."

"How so?"

As the other men fighting nearby began to halt their contests, John clamped Dawson's shoulder and leaned in. "She has not shown an interest in any man since Lord Neville's passing."

Her late husband. Every time Dawson thought of her as having been a married woman with a husband, his stomach soured. More than that, his chest burned with a disquieting jealousy.

"She has had months since his death, and 'tis no secret that many men from all over England have traveled to Lord Deighton's home in Thursford with the hope of winning her heart. But nary one has succeeded."

Why did that thought bring Dawson such perverse pleasure? "Perhaps she just needs more time."

"Her time ran out. Which is why she sought refuge in the priory and now why she is here with us."

"You can keep her safe. You don't need me."

John shielded his eyes from the sun before peering up at the closest tower in the embattlement that surrounded the keep. His men were on duty as usual and would alert them of any sign of danger. "I verily pray so." His brows gathered into a troubled pinch. "I shall do my best."

"And again, many thanks. I'm grateful—"

"I have discussed the matter with your mother, and we have come up with a solution that will protect everyone— including Lady Philippa. A solution that will give Lord Deighton no reason to attack us."

"Attack? Would he dare?"

"Yes, I fear he is planning on it. I have already heard rumors to that effect."

Dawson wasn't entirely surprised, not after the lengths Lord Deighton had taken to recapture Philippa. "So what is the solution? What will protect Philippa and stop her uncle?"

"You must wed her."

Wed Philippa? John couldn't be serious. But his expression was grave, not a hint of humor or hesitancy in any crease or crevice.

Several of the men close by had stopped their drills and were now eavesdropping on the conversation. Dawson bent in closer. "I cannot wed her."

"She may not agree to it in any case. But what harm can ensue from inquiring?"

"A lot of harm." A strange tight pressure was building in Dawson's chest. Marrying Philippa was ludicrous. First, he'd only met her. And second, he was leaving. How many times did he have to tell everyone that he was in the past for just five days? Of course, as his mum had reminded him, anything could happen to change that, especially if the Hamin hurt Acey and Chloe and they weren't able to administer the dose of holy water needed to wake him from his coma.

"Even if you must leave"—John dropped his whisper lower—"at least she will have your name and the marriage to keep her from having to wed the man of her uncle's choosing."

Dawson's ready protest fell away. Would marriage allow Philippa to protect herself and her inheritance from her uncle? After all, once she was married, what could her uncle do to her? Her land and wealth would belong to her new husband.

Dawson finally allowed himself another look at Philippa. She peeked up at him as though sensing the conversation was about her. When he didn't immediately shift his attention away as he had all the other times, she offered him a small smile, one that held invitation.

She really hadn't been interested in any other man until she'd met him? The knowledge was satisfying, again in a strange way. He had no right to care. No right to interfere in her life. No right to lead her to believe they had a future together.

But what if he could offer her hope of escaping her uncle's clutches? What if John was right that if they married, she would be free? He could do that for her, couldn't he? It wouldn't hurt him.

The trouble was that his body wouldn't physically leave the past. If he correctly understood how the time crossing worked, once he woke from his coma in the present day, his 1382 body would begin to shut down and eventually die.

The fact was, he'd leave her a widow for a second time, and she'd be back in the same precarious predicament with her uncle . . . unless Dawson made a show of leaving Barsham so her uncle wouldn't know he'd died and wasn't intending to return. If his mum and John could make certain his body wasn't discovered, then Philippa would technically remain married and out of her uncle's control, free to live her life the way she chose.

"Go talk to her." John gave him a firm push from behind.

Dawson's feet carried him forward. It wouldn't hurt to explore the options, would it? As he began to cross to the women, their conversations faded away. He could also feel the stares of the men following him.

Great. His entire interaction with Philippa was about to be observed by everyone in the courtyard. Apparently, without modern movies and TV shows, this sort of stuff was the entertainment.

His mum was assessing him too. Her face was unreadable, but if she'd already spoken with John about the matter, then she was likely expecting him to bend down on one knee right then and there and propose.

As he stopped several feet away, he was suddenly conscious of how sweaty and dusty he was. He most definitely needed his deodorant, a shower, and a spritz of cologne. Even without, he could at least use the proper manners the way the other men did when they interacted with women. Such formality would never fit in the modern age, but the respect was certainly a lost art.

He bowed his head toward Philippa. "My lady."

"My lord, you did well." The gray-blue of her eyes was especially light and pretty.

"Thank you, but I have a long way to go." He'd given the excuse earlier that his blindness had held him back from learning how to use a sword. And no one had questioned his healing, as if such miracles were to be expected.

She fingered the braid of flowers on her lap. Was she waiting for him to invite her to spend time together? Was that the next step?

"My lady, would you join me for another walk in the garden?"

"Yes." Her answer was slightly breathless.

Was she eager to spend time with him?

As if sensing his unasked question, she lifted her eyes to his and gave him a glimpse of the bright happiness his request had brought to her.

How was it that so simple a thing as a walk in the gardens could satisfy her? Was such simplicity another lost art? Whatever the case, her pleasure sparked something in him . . . perhaps an eagerness of his own he'd been attempting to dampen, but that he could no longer contain.

"Once I've changed, I'll meet you there."

She glanced at her cousin, seemingly seeking permission or a chaperone or both.

Joanna pursed her lips tightly as though debating his worth before giving a nod.

"Very well," Philippa said. "I shall be waiting."

A short while later, he strode down the garden path as he'd

done the previous day. She sat on the same bench, her hands folded in her lap, her posture perfect—the portrait of a lady, especially with the sunlight turning her hair to a golden brown and the flowers blooming all around her.

His heart betrayed him with a rush of affection. The longer he was in the past, the more his life was intertwining with hers. But he had to be careful. Couldn't forget that his time in the past was fleeting, that nothing could come of the feelings between them.

They had only a few days. And that would have to be enough for both of them.

- 20 -

"Am I being overly familiar, Joanna?" Philippa paced the circular top of the turret. The crenellations rose high enough to conceal her from anyone who might be observing from the bailey, although she wasn't embarrassed to have others know of her interest in Dawson. In fact, she was certain everyone was quite clear how much she liked Dawson . . . except for perhaps Dawson himself.

"Have no fear." Joanna was kneeling on the cushions and arranging a simple fare on the blanket. "He will join you erelong."

"He does not display his ardor the way other men do."

"And 'tis one of the reasons why you favor him. Because he is not trying to impress you."

Joanna was right. Dawson only displayed a hint of his desire on rare occasions. Most of the time, he interacted with her in nothing more than a friendly manner.

More than anything else they'd done, she'd enjoyed their private walks in the gardens each of the three afternoons they'd been at Barsham—walks which evolved into satisfying conversations about all manner of things.

She'd shared what her life had been like before her parents

had died, and he'd talked about growing up without his father and how difficult that had been. She'd spoken about the loneliness of not having siblings and how fond she was of her cousins, especially Joanna. And he'd talked about his sister, Sybil, of his memories of her when they were children, and how their relationship had been strained after his blindness. Philippa appreciated that he was honest about his struggles and about pushing Sybil away and how he regretted his treatment of her.

He'd told her more about his life, his time in the army, the injury that had brought about his partial blindness, and the friends who had stayed beside him through it all. And she'd shared more about her marriage to Robert, his mistresses, and how he'd hoped to have children with her but that she hadn't been able to bear him any.

She'd been disappointed when each walk with Dawson came to an end, and she'd counted the minutes until they could be together at the evening meal, where she'd enjoyed conversing with him again. Tonight, when the meal and festivities were over, Joanna had finally been the one to pull her aside and indicate that with the long summer night, Philippa needed to ask Dawson to watch the sunset with her from one of the towers. Thus, upon exiting from the great hall, she'd sent a servant to relay the invitation to him.

Even if she was being too bold summoning him to the top of the turret, she wanted to make the most of the time they had left. Always at the back of her mind was the countdown of how many days until he would leave. Today had been his third day in the past. That meant only two remained.

Unless she could convince him to stay . . .

She leaned against one of the merlons, taking in the western horizon and the lavender streaking the sky. "What can I do to sway him to tarry here at Barsham?"

"My lady?" Joanna paused in smoothing the wrinkles from the blanket.

"There must be something."

Joanna stood and slapped her hands onto her hips, her eyes flashing. "Do not even think about allowing him into your bed until he weds you properly."

Philippa cupped a hand over her mouth to hold back a gasp while glancing toward the open tower door and praying Dawson hadn't heard her cousin's brazen remark.

"You have witnessed women being lured into becoming mistresses because they gave away certain *privileges*"—Joanna dropped her voice—"before securing a vow."

"I do not intend to do so, Cousin." Heat enflamed Philippa's cheeks. "You misunderstood my query."

"I did?" Joanna straightened, her eyes widening almost comically.

"Yes. I shall not—" Even just whispering such words brought another rush of mortification. "I do not intend to allow any man into my bed outside the bounds of marriage."

"I should hope not."

Philippa fanned her face with her hand. "I only thought you might have advice for how to encourage him to like me better."

Joanna also began to fan her face, the discussion clearly one that would have been better left unspoken. "Are you suggesting you would like to share a kiss with him?"

"No, not at all." Robert had kissed her on a couple of occasions—unpleasant but short experiences.

"If he is inclined to kiss you, I shall give you leave to do the deed."

"If he is inclined . . ." Philippa slipped off her head covering, much too hot to wear it.

"If he attempts it, I shall look away and pretend not to see it."

Philippa hoped she could win him without having to tolerate a kiss. But if that's what he desired and if that's what would convince him to tarry with her longer, then she would do it.

At the heavy slap of bootsteps upon the stairway in the tower, Philippa pressed her hands to her cheeks with the hope of cooling them. In the same moment, Joanna hastened toward a slight shadow next to the door and flattened herself against the wall, clearly attempting to make herself invisible.

A second later, Dawson ducked through the low doorway. His keen gaze found Joanna first before it bounced to Philippa. She dropped her hands away from her cheeks, prayed he couldn't tell what they'd just been talking about. She didn't want to plant any ideas in his mind.

"Hi." The green of his eyes seemed to lighten a shade.

She could do nothing less than welcome him with a smile. "Are you ready for your third lesson on experiencing beauty?"

"So that is why you arranged for our meeting here?" One of his brows rose quizzically.

"Yes, of course." Did he suspect ulterior motives? What if

he thought, like Joanna, that she had less-than-noble purposes? Oh, heaven have mercy. What had she done? She would have to take extra care during their time on the turret to keep him from thinking she wanted him to kiss her . . . or more.

Although she was sorely tempted to fan her face again, she turned to the closest crenel.

"Come look." She squeezed into the narrow space of the dip in the embattlement.

He crossed and stood in the crenel next to hers, his hands behind his back. "What are we looking for?"

From the corner of her eye, she could see his profile—his hard jaw beneath the layer of scruff, his long, straight nose, the purposeful set of his lips.

As he shifted to glance at her, as though sensing her admiration, she gave the landscape her full attention. "The third way to experience beauty when life brings us darkness is to develop a habit of always giving thanks to Providence for everything—big or little, profound or mundane, old or new."

"Giving thanks." He sounded as though she'd asked him to wish on butterflies or blow on dandelion petals.

"'Tis more important than it sounds."

He was silent for several seconds. "Right. Then show me how it's done."

She expelled a breath and then inhaled an attitude of thankfulness. "I begin by gazing over creation and thanking Providence for everything within my view. Like this: thank You for the bright-green grass, the dozens of kinds of trees I cannot even name, the finches and martins and starlings, the wildflowers in their array of purple and white and yellow, the sky with a hundred hues, the sun that gives us warmth and light, and the chance to be alive hither on this turret with a kind man like Dawson." Her voice dipped with shyness as she finished her prayer of thanksgiving.

Dawson released a deep breath and inhaled, imitating her. Then he let his gaze sweep over the landscape. "Thank You for the scent of damp wood, the hint of smoke, and the spicy roasted aroma of quail. Thank You for the clucking of the hens, the snort of the horses, the clink of the chains in the well. And thank You for the chance to be alive hither on this turret with a kind woman like Philippa."

She turned to face him, unable to contain her delight at his efforts. She was more than a little surprised that he'd been such a willing participant in all her lessons.

"How did I do?" He continued to take in the scene.

"You are an astute and willing learner."

"Only because I have a good teacher."

She wanted to smile, but she bit it back. "If you discipline yourself several times every day to give thanks in this manner, you will see your outlook on life beginning to shift."

"Has it shifted your outlook?"

"Incredibly."

"So you were not naturally a positive person?"

"Perhaps more so than others. But I confess to harboring bitterness and disappointment all too oft."

He finally turned, crossing his arms and bracing his shoulder against the merlon. His brows were knit together and his expression grave. 'Twas one of many of his expressions she was learning to read. And this one always sent a shiver of delight up her spine because it meant he was concerned about her.

"What disappoints you?" he asked.

Should she use his query to tell him how she felt about his departure? If she did so, would he stay in Barsham longer? She gave a small shake of her head. She didn't want to manipulate him into staying.

"What?" he persisted.

She focused on the horizon and the glow of colors. "I shall be disappointed if we miss the sunset."

She could feel him studying her and waiting for more. But a moment later, he returned his attention to the sunset too. They stood in silence until the brilliant orb disappeared below the line of trees, leaving splashes of orange and red in the sky.

"'Tis the most beautiful thing I have ever seen."

"I bet you say that every time you see a sunset." His tone hinted at mirth.

"Perhaps." She closed her eyes and let the damp breeze from the North Sea cool her face. When she opened her eyes, she found him watching her, but he quickly made a point of looking at something else. It was the advance-and-retreat game they'd been playing for the past three days, and with every retreat, she longed for him to grow bolder, to take the game to a new level. Perhaps tonight he would finally do so.

She crossed to the cushions and blankets. As she sat, she spread her gown out to cover her legs and feet. "Tell me the most beautiful thing you've ever seen."

He continued to lean against the stone crenellation, propped up one boot, and then took her in with such intensity, she could almost feel each touch of his gaze from her face to her neck to her chest to her hands in her lap.

The tempo of her breathing picked up. She waited for him to answer her by saying something about her beauty. Other men would have done so if given the opportunity. But Dawson remained silent. And somehow his stare spoke loudly enough.

She finally smiled. "Come sit with me, Dawson."

"Is that a good idea?" His question was mirthful but charged.

What was he insinuating? That he wasn't sure he could resist her?

The very prospect sent a whisper of a thrill through her. "We have a strict chaperone. Now, come and see the stars make their appearance. 'Tis a wonder I could watch every night if the opportunity were afforded me."

She turned her sights to the heavens, still tinged with the remnants of the setting sun. A moment later he lowered himself to the cushion beside her.

Again, as all the other times, they fell into easy conversation. Soon the sky was dark and the stars emerged in abundance. Even then, he made no move to leave, and she was content to gaze at the stars and talk with him about anything and everything.

Somehow they both ended up lying with their heads on the pillows, their bodies stretched out, arms crossed behind their heads. He was telling her about the future with manmade stars called satellites that sent waves of communication here and there throughout the earth, that a person in one part of the world could press a button and communicate with someone else.

"Is that how you communicated with me the first few times we saw one another?"

"No, that was very different. That was the holy water, giving me a glimpse of you in the past. We call it an overlap."

"Overlap?"

"When two time periods join for a brief moment."

"Like they fold over each other?"

"Something like that."

"Well, however it happens, I neglected to thank you for coming to my aid that first night."

"You're welcome."

"I was in the process of working my way free from Father James."

"Yes, I could tell." His voice was wry.

She rose to one elbow. "Do you doubt my abilities?"

"Not at all." He was staring at the sky, giving her the opportunity to admire his features. Something about him beckoned to her, as though he was the miracle her soul truly needed and longed for.

"Do you think 'tis possible Providence brought us together at just the right time and the right place for a reason?"

"Since God is outside of time and space, I think He can do anything."

The slightly longer strands of his dark hair were mussed from the wind. And before she realized what she was doing, she combed a piece back.

The moment she did so, something changed in the air between them—something she couldn't explain, something she didn't understand, something that excited her nonetheless. She wanted to touch his hair again, actually had the urge to dig her fingers in and lose them there.

But before she could embarrass herself that way, she began to lower her hand. He captured it and in the next instant brought it to his lips. He pressed a gentle kiss to her fingertips and held it several long seconds—almost indecisively—before he flipped her hand over and planted a kiss at the center of her palm.

The instant his lips touched her there, she stopped breathing. The sensation was exquisite, beautiful, like nothing she'd ever known. When his lips shifted to her wrist and pressed warmly and firmly, her pulse throbbed faster. Was this his advance? Without a retreat? She hoped so.

His lips moved again, this time a little higher on her arm, and she drew in a trembling breath and closed her eyes, savoring the pleasure, drawing it out, letting it course through her whole body.

He kissed a spot halfway up her arm, this time at the bend. As his lips made contact with the tender spot, she couldn't hold back a gasp. Her eyes flew open to find that in the process of kissing her arm, he'd drawn her down against him.

He released her arm but didn't move. Instead, his eyes sought hers. The green was almost black, leaving no doubt he wanted her but that he was seeking her permission before doing anything more.

What exactly did he want to do?

As if seeing the question in her eyes, he slipped a hand to her neck, his fingers gliding around, sending more shivers of anticipation through her body. In the next instant, he guided her down, drawing her face nearer until their lips were almost touching and she could feel his breath.

She would let him kiss her if that's what he wanted. She bent the last of the distance, showing him her acquiescence.

As their mouths met, she wasn't sure what she was expecting—perhaps the hard, bruising quality of Robert's kisses. But Dawson's response was nothing like that. Instead, his lips were warm and soft, and he seemed to want to draw her into the kiss with him, guiding her lips to mesh with his, pressing and urging and nudging until she joined in the mingling.

The intimate tangle of their lips melted something inside her so that heat began to pool low, a heat that also emanated out, pulsing along every nerve and making every muscle tight with need.

Was this what kissing could be like? Should be like? How had she never known? After experiencing such intense attraction to Dawson, maybe that's why his kiss was so pleasurable—because she already desired him. Maybe it was also because he was so different from anyone else, so intellectually stimulating and interesting and kind.

Whatever the case, she didn't want to stop, and her yearning for him only swelled. She pressed in more urgently, but in the next moment he broke the kiss, framing her face with his hands and holding her back.

Her chest rose and fell rapidly against his. She could only gaze at his lips in dazed wonder.

His thumb skimmed the freckles across one side of her nose, then the other. His lashes were half lowered but couldn't hide the desire in his eyes—desire that matched hers.

She moved her hands to his face, letting her fingers glide over the stubble, over the hard lines of his jaw, up to his cheeks. He felt so good, better than she'd imagined. And she wanted to let her hands explore him wherever they wanted to go.

Was it possible that if she found such pleasure in kissing, she'd also find pleasure in other ways with him? Just because her intimacy with Robert had been uncomfortable, didn't mean it would be that way with Dawson—if this kiss was any indication.

But Joanna's warning from earlier resounded somewhere at the back of her mind. Her cousin had warned her about giving away intimacies meant only for the marriage bed. She hadn't worried about it before, but clearly Dawson made her feel things no one else ever had.

Of course, she had no intention of getting carried away. Joanna was still nearby and would never permit it.

But this passion with Dawson, it was too beautiful to do anything but enjoy.

Philippa combed back another strand of his hair, then bent closer so that her lips were almost brushing his. Then she waited for him to kiss her once more.

HE WAS GOING TO KISS HER AGAIN. He knew he shouldn't. But he was anyway.

She was the oasis to the parched wasteland of his soul. And now that he'd gotten a drink of her lips, the thirst inside him wouldn't be sated until he had more.

Her mouth hovered against his, and her breath teased him with her sweetness. He'd never tasted anyone or anything sweeter than her. Her fingers in his hair, the swell of her chest pressing his, the tickle of loose strands of her hair against his cheeks. His senses registered every detail of her. She was more real than anything else. And for the first time in his life, he felt as though he was truly alive.

With one hand on her cheek, he grazed his thumb down to her ear, to her neck, then to her collarbone. As he made a delicate trail to her shoulder, she sucked in a sharp breath.

Her soft sound of pleasure was all the invitation he needed to lift into her and taste of her lips again. This time she was ready. Not that she hadn't been ready before. But it had almost seemed like she'd never been kissed before. Yet she'd been married and surely was experienced in the ways between men and women.

He couldn't keep from quickly deepening the kiss, an insatiable need driving him. She made a moan at the back of her throat before she slipped her arms around his neck, as if holding him prisoner with no intention of letting him go.

The truth was, he didn't want to let her go. After the past three days of an endless undercurrent charging every moment they were together, he should have known this was where they'd end up—in each other's arms, kissing as though tomorrow didn't exist.

At a loud cough from the direction of the door, Philippa broke away with a gasp. She pushed up to her knees. Her gray-blue eyes were luminous, her lips parted and swollen, her face flushed.

He wanted to wrap his arms around her, pull her back down, and kiss her all night.

As though seeing the direction of his thoughts, she gasped again and sat back on her heels, putting more distance between them. Her chest rose and fell, and she pressed her hands against it, as if doing so would calm her breathing.

He let his lashes fall to half-mast, trying to bank his need, trying to gain control of the desire that had turned into a meteor, streaking through the sky and setting them on a collision course. Because, really, there was no other way for this relationship between them to end, was there? In a devastating crash that would hurt them both?

Unless he offered to marry her. . . Could he really consider such a thing?

John had spoken of it yesterday after their sword drills, as if the prospect was completely logical and acceptable. Clearly, marriages in the Middle Ages didn't come with the same set of requirements and expectations as modern marriages. Dating, love, engagement, and a fancy wedding weren't necessary. Other factors seemed to play a bigger part in the union. Factors like safety and security . . .

And, of course, if they were married, she'd have no reason to pull back from kissing him. They wouldn't need a chaperone. She wouldn't have to be embarrassed. And they could get carried away if they wanted to.

Yes, he wanted to.

She was even more beautiful in the moonlight, with the remnants of their passion making her glow.

"John thinks I should marry you." Whether right or wrong, the words fell out.

She lowered her hands to her lap and twisted at her skirt. If she was surprised by his statement, she didn't show it. In fact, she didn't reveal any emotion that could clue him in to her reaction to the possibility of marrying him.

"John believes if you marry, then your uncle will have to leave you alone, that he won't be able to exert any more control over you and your inheritance."

She plucked at a loose thread without meeting his gaze.

His chest seemed especially hollow, and the beat of his heart echoed there loudly. What was she thinking? Was she trying to figure out a polite way to tell him no?

"Listen, it's not a big deal." He pushed himself up so that he was leaning back on his elbows. "It's a crazy idea anyway." One driven by the passion of the moment. "Forget I said anything about it."

"No, Dawson. We need not forget about it." She continued to fiddle with the thread. "'Tis a viable option, to be sure."

Would she really consider marrying him? Heat speared him quick and hard. But just as soon as it did, he poured a mental bucket of icy water over his head. A marriage to her would be in name only. He couldn't sleep with her and then leave. It would be wrong, downright selfish, and unfair to her. Even within the bounds of marriage.

"'Tis possible if I marry, I might thwart his designs." She spoke quietly. "But he is cunning, and I cannot know for certain he will concede."

"If you marry, what choice will he have?"

She was silent, as though earnestly contemplating his suggestion.

A strange knot of tension twisted inside him. Was he really serious about this? Did he want her to say yes? If she did, would he have the guts to go forward with marrying her? Surely there was someone else she could marry, a man who would be able to stay with her in the Middle Ages and love her the way she deserved.

He pushed to his feet, sudden frustration coursing through him. "If you marry, you should marry someone other than me—"

"No." Her answer was so quick it sent another spear of heat through him. And when she peered up at him with both shyness and desire, he wanted to gather her into his arms and show every other man that this beautiful woman—the most eligible woman in all of England—belonged to him.

He gave a curt shake of his head. What was wrong with him? He had to do what was best for her and stop thinking about himself.

"If I marry, I would that it be you."

"I'm not the best choice—"

"I want you and none other." Her words came out in a rush.

She wanted to marry him and nobody else? Why him? She could choose other men who were honorable and worthy of her. Men better than him.

He hesitated and blew out a breath before he spun on his heels and stalked to the tower wall. He peered out over the grassy embankments to the dark forest beyond. What was he doing here with Philippa? He'd traveled to the past to help her, not to fall in love and marry her.

Fall in love?

He reached up and rubbed at the tension in the back of his neck. Was he falling in love with her already? It was too soon for that. He was probably confusing physical attraction, even infatuation, with love.

He could hear the swish of her gown as she rose, the hesitant patter of her footsteps as she crossed to him, the almost-imperceptible intake of her breath as she gathered the courage to speak. "Dawson?"

He knew if he turned, he'd only want to gather her close and kiss her under the starlight until they both forgot about the passing of time. But he couldn't do that, had to stay strong.

"What I feel with you?" She laid her hand on his back. "I have never experienced with another man."

"And what do you feel?" He tried to keep his voice even.

"I care about you more in the few days together than I did for Robert in the entirety of our marriage."

He closed his eyes to fight against the need to tell her that he cared more about her in their few days together than he'd ever felt for another woman. "Robert was a fool."

She released a soft laugh and let her fingers linger upon his back.

Her touch, as always, made him aware of her presence, her texture, her scent, her sounds. "There are other men who will recognize what a treasure you are."

"Perhaps. But you are the one I want."

Holy Mary and Joseph. He was losing his resistance more with every passing second.

"Why should I not marry a man I desire?" The hint of embarrassment to her tone told him this conversation wasn't easy for her, that she wasn't used to stating her feelings.

"You should marry such a man, but—"

"Then I choose you."

"But I'm leaving."

"Stay."

His muscles tightened with the need to tell her yes, that he'd stay, that he'd be with her, that he'd do whatever she wanted.

She trailed her fingers to his arm and made a move to twist him around so they were facing. Instead of giving in to the pressure, he drew her arm around his torso, pulling her close to his back so that she was embracing him from behind.

She held herself stiffly, as though she didn't quite know

what to think. Then she slipped her other arm around his waist, hugging him from behind and resting against his back. As she clasped her hands together at his navel, he laid his arms over them.

This was safer. He'd be able to resist temptation much better if he wasn't staring at her lips.

"Will you think about staying?" she asked.

"It's out of my control, Philippa." Why not simply tell her the truth? She'd accepted everything else he'd said so far about the holy water and the time crossing. "My friends are planning to give me a dose of holy water at the end of my fifth day in the past. The dose will wake me and bring me back to my normal life."

"Is there nothing you can do to stop them, a message you can send to tell them you want to remain here?"

He wasn't sure how an overlap from the past to the present would work. After all, he was in a coma, so there likely wasn't a way for him to communicate with his friends. Besides, if his present-day body was at the hospital in Norwich, then he'd have to travel to the vicinity of Norwich here in the past. Even then, he had no guarantee Acey and Chloe would be there when he overlapped.

He expelled a sigh, staring unseeingly into the night. "There's nothing I can do." And if he could think of a way to delay his friends, he'd only endanger them all the more with the Hamin. They wouldn't be safe until he used the information from Mum—as sparse as it was—to track down the Hamin's headquarters in Norfolk.

"The truth is, I have to go back and help capture a group of terrorists. If I don't, my friends will likely be attacked by them next."

It was Philippa's turn to sigh.

He could admit, the longer he was in the past, the more he wanted to remain. A powerful energy seemed to be pulling him to build a life in this place where he could be with his mum and sister and get a second chance with them. He'd also relish the opportunity to stay longer and get to know Philippa better.

She hugged him tighter. "Is there a way you can come back once you are finished with saving your friends from this group?"

Was there? His thoughts returned to all Lord Burlington had relayed to Chloe. If Dawson remembered correctly, once he ingested holy water to return to the present, his 1382 body would have a difficult time surviving because people could only live for a few days without IV fluids, oxygen, and other life-sustaining measures after their bodies became comatose.

Essentially, at some point—whether sooner or later—the person would begin to die in both eras, since the body wasn't able to sustain the energy needed to span two eras simultaneously forever. A person could continue to live, but only if given more holy water at the right time.

So, while it was possible for him to cross back again, he'd need the holy water to survive. Even then, it was risky. What if his past body died before anyone administered the holy water? What if they didn't have any holy water to give him?

He'd known from the start that making the time crossing would be complex and dangerous. He'd just never expected it to get this complicated.

"Now that I have you in my life, I cannot picture a future without you." Philippa's whisper wrapped around him tighter than her arms.

After he returned to the present, he couldn't imagine any other woman he'd ever want as much as he wanted Philippa. Of course, good women still existed in modern times. But how could anyone compare with this positive and encouraging woman?

Why would he want to exist in his other life without her? What would he have there to live for? Yes, he had friends. But his family was here, and so was this woman he was growing to love. Yes, love. Why not return to the past to be with her?

"If you'll wait for me," he whispered, "I'll do my best to return."

"I shall wait forever if need be." Her voice contained a smile, and she sidled around, making her way under his arm until she was standing in front of him, her lips curved and her eyes filled with happiness.

The idea of being together, possibly forever, sent a waft of happiness through him too. And desire. Lots of desire. He slid his hands to the small of her back and guided her closer. "I was holding you behind me for a reason."

She came willingly. "What reason could you possibly have?"

"So that I wouldn't do this." He angled down and took possession of her lips. This time there was no hesitancy on her part, no need for him to show her how to kiss. She'd learned the lesson well from their first time, and now she met him with an eagerness that matched his.

If he'd thought he'd been thirsty for her before, this time he craved her more than life itself. And he knew there was no place he wanted to be, either in the past or the present, except by her side, holding her and kissing her like this.

He delved deeper, pressing against her harder, pinning her to the tower wall. She released a soft moan before opening her mouth wider, giving him all the deliciousness he wanted, her fingers digging into his back.

A moan of his own rose swiftly, the need for her consuming him, fueled by her passion, so innocent and yet so strong.

From the tower doorway came first a throat clearing, then coughing. Their chaperone.

He had to put an end to the kiss, couldn't let himself get carried away, had to be grateful for Joanna watching over Philippa and guarding her reputation—even if he was slightly irritated.

He needed to guard her reputation too, had to respect and honor her, because he cared for her too much to allow himself to use her in a moment of passion. With the steely self-control he'd developed in his early days in the army, he released her and took a step back.

With an almost dazed, dizzied expression, she touched her lips, perhaps in an attempt to recapture the kiss.

His gut hardened with the need to recapture the kiss too, but he moved another foot away.

"Yes," she said breathlessly.

He quirked an eyebrow.

"Yes, I shall marry you."

Was that the best thing for her? Would it protect her from

her uncle's scheming, especially during the time he was gone back to the present? "But what if I'm unable to return?"

"You must. We shall make a plan to ensure it."

His heart gave a leap of hope. Was it really possible that his whole life could change so drastically, that not only would his sight be restored and he'd cross into the past, but that he'd have the gift of this incredible woman in his life?

He wasn't sure, but he wanted to find out. The only way to do that was to talk with his mum and John about the options. He glanced to the position of the moon. It was too late to meet with them now. But he'd do so first thing tomorrow and enlist their help so that he could be with Philippa forever.

In the meantime . . . he put several more feet between them.

"Do not go." She held out a hand in invitation, her eyes beckoning, even her lips parted with readiness for more.

He knew she wasn't inviting him to share anything beyond more kisses. Even though she'd been married, she was too innocent, didn't realize the chemistry between them was incredible, even sizzling. And if he stayed, he might not be able to stop at just kissing.

He had to go. He backed up until he stood in the door to the tower stairs.

She didn't move from where he'd pushed her against the wall. And just the memory of his body pressed against hers nearly sent him careening across the tower to her. Instead, he gripped the doorframe. "I cannot kiss you again and hope to remain sane and in control."

At his confession, her eyes widened, and her lips turned up

with the delectable hint of a smile, one that only made him want to cross and kiss her all the more—quite a lot more, actually.

He scraped a hand down his face, over his mouth and chin, as if that could somehow wipe away his needs. But he suspected he'd never get enough of her.

Without another word, he forced himself to walk away and down the tower stairway. He just prayed he would be able to find a way to be with her. He wasn't sure how, but he would do anything to make it happen.

~ 22 ~

SHOUTS AND THE HURRIED SLAP of footsteps woke Philippa from her dreams—dreams in which she was still lying beside Dawson and kissing him.

Gentle hands shook her, but she burrowed deeper underneath her cover. She wasn't ready to leave that blissful place where just the two of them existed, where he held her and kissed her so tenderly one moment and so ardently the next.

She'd never known what she was missing until she'd met Dawson. Not only had she never understood how pleasurable a man's physical touch could be, but she hadn't known a man was someone she could enjoy being with, even long to be with.

But with Dawson . . .

She sighed again, dragging her pillows over her head to block out reality a while longer. All she wanted to do was dream about him.

After he'd descended from the tower last night, she'd actually loathed his leaving. She'd wanted to stay with him all throughout the night, but Joanna's presence had prevented her from racing after him and throwing herself at him. In fact, one look at Joanna's pursed lips and narrowed eyes had squelched any thought of attempting to persuade Dawson to kiss her again.

Oh, how he could kiss. And oh, how she wanted to kiss him more as soon and as oft as possible.

Should they get married forthwith? Today? Even this morn?

The very prospect made her heart beat faster.

At another shake against her shoulder, she shifted her pillows and opened her eyes. She expected to see Joanna. Instead, Lady Wilkin leaned over her, serious green eyes fixed upon her. "My lady, I regret to wake you in such a manner, but your uncle arrived in the night and has laid siege to Barsham."

All the warmth in her blood drained away, leaving icy cold in its stead. She sat up, brushing her loose hair out of her face. So, Uncle had finally discovered her whereabouts. She'd known eventually he would. And she'd expected him to pursue her. She just hadn't anticipated he'd arrive so hastily or that he'd wage war against Lord and Lady Wilkin.

A new sense of panic pumped through her, and she thrust aside the cover. "I must find a way to leave Barsham. Are there any secret passageways out of the fortress?"

Lady Wilkin placed a hand on her shoulder as though to steady her and lend her strength. "You need not leave. But I do suggest you wed Dawson anon."

She'd wanted to get married just moments ago, but not under such dire circumstances, with Uncle Hugo having come to Barsham with the intention of attacking and taking her by force if necessary.

"I cannot bear to think of the distress I shall cause to you and your husband's household by my presence here."

"Once you are married, we shall alert your uncle of the news."

"Do you think such news will deter him?"

"If you are legally wed, how can he pursue you for his own gain?"

Philippa nodded and yet hesitated.

Lady Wilkin smoothed a lock of Philippa's hair off her face, her eyes turning tender. "Dawson told us already this morn that the two of you agreed upon marriage and that he has decided to come back, that he wants to be with you."

"Do you think 'tis possible?" She wasn't sure what was needed to secure his return, but she'd do whatever she must for that to happen.

"I have set aside some ampullae of holy water from the spring at the priory. When the time comes, we will use the water to revive him."

Philippa expelled a taut breath and whispered a prayer of thanksgiving. In spite of Uncle's threat, she still had much for which to be grateful.

"So, shall we proceed with the wedding?" Lady Wilkin's mouth curved into a semblance of a smile.

"Now?" Philippa glanced down at her thin linen chemise.

"Yes, now."

Joanna stood nearby, already dressed and groomed, clearly prepared for the turn of events.

Of course, Philippa hadn't been able to stop talking about Dawson after retiring to bed with Joanna. And they'd whispered late into the night about him and how he made her feel things she'd never known were possible. Even though Joanna had once experienced some of those feelings with Lance, she'd never kissed him, never had a pool of warmth

244

form in the pit of her stomach, never wanted to brazenly press against him.

Philippa had tried to explain the new sensations to Joanna, had tried to describe her desires. But ultimately, everything with Dawson was so new and different that nothing had been quite adequate to depict the way she felt. If she had to assign one word to her feelings, she'd say *love*. She'd never loved before, but this had to be close to it.

"Will you agree to a wedding?" Lady Wilkin's voice contained an urgency that told Philippa she didn't have time this morn to daydream.

Joanna gave a nod as though to encourage Philippa to accept the offer of marriage. After all, they'd already discussed the benefits and possible repercussions of a union with Dawson. And Joanna was of the mind that Philippa would be happiest if she broke away from Uncle and started a new life with Dawson.

Philippa pushed up to her knees. "Very well. I shall agree."

Before Philippa could speak further, Lady Wilkin motioned past the bed curtains toward the door, which was wide open. A crowd seemed to be tarrying in the hallway, and in the next instant, Lord Wilkin stepped into the chamber followed closely by Dawson. Their faces were grave, and they were in the midst of what appeared to be a serious discussion.

As Dawson's gaze landed upon Philippa kneeling in the center of her bed, he halted suddenly and ceased speaking. He took her in, starting with her unruly hair swirling in abandon over her shoulders and hanging unfettered to her waist. Since she was wearing naught but her chemise, she was grateful for the curtain of her hair to shield her indecency.

Even so, she hugged her arms over her chest and wished to draw her cover around her.

Others had begun to congregate inside the room—Lord Wilkin's knights, guests, sons, and other relatives who were visiting or living with him. A priest circled around them all and came to stand beside the bed next to Lady Wilkin.

"Are we ready?" The priest directed his question to Lady Wilkin.

In turn, Lady Wilkin held out a hand toward Philippa. "'Tis time."

She glanced to her chemise. "Shall I not change into more appropriate attire?"

Lady Wilkin bent close enough to whisper. "Since you will wed and consummate your union directly after, there is no need . . ." Lady Wilkin had the grace to blush.

Her own cheeks heating with embarrassment, Philippa could only grab at the cover and draw it around her shoulders. Of course they must consummate if they wanted their marriage to be considered true and honorable. But the prospect of doing so immediately following their vows was not the way she'd expected to start her morn.

What did Dawson think of all this? Was he in agreement?

Her eyes found his. His look smoldered so hotly she had to drop her gaze lest everyone in the room see such brazen desire, not only from Dawson but also from her. For just the prospect of knowing how much Dawson wanted her only stirred fierce longing inside her.

"They are indeed ready." Lady Wilkin was now smiling,

her gaze darting back and forth between Philippa and Dawson, clearly sensing their attraction and delighting over it.

Philippa allowed the lady to help her to her feet—bare feet. And as she moved toward Dawson, she clutched the cover around her to provide a measure of decency, at least until the ceremony was complete.

As she reached Dawson's side, he leaned in. "Are you certain this is what you want?" His eyes still radiated with unmistakable desire . . . and something else she couldn't name but that seemed to encompass her with affection and devotion.

"Yes." She wanted to be with him more than she'd ever wanted anything else.

She went through the motions of the wedding ceremony, led by the priest and witnessed by at least two dozen people who had gathered around them. Dawson spoke his intentions with such sincerity, she could sense the marriage meant more to him than just saving her.

As the time came for her to speak her vows, she knew the marriage meant more to her than that too. "I, Philippa, take thee, Dawson, to be my wedded husband, to have and to hold from this day forward, for better, for worse, for richer, for poorer, in sickness, and in health, to love, cherish, and to obey, till death us do part, according to God's holy ordinance; thereto, I give thee my troth."

She desperately prayed that they would have many days to love and cherish each other. But with Uncle's army surrounding Barsham Castle, she didn't know what the future would hold. 'Twas best not to think on it and to instead make the most of every moment they did have.

"The ring?" The priest directed his question to Dawson.

He dug into his pocket and pulled out a band bejeweled with what appeared to be small diamonds. It was stunning and unlike anything she'd ever seen before. Where had he gotten it?

As if sensing her question, he glanced at his mother. "The ring belonged to Mum before her marriage to John."

Lady Wilkin nodded at Philippa warmly, as though she'd handpicked Philippa to be her new daughter-in-law herself.

Dawson placed the ring on the prayer book the priest was holding out. The priest spoke a blessing over the ring, then motioned for them to place their hands together on the book while he prayed.

After the prayer, Dawson took up the ring and slid it on her finger, repeating after the priest: "With this ring I thee wed, with my body I thee worship, and with all my worldly goods, I thee endow. In the name of the Father, and of the Son, and of the Holy Ghost. Amen."

The band was loose, but not enough that it would slip easily off. She admired it upon her finger, seven diamonds in a band of gold. Seven, the number of perfection. Was this a sign that Providence was pleased and would make a way for them to remain together?

The rest of the ceremony passed quickly, and within minutes the priest was issuing the benediction and the sign of the cross.

After the final word, most people lingered, primarily men who were talking strategy with Dawson. A maidservant was already busy at work preparing the bed with fresh sheets and covers, while Joanna and Lady Wilkin had turned their

JODY HEDLUND

attention to Philippa. Joanna brushed her hair, while Lady Wilkin clasped a matching diamond bracelet and necklace to her attire.

When finished, Joanna stripped away the cover to which Philippa had clung throughout the ceremony. She knew well the customs involved in putting newlyweds in the marriage bed. The guests would make sure the husband and wife were undressed or at least in their night garments. Then they'd watch the couple lie down together in the bed. The priest would say a prayer. Finally, everyone would exit the room and allow the newlyweds privacy.

Now, as Philippa stood only in the thin summer chemise, a strange tremble worked up her legs and into her stomach. She wasn't frightened the way she'd been on her wedding night with Robert.

But as Joanna and Lady Wilkin led her to the bed and settled her on one side, her nerves drew taut. Whether she liked it or not, this was her duty as Dawson's wife, and she wouldn't shrink from it. Maybe with Dawson, with the passion they already shared, the time together would be less awkward than it had been with Robert. After all, the kissing had been different.

Lady Wilkin finished tucking the cover around her, leaving her shoulders showing and hair hanging in waves around her. Then with a satisfied smile, she straightened. "Dawson, your bride is ready."

~ 23 ~

DAWSON STEELED HIMSELF, straightening his backbone and tensing his muscles. As much as he wanted to avoid lying beside Philippa, he had no choice.

After awakening in the early hours of the morning and discovering Lord Deighton's army encamped around Barsham, Dawson had realized he had to wed her, not only to save her but also to save his mum, John, and the rest of the people living in Barsham.

He'd gone directly to Mum and John and let them know his decision. They'd both agreed with him and explained that the wedding must take place as soon as possible, along with the consummation of their marriage.

He'd argued with Mum that he hadn't known Philippa long enough to sleep with her. But his mum had told him that he'd had more time to get to know Philippa than many noblemen had with their future wives, that sometimes unions took place without either the bride or the groom having the chance to speak to each other previously.

Dawson had tried to reason with her that anything could happen in the traveling between the past and present. What if he never came out of his coma and didn't make it back to either place? But his mum insisted that even if he died, the marriage would help Philippa, especially if they kept his death a secret.

In the end, despite all his arguments, he'd reluctantly agreed to his mum's instructions that at the very least he had to get into bed with Philippa. "What you do after the door is closed is up to you," she said. "But if you care about her, then you'll make her yours and give her uncle no doubt that you are truly married."

Make her yours. The words sounded so archaic coming from his mum, who'd always been adamant about women's rights and their equality to men. The mum he'd once known wouldn't have insinuated that Philippa would become his when they were married, that he would have the power over her simply because he was a man.

He'd shaken his head, tried to explain to his mum that he wanted Philippa to be his equal, that she wouldn't belong to him any more than he would belong to her.

But Mum had pressed her lips together and told him that in this case, if he didn't possess Philippa, her uncle would still claim the young woman.

For now, he had to put on a good show for their witnesses, but later, when everyone left, he'd assure Philippa he had no intention of forcing her to be with him. He'd never been a one-night-stand guy, had always tried to pursue women respectfully, and that's what he intended to do with Philippa.

If he survived the coming week and was able to make it back to the past, then they'd have more time together, and he'd win over her heart before he won her body.

The room had grown silent, the dozen or more witnesses having tapered to silence. He could feel their eyes upon him. And he wanted to squirm with the awkwardness of the entire situation. This bedding custom of the Middle Ages was the strangest thing he'd come across yet. If he could survive this, surely he'd be able to survive anything else the past would throw his way.

With a deep breath, he finally pivoted. He didn't dare let himself look at Philippa in bed. He'd already made that mistake once when he first arrived in the room and caught sight of her in her nightgown with her long hair tousled with sleep. She'd been so exquisite and enticing he'd forgotten how to breathe. All he'd been able to do was stand and watch her like an idiot.

Now, as John moved to his side and began to assist him out of his weapons belt, Dawson forced his gaze to his garments— the oddly fitted trousers and doublet he'd borrowed from John—and began shedding everything, until he stood in his underdrawers. He'd already made it clear to his mum and John that he didn't care what other men in the Middle Ages did, he wasn't climbing into bed naked. The situation was uncomfortable enough as it was.

Was Philippa watching him? What did she think of this weird custom of bedding the newlyweds? Was she as embarrassed as he was, or was she used to the frank approach to sex?

Still avoiding looking at her, he quickly crossed to the bed and slid onto the feather-stuffed mattress beside her. As he situated himself, he tried to keep from brushing against her, taking care that not even their shoulders and arms grazed. God knew he wasn't a saint. If he allowed himself the pleasure of touching her, he wasn't sure how his self-control would hold up.

As the priest moved to the end of the bed and began another prayer, Dawson bowed his head, but from the corner of his eye he could see that everyone was watching him with Philippa. If he was as stiff as a brick wall in bed with her, would they begin to call into question the validity of their union? Enough that her uncle would force an annulment?

Beside him, he could feel Philippa move. Her fingers. They were trembling. Was she simply nervous about having to undergo this strange ritual, or was she anxious about the coming time with him? He wished he could stop everything and order everyone out right then and there so he could reassure her that she had nothing to worry about. But for the moment, he was as trapped in this situation as she was.

Underneath the cover, before he could reason himself out of the connection, he reached for her hand and clasped it within his, hoping she would understand his offer of assurance.

She stiffened for only a moment before letting her hand relax within his.

"Bless Lord and Lady Huxham," the priest said. "May they be fruitful and multiply, according to Your command in Scripture. And may they forever live as Your stewards in both this world and the one to come."

As the priest brought the prayer to a close and spoke the Amen, Dawson whispered a silent plea for strength to make it through his final two days in the past with integrity. He had today and tomorrow left. It wasn't long. But it was enough to make mistakes if he wasn't careful.

"Lord Huxham." John approached the bed and bowed. "We wish you and your bride many happy years."

"Thank you." Holy Mary and Joseph. He hadn't thought the situation could get any more awkward. But apparently it could. He wished everyone would go away already, but unfortunately, it took several more agonizing moments before people began to make their way out of the chamber.

Joanna was the last to leave, pulling the bed curtains closed with a slight smile directed at Philippa.

They lay unmoving in the shadows of the thick tapestries that surrounded the bed on three sides as Joanna's footsteps crossed the room. The door opened and then, a moment later, it closed.

When silence descended, Dawson peeled back one of the curtains to get a peek at the room, making sure they were really alone and that no one remained.

The large wardrobe was open but mostly empty. The chairs on either side of the cold hearth were deserted. A tray of berries and a bowl of cream sat upon a table near the door. Beside it were two goblets and what appeared to be a bottle of wine.

No doubt his mum had left them for Philippa and him. Even though the circumstances for the marriage had come about in an unlikely way, he'd sensed his mum's excitement that he'd decided to stay and marry Philippa. She wanted them to be together as a family as much as he wanted it. And she probably viewed a marriage to Philippa as the insurance that would motivate him to return to the past.

His mum was right. Now that he had Philippa, he'd do anything to stay. The more he was with her, the more he couldn't imagine going away. Not even for a few days.

"Looks like we're finally alone." He let the bed curtain fall back into place.

She shifted, her body stiff. Her fingers were no longer trembling, but they were cold.

"Listen, Philippa." He brushed her hand with his thumb, wanting to do more, but knowing just how easily passion flared between them. "I don't intend to sleep with you right now."

She drew back, clearly not expecting the declaration. "You must do it—"

"No." Was she insinuating that he was the one who needed to do this, as if it was an act a man must perform with no pleasure for the woman? That wasn't right.

"Dawson, 'tis necessary. And I understand what must be done." Her voice dripped with an embarrassment that told him all too clearly that she hadn't taken pleasure in sex—that she'd seen it as her duty, and that she would continue to see it as her duty now to him. "I have endured this before."

"Endured?" He twisted to face her, frustration carving a path inside him. "Is that what you did with Robert? Endure?"

She hesitated, her exquisite face pale against her pillow, highlighting her freckles.

Was she afraid of him? He hated that thought, hated that she had a mistaken view of what the marriage bed was supposed to be like.

All the more reason he needed to wait. He pushed the covers off and climbed out of bed. He stalked over to a peg on the wall where someone had hung his clothes, then grabbed the long tunic and stuffed his arms in, bringing it down over his head.

A moment later as he pulled up his leggings, Philippa's flowery perfume from behind stopped him before she placed a hand on his arm. "I did not mean to offend you, my lord."

The frustration only pulsed harder through his veins. This wasn't her fault. "Don't call me *my lord*, Philippa. I'm not a lord over you or anyone. We're equals."

Her hold wavered as though she didn't know what to make of his rant.

"Where I come from, women aren't considered possessions or property to be sold and traded at will. Instead, women have the same rights as men—or nearly so."

"I see."

Did she? He spun to face her. And the moment he did so, he realized his mistake. In the flimsy nightgown with her hair unbound and her wide innocent eyes watching him, she was more beautiful than ever.

His breath got lost somewhere in his chest, and he wasn't sure he had the power to walk away. He had to bring an end to the conversation quickly and put distance between them. "Our marriage, I want it to be different from your other one." It was odd to speak of himself as being married. He never would have imagined it only a week ago. And Acey and Chloe would be shocked when he told them.

Philippa tilted her head slightly, a sign—he was learning meant—she was thinking.

Was she comparing him to Robert? How could he prove he

was different? That they would be different together? He lifted a hand and stroked a strand of her hair. "Did you have the kind of relationship with Robert where you could talk openly about things like this?"

"No, we rarely spoke to one another."

"And did he touch you this way?" Dawson combed his fingers more deeply into her hair, staying gentle.

"No. Never." Her voice was breathless, and her chest rose and fell with a giant intake.

"What about his kisses?" His attention dropped to her lips, slightly parted as she struggled to breathe.

She shook her head, even as her attention came to rest upon his mouth. The gray-blue warmed into the haze of a hot summer sky.

His blood burned, as if the temperature in the room had suddenly spiked. He shouldn't kiss her right now. They weren't completely clothed. They were alone. And their defenses were down—at least his were.

But a short kiss wouldn't be a big deal, would it? He could prove his point with a kiss.

He tugged at her hair, winding his fingers in tighter and deeper.

She closed her eyes and swayed toward him. In the same motion, he bent in and seized her lips the way he'd wanted to do since last night. He wasted no time in taking the kiss deeper, moving faster, lighting a fuse that rapidly crackled like the wick of a stick of dynamite.

She responded almost as forcefully, rising on her toes, wrapping her arms around his neck and pressing in. Gone was the initial timidness of her first kisses. Instead, he could feel her hunger, which only made the fuse burn and spark more intensely.

The warmth of her body, the softness of her flesh, the urgent press of her chest—he tightened his hold, sliding his hands to the back of her neck, wrapping her hair up, weaving his fingers among the strands, and losing himself in her.

When she made a soft groan, he had a desperate urge to sweep her off her feet, take her over to their bed, and show her that she didn't have to *endure* anything with him.

But if he did that, he wouldn't be respecting her the way she deserved. No, for now, he had to stay strong in his resolve to wait, give her time, help her understand they were equals in everything, including in the bedroom.

He started to back away.

She released a huff of protest and clung to him.

Closing his eyes against the sharp need to kiss her again, he drew her head against his chest, tucking it under his chin, keeping her face from his view because if he saw her lips, he'd lose himself, wouldn't be able to stop.

"Did you have to endure our kiss?" His voice came out raspy.

She shook her head. "I have to endure *not* kissing you."

"Good." His mouth curved up. "When the time comes for us to share the marriage bed, I want you to feel the same way about that as you do about our kissing."

"I am not sure that is possible."

"I promise it is."

"Then you will have much convincing to do since I cannot

fathom anything better than kissing you."

The conversation was heating his insides more than he wanted to acknowledge, and he needed to shift the course of the discussion before he let his thoughts wander too far.

"I have never met a man like you, Dawson." She burrowed into him, clearly satisfied to be in his arms.

Pulling her with him, he leaned against the wall, trying to calm his runaway pulse and cool his hormones. "And what kind of man do you say I am?"

"You are considerate and gentle. And you seek my happiness and pleasure ahead of your own."

He loved hearing her frank observations, but the truth was, he still had a lot of growing to do. As strange as it was to admit it, he was glad God had allowed the recent trials. That night of the attack by the Hamin had been brutal. But it had given him an awakening—along with Sybil's death—to see that he was stuck and needed to push through his grief instead of avoiding it forever.

Maybe part of the reason God had given him this trip to the past was so he could meet Philippa, witness her courage, and learn from her the lessons for seeing beauty in difficulty.

He pressed a kiss to the top of her head. "In this moment, I propose we start out our marriage with your lesson number three, reminding ourselves of the many things we have to be thankful for."

She pulled back just enough so she could peer up at him. Her eyes brimmed with a joy that sparked happiness inside him. "I like that idea very much."

"Then you go first." He guided her head back to his chest.

She began the simple prayer. "Thank You for this wedding day and for my new husband, who is everything I could ever ask for and more."

He offered his own silent prayers of thanksgiving, hoping the brightness and beauty of being with her would last as long as possible but sensing dark storm clouds were waiting for him just over the horizon.

~ 24 ~

SHE WANTED DAWSON TO KISS HER AGAIN, but he kept his distance and refrained. Although he'd said they were equals, she didn't have the courage to approach him and pull him down into another kiss, even with everything inside her longing to do so.

Instead, they sat in the cushioned chairs near the hearth and ate berries and cream and sipped mulled wine. He was only half dressed in his simple tunic and leggings, and she'd donned a light cloak to cover her chemise. Even with her feelings for him distracting her, she found herself enjoying their time together as she always did, answering his queries about her uncle and his connections to other nobility.

Finally, he glanced toward the open shutters, as if he could gauge the time of day. The sunlight from earlier had disappeared, clouds having swept over Norfolk to bring the summer rains that were necessary for the crops.

"I think it's about time for us to show ourselves to your uncle and let him know that we are married."

"Would Lord Wilkin send word to my uncle of the news?"

"Yes. But everyone agreed we should make an appearance so your uncle can see that you're willingly standing beside me and haven't been coerced into our union."

She dipped a ripe strawberry in the cream and took the moment to play coy, taking a dainty bite and pretending innocence. "And what, may I ask, will convince him most that I have not been coerced into becoming your bride?"

He sat forward, leaning his elbows on his knees so his tunic stretched across his shoulders. His lashes lowered halfway, but she could sense his regard, his desire, even his need.

She loved when he looked at her that way. She took another bite, letting her lips linger longer this time.

"What do you think will work to convince him?" Even his tone, though partly playful, hinted at something more.

"I am not entirely sure." This time she let her gaze purposefully drop to his mouth while she finished the last of her strawberry.

His lips tilted into a grin, one that was rugged and daring and much too appealing. If she'd believed she had an advantage over him, his self-assured smile spoke loudly enough that she had none. Even though she might try to wrap him around her finger, he would only let her if that's what he wanted.

She liked that he was strong, that he wasn't completely enamored of her the way other men were. Joanna had been right about that.

A simmering in his eyes told her he had a response, and she held her breath, waiting for him to speak his suggestion, hoping it was the same as hers. But before he could say anything, a firm knock resounded against the door.

"'Tis I, Lady Joanna. I have been sent by the lord and lady to assist Lady Huxham for the meeting with her uncle."

Lady Huxham. The sound of it from Joanna's lips warmed Philippa. She was Dawson's wife. They'd spoken irrevocable vows, pledged their lives to each other, and promised to love and cherish one another until death. Even if they hadn't yet made their marriage completely official, she felt a connection to Dawson that was only growing stronger.

Although she tried to understand his reasoning for waiting to consummate, she could admit to a lingering worry that Uncle would discover the truth and force an annulment. Regardless, they must now face him. In the process, she would pray he'd accept her decision of marriage and relinquish his need to use her wealth for his own purposes.

· ● ·

Within the hour, Philippa was standing beside Dawson at the top of the stone steps leading into the front entrance of the keep. Joanna and a maidservant had assisted her into her lavender gown and fashioned her hair underneath an opaque head covering.

Dawson was freshly groomed, his hair combed back, the layer of scruff on his face trimmed. With another fashionable outfit, including a doublet of black velvet trimmed with silver, he held himself with the bearing of an important man.

She'd prayed Uncle would take one look at Dawson and realize he'd lost the fight for her, that he could no longer control her and he might as well put his scheming to an end. With Lord and Lady Wilkin, Lord Wilkin's sons, as well as a dozen other men of diverse ranks standing in the bailey, her uncle wouldn't attempt to capture her. Not with so many people present. And not with Lord Wilkin's fighting men in position on the embattlements.

Dawson was studying the soldiers in their strategic spots circling the keep, most with bows and arrows at the ready. He hadn't smiled once since they'd stepped outside, almost as if the sight of the armed men inside the castle as well as outside was a reminder of how volatile the situation was.

Under the canopy of heavy clouds, a retinue of Uncle's soldiers rode through the main gatehouse and up the path toward the castle. Philippa searched for her uncle, a large man who was usually easy to spot wearing a felt chaperon over his balding head. But he wasn't among the group, and his absence didn't bode well.

Had he remained behind with his army of men and horses amassed along the perimeter of the castle? Already she'd heard frightened whispers that a siege engine was being constructed.

She'd hoped like everyone else that this hasty marriage to Dawson would avert disaster. But if Uncle refused to meet with her and was preparing for an attack, then their efforts were likely for naught.

A warm wind blew from the north, bringing with it a faint mist. Even so, she shivered, praying for peace, knowing she would never be able to stand silently by and watch her uncle bring ruin and destruction upon Barsham Castle and to the generous Wilkin family.

Dawson lifted his hand to the small of her back.

Had he noticed her shiver? As she lifted her gaze to meet his, the green of his eyes was serious. And yet, amidst the gravity of the situation, he seemed to be asking if she was alright.

His fingers grazed her, his touch bringing her assurance that she wasn't alone this time, that he was on her side and would fight for her. She wanted to reach for his hand and clasp it in hers, but she held herself with a measure of pride that would hopefully display her confidence to her uncle's men and her unwillingness to be intimidated by them.

As the knight at the forefront of the retinue halted his horse, the other knights reined in behind him. In their plate armor and great helms, she couldn't distinguish any of the men. But she guessed the leader of this band was her cousin, Joanna's older brother Norman.

"Greetings." Lord Wilkin's voice rang out over the now-silent gathering, the only sound the flapping of the flags flying from each of the four corner towers of the keep. "We thank you for agreeing to meet with us and come to a peaceful agreement—"

"The only peaceful resolution Lord Deighton will accept is the full return of his niece with an annulment in hand." The powerful voice behind the helm did indeed belong to Norman.

Beside her, Dawson stiffened, his fingers on her back curling into her more possessively.

"She is lawfully wedded in the sight of God and man." Lord Wilkin's answer contained a decisive bite.

"Lord Deighton is her guardian and advisor in the matters of marriage." Undoubtedly Norman was conveying the exact words Uncle Hugo had instructed him to speak. Norman, like his brothers, did not have the inner fortitude to disobey his father, unlike Joanna, who bore the strength of her mother—at least, Philippa wanted to believe she and Joanna both had inherited their mothers' strength.

"As guardian, Lord Deighton has received word from the king that he has granted his favor upon the union of Lord Kempe to Lady Neville." Norman held up a folded parchment with a crimson wax seal and then held it out toward Lord Wilkin.

One of Lord Wilkin's sons stepped forward, retrieved the parchment, and delivered it to his father. From where Philippa stood, she couldn't make out the exact nature of the seal to ascertain if it truly belonged to King Richard II.

However, as Lord Wilkin unfolded and read the missive, his lack of immediate response told her what she needed to know. It was from the king. Her uncle had likely instructed Lord Godwin Kempe to go before the king and ask permission for the marriage. Although such permission wasn't required, the king had probably been pleased with Godwin's request, especially if Godwin made sure the king knew of the advantages of the union to the wealthy, widowed Lady Neville.

Now that the king had granted his approval, how could anyone resist it? Certainly Lord Wilkin wouldn't be able to.

Philippa drew in a shaky breath.

Dawson leaned in against her ear. "What's wrong?"

"With the king's missive," she whispered back, "my uncle has trapped me."

Dawson shook his head, his eyes turning dark. "No."

"If I refuse to do as he wants, he will beseech the king for reinforcements." Lord Wilkin would already have a difficult time withstanding her uncle's forces. He'd have no hope if the king's reinforcements came. Essentially, Lord Wilkin had no choice but to concede to Uncle so that he didn't find himself an enemy of the king.

Lord Wilkin passed the missive back to his son, who in turn handed it to Norman.

Norman folded it carefully. "Lady Neville must renounce her hasty union to this imposter. Then she must depart with us anon."

Dawson wrapped his arm around her more securely, and he responded to Norman before she could. "Philippa is my wife. She chose to marry me of her own will, and now we are lawfully married. You're too late to change that."

"You made a mistake." Norman's response, as before, sounded rehearsed. "You did not know of the king's decision regarding Lord Kempe and Lady Neville. But now that you are aware, you must set the wrong to right."

"There's been no wrong done here." Dawson spoke forcefully. "Except that of Lord Deighton attempting to use Philippa for his own gain."

Through the eye slits of his helm, Norman held Dawson's gaze. "Perhaps 'tis you, an obscure nobleman with nothing to his name, who is using Philippa for gain."

"I didn't marry her for her land or wealth. In fact, they mean nothing to me." Dawson didn't back down, didn't look away from Norman. "I married her because I love her."

He loved her? Philippa's heart tumbled over itself before racing forward at twice the speed. Was he simply saying so to deter Norman? Or did he really mean it?

She waited for him to look at her so she could read the truth in his eyes. But he was locked in a battle of wills with Norman.

"Affections come and go," Norman stated.

"My love for Philippa will never go away. I'll love her to the day I die." When Dawson's gaze dropped to hers, the normal shadows in his eyes were gone, and the green woodland was alight . . . with love.

How was this possible? That he could love her already?

He gave her a tender squeeze, as if to reassure her, then turned his attention back to Norman. "Even if I can't have Philippa, I still wouldn't let you take her away. No man should dictate her future. She has a right to choose the life she wants."

She appreciated that Dawson was willing to defend her, to defy convention, to rebel even against the king for her. But as much as she wanted to be with him, as much as her heart ached to be his, as much as she wanted to explore their blossoming love, if she refused to go with Norman, she would turn everyone into enemies of the king and bring them great censure and hardship as a result. She couldn't willingly do so.

From the corner of her eye, she glimpsed Lord and Lady Wilkin in a whispered conversation, their worry creasing their foreheads. They were too kind to hand her over to these knights and her uncle.

She would have to surrender herself. But could she really do so? Now, when she'd just married a man whom she loved? Loved. Yes, she loved him in return.

Their future together was uncertain with his imminent departure. But they had a plan for him to return to her. Could she really give that up? Give him up?

- 25 -

DAWSON COULD SENSE PHILIPPA WAS WAVERING, that she was considering going back to her uncle to protect everyone from retributions from the king.

After how hard she'd worked to free herself, after all she'd done—including marrying him—she truly had no wish to go with her uncle. But she would do it anyway. She was a sweet and sensitive woman who wouldn't be able to insist on having her way when it would put others in jeopardy.

She opened her mouth to speak, but he caressed her arm, causing her to pause and draw in a breath. He wasn't being fair by using physical touch to disarm and distract her, but at this point, he gave himself permission to do whatever it took to save her. In fact, he leaned in and brushed his lips against her ear, lingering a moment longer than necessary.

Again her breathing wavered. As with every other time they'd touched, she wasn't good at hiding her reaction to him.

He should have been embarrassed at making such a public declaration of his love for her. Especially with his mum there to hear it. He probably sounded like a lovesick fool. But the moment he'd spoken the words, he knew they were true.

He loved Philippa as he had no other woman.

Yes, the love had developed quickly. But he was twenty-nine and had lived a lot of life in those years. He didn't need to sort things out for months, even weeks, to know how he felt about her.

He pressed a deeper kiss to her ear, felt her melt against him. "I'm not letting you go, Philippa." He didn't care that his whisper was filled with passion. He wanted her to know exactly how he felt about her.

"I cannot bring harm to everyone here," she whispered in return, her eyes welling with tears and desperation.

"We'll talk with John and Mum. They'll help us come up with a plan to fight back."

She hesitated.

"We have to at least try. We'll tell your uncle we need until tomorrow before making a decision."

She bit at her bottom lip, then nodded.

Dawson allowed himself a breath of relief before he straightened and faced the lead knight who'd spoken for the group. "Inform Lord Deighton we will have an answer for him by tomorrow."

The knight at the forefront shook his head curtly. "You must bring Lady Neville to our camp at daybreak. If not, we shall take that as a sign of your rebellion against Lord Deighton and the king."

The knight's arrogance rubbed Dawson the wrong way, so he didn't bother with an answer. Instead, he pressed his lips together and watched as the knight reared his horse around and kicked it into a trot. The other men followed suit, exiting the bailey. Within minutes the hoofbeats faded, leaving a heavy silence behind.

JODY HEDLUND

John was the first to move. He pivoted and started up the steps at a jog with a glance toward Dawson. "Meet me in my chamber. We have much to discuss."

Dawson nodded and began to guide Philippa inside, keeping his arm around her, needing her now more than he had in the bedroom earlier. Somehow the thought that she might be ripped from him and forced to marry another man only made him want her more.

As he started down the passageway that led to John's chambers, Philippa dragged him to a stop. "Surely I cannot go with you to the meeting."

Though servants and other guests milled about, Dawson didn't care. He lifted her veil aside. With her hair coiled and pinned up, her slender neck was his for the taking. And take it he did. He bent down and kissed the spot where her shoulder and neck met.

She released a soft gasp. "Dawson." Although her whisper might have been meant as a chastisement, it came out sounding like a plea for more.

He answered the request with another kiss against her neck before he pulled back. "This is your life we'll be discussing, and you deserve to have a say in what happens."

Her eyes were round with both desire and tenderness. "Did you mean what you said a moment ago outside?"

He knew what she was referring to. Perhaps because his time left in the past was so short, conventions were falling away, giving him the freedom to speak his mind and bare his truest self. He drew his knuckles across the line of her jaw down to her chin. "I meant it."

"Are you certain—"

He laid a finger across her lips, wishing he was cutting her off with his lips instead. But if he kissed her, he'd only stir up his longing for more and make it nearly impossible to do anything but sweep her up into his arms and carry her back to her bedroom.

As though she saw the heat in his eyes, a small smile played upon her lips. "I believe I feel the same." Her confession was a whisper, but it jolted through him as if she'd shouted it, especially as she lifted her lashes and gave him a clear view of her love.

It only made him more desperate to find a way to be together against all the odds that conspired to tear them apart.

• ● •

They closeted themselves in John's chamber for hours and discussed every option available to them. None were very good. But his mum was an intelligent woman, and from her years of working in counterterrorism, she was meticulous in every detail. Dawson appreciated her skills, seeing a side of her she'd always kept hidden. She was savvy, sharp, even deadly, reminding him of Sybil.

By evening, they'd plotted every detail. Rather than dine in the great hall with everyone else, they opted to stay in the solar, and the servants brought trays of food laden with fruit, nuts, bread, cheese, and cold cuts of meat.

Philippa didn't join in the meal. Instead she paced to the window, her shoulders stiff with the resistance that had been growing throughout the day.

Dawson paused in the middle of chewing a piece of dark meat that tasted like chicken but was probably some other kind of fowl. Although the food was simpler than what he was used to, he was surprised at how tasty most if it was—seasoned with the herbs that grew in the gardens he'd walked with Philippa.

The solar was spacious with a long dining table and benches, several other comfortable chairs, and smaller tables. The cushions and tapestries and embroidered wall hangings gave the place a homey feel, and he guessed this was where his mum and John retired when they wanted time alone from the busyness of the rest of the castle.

It had provided a quiet haven, one they would soon leave behind.

Philippa stared out the window. "No matter where I go, I shall eventually become a burden to whoever harbors me."

Dawson swallowed his mouthful. "Your uncle will get tired of chasing us."

She shook her head, having discarded her head covering, giving him full view of her graceful neck and delicate shoulders.

Although he longed to cross to her and plant kisses all over her soft skin, he held himself firmly back as he'd had to do for the past long hours.

"You do not understand, Dawson." Her shoulders heaved as she expelled a tense breath. "My uncle is not a man who is easily dissuaded."

"And I'm not a man who easily surrenders." He had no intention of letting her turn herself over to her uncle and then attempt to escape on her own, as she'd done when she'd run away to Walsingham Priory.

"You should be safe in Canterbury with Sybil." Mum nibbled on a piece of thick white cheese. "Even if Lord Deighton learns of your whereabouts, the outbreak of the plague will likely deter him from traveling there."

Dawson wasn't keen on exposing Philippa to the plague. But they needed to go. Mum and John expected they would be able to stay with Sybil for several weeks before it became too dangerous. From there, they could easily reach the coast and sail to the Low Countries. John had given him the name of a friend in Amsterdam who would welcome them in.

Staying one step ahead of Lord Deighton wasn't an ideal way to live. But Dawson hoped the man would get tired of the chase, give up hope of manipulating Philippa, and finally admit defeat. At the very least, they would draw her uncle and his army away from Barsham. Lord Deighton wouldn't dare attack the place once he learned Philippa was gone. And hopefully John and Mum and all of Barsham would be spared any repercussions for coming to Philippa's aid.

The one unknown over the coming twenty-four hours was what would happen to him as Acey and Chloe administered the holy water to revive him. Ideally, he and Philippa—and Joanna—would already be in Dover and have a room when he fell unconscious, possibly with a scrivener who was friends with Nicholas and Sybil.

But if it happened on the boat as they were sailing toward the southern coast of England, then the two women would have to transport him to the room. Once there, Philippa would need to wait three days before administering one of the doses of holy water that would bring him back to the past.

After the first dose woke him and he took the second dose to keep himself alive, then they'd make their way toward Canterbury and Reider Castle, where Sybil lived.

Yes, it was a risky plan, especially as they tried to keep their whereabouts a secret from her uncle. But Dawson would do anything to keep Philippa safe and free. Anything, even give up his own life if necessary.

As though hearing his inner declaration, she pivoted, her hands crossed over her heart. "No."

He arched one of his brows.

"You will stay here. And I shall go with Joanna."

He pushed away from the table and stood. Wiping his fingers on his leggings, he crossed to her, his footsteps thumping in time to the hard pounding of his pulse.

Her eyes rounded, and she took a step back, then bumped into the wall. "You must go to your home, stay there, and forget about me."

A growl of protest worked its way up his throat.

She pressed herself against the wall as if she could escape through the stone. "'Tis the safest and best course for you, Dawson."

As he halted before her, he didn't care that his mum and John were still present. As with earlier, he'd lost his inhibitions and was bolder and braver here in the past, where the sand in the hourglass was nearly spent. He pressed his hands to the wall on either side of her head, boxing her in. Then he stooped and did what he'd been waiting to do all day—he started a dance of their lips, twisting and tangling to a melody of her soft murmurs of pleasure.

She grabbed fistfuls of his doublet and clung to him as she rose into the kiss and joined in orchestrating the wild steps of their dance.

As quickly as he started the kiss, he broke it and stepped back, forcing her to release him.

Her hands trembled as she flattened them against the stone. Her lips quivered. And her eyes brimmed with tears.

"The safest and best course for me is to be wherever you are." His breathing was ragged. "That's all I could wish for." And it was true. Yes, he still needed to go back to the present and complete his mum's mission in eliminating the Hamin so they could no longer hurt innocent people. But once he finished, all that mattered was being with Philippa wherever she was.

"What if I bring harm to you?" she asked tremulously.

Now that he'd kissed her again, he wanted to grab her once more and kiss her and prove to her that everything would be alright as long as they were together. But that was unrealistic. He couldn't guarantee her anything beyond the moment at hand.

"I once had a good teacher who showed me that we can always find ways to see beauty amidst our difficulties."

Her lips didn't move into that half smile that made his heart melt.

He reached under his shirt and took out his dog tags hanging from a chain. He hadn't taken them off since he'd left for Afghanistan. He lifted the chain from around his head, then slipped it over hers. Yes, he'd given her his mother's ring, but in placing his dog tags on her, he was transferring his identity. No one would ever be able to question that they belonged together. "No matter what hardships might come our way, we said we'd wait for each other. Right?"

She hesitated. "Right."

He tugged on the dog tags around her neck. "Good, then. Hold on to these for me."

She nodded and clutched the small metal plates while studying his face intently. Was she memorizing it? Because she didn't expect to see him again after today?

He refused to memorize her face. Doing so was too final. Instead, he'd keep holding out hope that somehow, someway in the end they'd find a way to be together.

~ 26 ~

PHILIPPA SLOWED HER STEPS as the end of the long tunnel under Barsham Castle loomed ahead—an iron gate locked with chains along with a solid oaken door that was also barred and locked.

Bending low, Lord Wilkin led the way with Dawson behind him, the two having spoken in hushed tones during the past hour as they hiked.

The passageway wasn't unusual. Some castles had been built with secret tunnels that allowed for escape during an attack or siege. According to Lord Wilkin, this particular tunnel led directly north toward the coast. They would still have many miles to cover over the night before reaching Lord Wilkin's merchant friend, Bollinger, at Wells-next-the-Sea. But they would be sufficiently on their way.

Bollinger oft transported goods from Norfolk to London as well as to towns along the southern coast. Thus, the trip wouldn't raise suspicions of anyone in the area, and they should be able to sneak away without drawing undue attention.

Lady Wilkin had trudged through the passageway with them, taking up the rear behind Joanna. Now upon halting, Lady Wilkin sidled beside Philippa and pressed a leather pouch into her hands.

"You must guard these with your life," the noblewoman whispered. "They are the last of the holy water I have."

"My thanks." Philippa grasped the bag, feeling the outline of two of the same type of ampullae she'd placed in the alcove for Dawson. She slipped the strap over her shoulder and then tucked the pouch underneath her gown against her chest where the holy water would be safe. For Dawson. When the time came to ensure that he remained with her.

"Godspeed." Lady Wilkin gripped Philippa's hands.

Though the darkness was broken by the torchlight, the shadows were deep and heavy, reflecting the shadows in Philippa's heart. For once, she saw no beauty in their situation, not while she was bringing so much peril to Dawson.

She'd implored him numerous times to remain behind at Barsham Castle. But he insisted on traveling with her. She finally relented, especially when Lord and Lady Wilkin hinted at the threat that might await Dawson if he stayed. Her uncle, cousin, and their men would endeavor to capture him and perhaps eliminate him, ensuring she was indeed a widow once again.

"Remember. Do not give him the holy water until he has been unconscious for about three days and is near to death." A thread of worry laced Lady Wilkin's voice. "Or unless his breathing seems to be stopping."

"Have no fear. I shall watch him carefully."

Lady Wilkin's hands trembled against Philippa's. "I know my son well, and he's never loved anyone as he loves you."

"And I love him." Deeply. Oh so deeply. But she couldn't say that for fear doing so would unleash tears she couldn't shed right now.

Ahead, the chains rattled as Lord Wilkin began the process of unlocking them. They didn't know what would be awaiting them once the door was opened. There was always the possibility that one of the locals had informed Uncle Hugo of the escape passageway and directed him to the exit. Uncle's men could attack the moment they stepped outside into the dark of night.

Lord Wilkin had reassured them that very few people knew about the tunnel, that his kin had purposefully kept it secret so an enemy attacker wouldn't discover it.

Philippa prayed he was correct. Even if so, Uncle would have patrols circling the countryside in expectation of an attempted escape like this. While his men wouldn't know exactly where a tunnel might lead, they would certainly have some ideas.

Lady Wilkin squeezed Philippa's hand one last time. "If anything happens, you must seek Sybil's help immediately."

"I shall do so."

Before Philippa could say anything further, Lady Wilkin gathered her into an embrace and whispered, "I could not have asked for a better woman for Dawson than you. I am thankful Providence brought you both together."

For a moment, Philippa settled into the embrace. She hadn't experienced a motherly hug in too many years. Not since her aunt had died. Lady Wilkin's fortitude seemed to flow into her, as if the kind woman understood just how difficult the coming days would be and wanted to prepare her.

Lady Wilkin gave Joanna a hug too, along with a bag of provisions. Then she proceeded to embrace Dawson, clinging to him and sniffling back tears.

"Don't worry, Mum. I'll be fine."

Lady Wilkin finally pulled back and brushed her hands over Dawson's face. Was she doing so for the last time? Philippa hoped they would reunite someday. But what if the farewell was final?

As Lady Wilkin stepped away and clasped her husband's hand, Dawson's attention shifted to Philippa, as it did frequently. The slightest touch of his gaze always seared her, made her keenly aware of him. But this time, instead of wishing she could wrap her arms around him and kiss him, she wanted to wrap her arms around him and drag him away to a place where they could be safe together. Did such a place exist?

"Ready?" Lord Wilkin whispered.

Dawson reached a hand toward Philippa, while with the same motion she took hold of Joanna's. With Dawson's keen sense of direction and ability to utilize his senses to get around in the dark, Philippa knew he would lead them well, the same way he had the night he'd helped them escape from the priory.

In the next instant, the torchlight was extinguished, and darkness crowded around them. The faint rattle of the door opening was followed by a whoosh of air.

There were no more farewells. Dawson tugged her hand and led her forward. The moment the three of them were outside, he wasted no time in ducking through the thick brush and hedges that concealed the secret door. Even though she could make out the faintest outlines of trees and stones, she held tightly to Dawson's hand and Joanna did the same with hers.

The woodland was silent, and they appeared to be alone. But even though they witnessed no torchlight in the vicinity, Dawson moved as quietly as he could, careful to lead Joanna and her through the easiest terrain.

They traveled for some distance before he halted and stood absolutely still, listening to the sounds that only he could hear. "Guards are passing to the east," he finally whispered. "We'll wait here until they're gone."

After resting for long minutes, Dawson started off again. He guided the way, stopping occasionally to listen or switch directions. They walked for several hours through both fields and woodlands before the tension seemed to ease from his hold.

When the first hints of an overcast dawn lit the sky, he slowed his pace, and as they neared Wells-next-the-Sea, he found a secluded spot for them to hide while he crept ahead to locate Lord Wilkin's friend.

They had no guarantee the merchant would be available or if he'd be willing to take them to Dover. If not him, Dawson had a pouch of silver from his mother he could use to buy passage on another vessel.

The respite in the sandy brush seemed endless, but upon his return less than an hour later, he brought good tidings—Bollinger was willing to transport them.

"He and his crew will set sail from the quay of East Fleet," Dawson said, the daylight revealing the relief in his eyes. "Then he'll meet us just north of town at the first large sandbar—one in the shape of a cross."

After taking a circuitous route around the village, they

crouched in a hedge but a hundred feet from the shore north of East Fleet where it curved and began its flow north into the sea. The edge of the village of Wells was still in sight, though shrouded in a low fog that wound around weather-beaten cottages and several sturdier brick buildings.

"I see the ship." Dawson waited tensely, peeking out from the brush to the waterway. "He said he'd keep his sail at half-mast."

"Let us pray Bollinger is trustworthy," Joanna said.

Philippa crawled next to Dawson and watched a cog fast approaching the sandbar. "Praise be." They'd made it. Within minutes, they'd be boarding the vessel and putting out to sea far from Uncle and his reaches. They would have a respite from him. But for how long?

She bit back a sigh at the prospect of having to run and hide like this again, perhaps many times over the coming weeks.

Dawson's shoulder brushed against hers as he glanced up and down East Fleet, making certain the way was clear of danger. Then he reached for her hand, circling his fingers around hers. "Time to go."

She didn't hesitate. As before, she grasped Joanna and let Dawson lead the way out into the open. They wouldn't be exposed long since the cog was nearing the sandbar with several sailors at the oars, directing the flat-bottom boat.

At shouts from near the village, Dawson stiffened and picked up his pace.

Philippa strained to see through the fog. Had someone spotted them?

"Hurry." Dawson's call was tense and urgent.

"Who are they?" Joanna asked.

"I don't know." He cast another glance toward the village. Three armed men on horseback were riding low and hard toward them.

Were they Uncle's men? Perhaps one of his patrols? Uncle had probably sent men to Wells-next-the-Sea, which was the closest sea town to Barsham and the most likely place for them to attempt an escape from Norfolk.

Whatever the case, they couldn't tarry.

By the time they reached the sandbar, they were practically running. Dawson paused to help them down an embankment, his gaze darting between the cog and the knights drawing closer. His handsome features were taut, and his brow creased.

A sailor at the stern of the cog was calling and motioning to them. He'd obviously seen their pursuers too.

Dawson took hold of both Joanna's and her arms as they started through the thick sand, urging them ever faster. They were only halfway to the cog when the soldiers halted at the embankment behind them.

Philippa's pulse raced frantically. Surely the knights wouldn't be able to catch up. She hadn't worked so hard to gain freedom only to fall into her uncle's clutches again.

A gust of wind buffeted them and brought with it the patter of rain. Ahead, the sailor, probably Bollinger, was leaning over the side of the ship, preparing to help them climb aboard.

She pushed herself to go faster, but she slipped in the sand and fell to her knees. The impact left her breathless and forced her hand from Dawson's.

Dawson halted and lifted her back to her feet. As he did so, his eyes widened upon the knights, and he thrust her toward Joanna. She stumbled again but her cousin caught her.

"Run!" Dawson waved his arm at the two of them. The wind whipped at his garments and the rain slapped at him harder. "Get on the ship!"

Philippa's muscles burned with the effort of slogging through the sand and trying to stay abreast of Joanna. With only a dozen paces to go, the sand turned flat and solid with the dampness of the sea. Once again, she stumbled and nearly fell, but she plunged ahead into the water, heedless of her slippers and skirt.

"Make haste." Bollinger reached a burly hand toward her, grabbed her arms, and hoisted her upward. Another sailor stood beside him and took hold of Joanna, lifting her in the same manner.

The rain came down in earnest, as though attempting to encumber their escape. But the sailors were strong, and within seconds she and Joanna were sitting upon the hull, gasping for breath. She turned, expecting Dawson to be climbing in beside her. But he wasn't there.

"Go, go, go!" Bollinger shouted at the men at the oars, even as he reached for the sail at half-mast and rapidly raised it, the wind catching the square canvas and pushing the cog away from the sandbar.

Philippa scrambled to her knees. "Dawson?" She choked out the word past her heaving breath.

Joanna leaned against the side of the cog, closing her eyes

and trying to catch her breath.

"Where is Dawson?" Philippa wiped the rain from her eyes and scanned the deck, desperate for sight of him. She pushed unsteadily to her feet so she could assist Dawson out of the water and into the boat. But as she searched the water then the shore, her pulse slammed to a stop.

He was at the center of the sandbar, his sword in one hand, his knife in the other. And he was squaring off with the knights trying to get past him and reach the cog.

Dawson lunged at one man while swinging at another, forcing them back, and in the process giving the cog time to escape. The problem was, he was sorely outnumbered against well-trained knights who could easily cut him down.

"No!" Horror swelled within her, and she leaned over the boat to jump out. She would hand herself over to her uncle's men before she let Dawson sacrifice himself for her. Could she reach him in time?

Before she could drop back into the water, fingers closed around her arm and yanked her backward.

"Unhand me at once!" She twisted to find that she was wrestling with Joanna. "I shall not leave him behind."

Joanna didn't respond except to wrap an arm around Philippa's waist and drag her farther away from the boat's edge. Philippa thrashed, struggling to free herself. But Joanna's grip didn't waver.

"Please!" Philippa strained toward Bollinger, desperate to save Dawson. "We have to go back for my husband."

Bollinger was in the process of securing the sail and shook his head. "He gave me specific instructions to get you away regardless of what befell him."

"We cannot just leave him!" She didn't care what Dawson had plotted with Bollinger. And maybe even secretly with Joanna. Philippa had to find a way to save him.

Through a curtain of heavy rainfall, she could still make out the battle on the shore. A soldier slipped past Dawson and ran toward the cog. But even as he hurried into the water, Dawson threw his knife, impaling the man's back. Shock and pain rounded the knight's expression as he dropped to his knees in the water.

Dawson didn't have the chance to turn around and resume the fight with the other two. One of them slashed him across his back, and the other ran toward him, sword lifted.

"No!" Philippa screamed, but the wind and rain ripped the word away and tossed it out to sea.

Even with the distance and the rain standing between Dawson and her, she thought she caught his eyes, glimpsed the love there, before the sword drove into him from behind.

He wavered, then toppled face-first into the sand, the blade of the sword thrust deeply into him.

Philippa sagged, a sob slipping past her lips. Even as the two knights raced to the tip of the sandbar, she watched Dawson, praying he would stand up and keep fighting.

"Row faster!" Bollinger called.

Uncle's knights splashed out until they were waist deep. But the cog was moving too quickly. There was nothing more they could do, at least for now.

And there was nothing more she could do either but pray Dawson would push himself up and live. But as the knights returned to the shore and retrieved their weapons, including the sword in Dawson's back, he didn't move. They gathered their companion and tossed him over one of the horses. Then they came back for Dawson and did the same.

As the cog moved out of East Fleet and into open sea, the fog swallowed the knights, finally taking Dawson from her view. Philippa broke free of Joanna, slid to the hull, and buried her face in her hands, letting her tears mix with the rain, weeping for the man she loved and praying that Providence would provide another miracle, this time to save Dawson.

- 27 -

DAWSON GROANED. As he rolled over, he braced himself for the searing pain. He knew he shouldn't have turned his back on his remaining opponents, but he'd had to do something to slow down the knight who'd rushed past him, had to stop him from getting to Philippa.

"He's stirring," came a woman's voice.

"Mum?" he murmured. Had she heard of the attack and come to get him? Maybe she'd brought him to Barsham to tend his wounds.

"He *is* awake." The whisper—this time a man's—was faint but contained a thread of excitement. "The holy water worked."

Dawson flexed the muscles in his back, but the pain was gone. His mum must have found more holy water to heal him. The moment the sword had sliced into his flesh, he'd guessed it was deep. And the other wound . . .

His mind was hazy, but he distinctly remembered the burn as another sword pierced him. After that, everything had gone black.

What had happened to Philippa? His heart twisted with his last picture of her standing in the cog, Joanna struggling to restrain her, the rain streaking her face. She'd been wrestling to get free, probably hadn't wanted to leave him behind, which was why he'd made sure Bollinger and Joanna both knew they had to go on without him.

"Did she get away?" he whispered.

"Did who get away?" a woman's whisper replied. Chloe's whisper.

Dawson's eyes flew open at the same time he registered the beeping of a monitor, the whirring of oxygen, the drip of an IV. His nose tickled with the overload of smells—antiseptic, chlorine, burned coffee, a woman's perfume, breath mints. He stared at the sterile white ceiling of a hospital room, the curved tracks for a curtain, and a modern electric light.

He was back in the present.

Disappointment surged in like a suffocating wave, and he closed his eyes, wishing that he could be transported back into the past where he could be with Philippa.

But even with his eyes closed, the present day didn't disappear.

He could feel the hospital bed beneath him, the flimsy gown he was wearing, the stickiness of the tape on the back of his hand over the pinch of his IV.

A stab of pain sliced through his chest, this time right at his heart. He needed her. His wife. The woman he loved more than his own life. How could he possibly go on without her? Even just for a few days? He missed her fiercely already, and he'd only been back . . . how many hours had it been?

"Hi, guys." His voice came out raspy.

"Hey," Acey replied quietly.

"Welcome back," Chloe whispered.

Dawson pried open his eyes again and this time shifted his head to find his two friends sitting in plastic chairs beside his bed. Their clothes were frumpy and wrinkled and their faces weary with dark circles under their eyes. Had they been at his bedside the entire time he was gone?

"How long have I been out?"

"Almost five days," Chloe responded with a knowing gleam.

Dawson did the calculations. It had been the morning of his fifth day when he'd escaped to the coast with Philippa. Did that mean the current time was late afternoon or evening?

He peered past the curtains hanging over the window to find that the day wasn't yet expired.

Why hadn't they allowed him to stay until the end of the fifth day?

"Your vitals were crashing," she whispered, clearly sensing his question.

Had he started dying when he'd been attacked by the knights on the sandbar?

"How are you feeling?" Acey sat forward and surveyed the open door before he passed Dawson a note.

Dawson picked it up and scanned it: *You could use the concussion from your accident to explain that your eyesight has returned.*

Acey raised a brow in question.

Clearly the Hamin were still keeping close tabs on everything that was happening with them, enough that Acey wasn't taking any chances of relaying the suggestion verbally.

Acey's suggestion was a good idea. But even then, once the Hamin learned of his eyesight returning, they wouldn't attribute it to his accident for long. They'd guess he'd been healed from the holy water. And once they did, they'd come after him.

He had to chase after them first. As much as he wanted to wallow in missing Philippa, he had to finish what he'd set out to do—take down the Hamin once and for all. No, he wouldn't find his mum with the Hamin the way he'd hoped when he'd decided to go into the past. He knew with finality that she was gone from the present, and there was nothing he could do to bring her back. Not that he'd even want to anymore, especially since she was happy in her new life with John.

He locked eyes with Acey, then Chloe. He had a lot to tell them. In fact, they were never going to believe half of it. He hoped they could see what he couldn't say aloud at the moment—that he'd gone back, and it had changed everything about his life. *Everything.*

And now he had possibly three days before his comatose body in the past would begin to fail and die. Maybe less, depending on what had happened to him after he'd been injured on the sandbar. The best-case scenario was that the knights had left him behind and friendly villagers had come to his rescue.

But if the knights had taken him—which he suspected was the case—the next best option was that they worked out a deal with Mum and John for his return. If Philippa's uncle, Lord Deighton, refused to surrender him right away, things might go poorly. Without anyone to tend his wounds, how long would he last?

Panic began to churn in Dawson's gut. Would his 1382 body die before anyone could save him with holy water? *Please, God, no. Please.* If that happened, he'd never get to be with Philippa again. The prospect was too awful to consider.

He had to think positively—like Philippa would. God had already brought them together. Surely He would allow them more than just five days to be with each other.

Mum. Yes, Mum and John would learn of what had transpired. Mum would realize the urgency of the situation and attempt to get him back into her custody. Of course, Mum would have to find more holy water since Philippa would have the last of her supply. No doubt Mum would sneak into the tunnels beneath the priory and make her way into the crypt. Joanna and Philippa had claimed there wasn't much left. But Mum would find a way to get enough to fill two ampullae.

Acey waited, likely seeing his mounting anxiety. No doubt his friend was expecting him to snap, fall apart, or something.

If Philippa were here, she'd tell him he needed to pause, take a deep breath, and find the things that made him thankful—like the fact that he wasn't dead yet, that he'd made it back to the present at all, that he'd experienced more than most people, that he had such good friends who'd stuck by his side.

He expelled the tightness in his chest, then attempted a grin—one that felt only half forced. "Guess we better call the doctors in. They'll be in for a surprise, won't they?"

• ● •

The various specialists who came to inspect him all confirmed that his vision impairment was gone—as if he needed them to tell him that. But he playacted as he had before, listening and nodding to their medical explanations for how the brain injury could have brought about the changes.

When he was discharged the next morning, Acey quickly realized they were being followed. Without a word, he drove straight to the National Counter Terrorism Security Office in London. After entering the building, they didn't leave and spent the better part of the day meeting with some of Mum's old colleagues, who'd worked with her in tracking the Hamin.

Dawson was as honest with the agents as he could be. They were experts in the Hamin just as his mum had been, and they knew of the legends that claimed the holy water could heal any disease. They'd heard stories of miraculous recoveries taking place among some ultrawealthy elites, particularly in the Middle East. Thus, his mum's coworkers weren't surprised to learn he'd gained back his sight after drinking a bottle of holy water he'd discovered in Canterbury.

He didn't feel comfortable trusting them with the knowledge about the time crossing. And if they already had previous information about it, they clearly didn't trust him enough to say anything either.

Instead, he explained that he, Acey, and Chloe had gone on an adventure that had led them to uncovering more about the Hamin. He told them he'd discovered the information about his mum's connection to the Hamin while living in his mum's town house in Fakenham as well as during the trip to the old priory in Walsingham.

He gave them all the clues his mum had relayed—details that might help them locate the Hamin's whereabouts in Norfolk. Then they worked out a plan that would hopefully take the Hamin by surprise.

Dawson wanted to go along and so did Acey. But the agents insisted the three of them remain at the London headquarters until the operation was complete. Though disappointed in not being a part of the mission, Dawson was just grateful the agents had taken him seriously.

Now, twenty-four hours after waking up from his coma, Dawson rested with Acey and Chloe in a private suite within the Counter Terrorism offices. Acey and Chloe were sprawled out together on a sofa watching TV, and Dawson sat at the table, drumming his fingers as he'd been doing off and on for the past few hours.

That and pacing.

Even though he had no energy, he stood and stalked to the door, stared through the peephole, then returned to the table. He picked up the bottle of water, took a swig, then walked back to the door.

Thankfully, Acey and Chloe were staying silent about his going stir-crazy. And they'd also stopped bugging him to eat something from among the snacks piled on the table. He had no appetite and hadn't since he'd come out of his coma yesterday evening.

"What's your bet?" Dawson peered out the peephole again. "Did the agents attack successfully, or did the Hamin have too much notice and get away?"

"I hate to be the naysayer." Chloe sat up with a yawn. "But I think our coming here was a big clue to the Hamin that we had information to share."

Acey rubbed at the stump left of his leg, his prosthesis discarded on the floor. "I don't know about that. It's possible they thought we were seeking protection."

"That's what I'm hoping." Dawson rolled his shoulders to ease the tension, but exhaustion and anxiety clung to him anyway. "It probably didn't take much probing at the hospital for them to learn about my healing. If they think I'm afraid of them, then it would make sense for me to ask for help."

A strange wave of dizziness hit Dawson. It was so staggering that he had to grab the door to keep from falling.

"You're tired, Dawson." Chloe's tone contained a gentle rebuke. "You need to sit down and rest and stop worrying."

Was that really it? Was that why he was weak? He wanted to believe so, but an uneasy premonition had been growing. He kept replaying his last moments on the sandbar fighting against the knights. He'd known he hadn't had a chance against them, that all he could do was attempt to slow them down. Most likely he'd sustained mortal wounds. Without modern medicine and proper medical treatment, how long would he last before his past body died?

Probably less than the three days he'd assumed he'd have, maybe not enough for his mum to save him.

The fact was, he was probably going to die as a prisoner of Lord Deighton, and it might happen soon, especially if his current physical symptoms were an indication.

Was there anything more he could do to keep himself alive there a little longer? He sifted through every option, but helplessness washed over him.

He had no control over what happened to his body in the past. He was at the mercy of the people there. After he breathed his last, Lord Deighton would throw him into a grave or toss him to the wild animals. He'd have no chance of reviving and finding Philippa. His connection to her would be severed.

The thought made him sick to his stomach. He pressed a fist into his gut and tried to fight off the despair.

"Are you thinking of Philippa again?" Chloe was watching him, her expression earnest. Not once had she doubted him when he'd finally recounted the details of his five days in the past. He hadn't wanted to say anything at the hospital or during the drive to London in case the Hamin were listening. So he'd waited to share his experiences until they arrived in the suite and had privacy.

Of course, Acey had listened just as openly as Chloe, but Acey hadn't been there when he'd had all the overlaps, and Dawson sensed his buddy was having a harder time accepting his tales, especially the part about marrying Philippa. Regardless, he'd told them the truth about meeting her, the attraction that had quickly developed, and then the hasty marriage to protect her.

"I don't think I'll make it back to her." Just saying the words tore his heart out, and the pain in his chest was excruciating. He doubled over to ward it off.

"Dawson?" Chloe was on her feet and rushing toward him.

He'd told his friends all about his desire to go back to 1382. He'd already instructed them not to give him the second ampulla of holy water to resuscitate him when he started to deteriorate in a couple of days. But if he was dying right now in the past and no one was there to keep him alive, then he needed Chloe and Acey to give him the holy water, or he'd end up passing away in both eras.

A part of him didn't want to live if he couldn't be with Philippa. He couldn't fathom a future without her in it. The prospect loomed darkly ahead, worse than blindness.

Yet, if he allowed himself to stay alive in the present, was there a chance—even if slim—that he could eventually find a way to cross back to the woman he loved?

"I love her." He stated the words again as he already had, but this time with more force, as if that could somehow make things work out, maybe convince God that he deserved to go back to her.

Chloe rested a hand on his back. "She must have been someone really special if she won you so completely."

She was more than special. She was the most incredible woman he'd ever met. Once she got news of his death, she would be heartbroken. And he loathed the prospect of hurting her and causing her grief.

But what choice did he have? He'd have to return completely to the present. But hopefully she'd understand he hadn't wanted to leave her and would fight to return. He'd pray that she wouldn't give up the fight against her uncle and that she'd wait for him to make his way back.

He started to straighten but then wavered. For a moment,

the room faded from his view. His chest pinched hard, and tremors rolled up and down his left arm.

Chloe grasped him. "You need to lie down, and I'm not taking no for an answer this time."

"This is more than you being tired." Acey stood and reached for his cane, his voice radiating concern. "What's up, man?"

Dawson couldn't keep from leaning heavily against Chloe and clutching his chest. He had to tell them before it was too late and he fell unconscious. "My body in the past is already dying." The words came out in a strangled whisper.

Acey was at his side in the next instant.

Dawson felt his eyes roll back in his head, and blackness hovered close. "The holy water—I need it—"

The world—both past and present—disappeared, and he fell headlong into oblivion.

~ 28 ~

As Philippa's feet touched the ground within the inner bailey of Reider Castle, her knees buckled, and she would have collapsed if not for the quick reflexes of her traveling companion, a fatherly man who'd sheltered Joanna and her after they'd disembarked in Dover.

"My thanks, Walter." She tried to bestow upon him a smile, but over the past four days of traveling, she'd lost the ability to make her lips curve upward.

"You need not worry any longer, my lady." Strands of brown hair stuck out from Walter's simple coif and were plastered to his overheated and red face. His robes, especially the sleeves, were stained with ink, as were his fingers—the consequence of his work as a scrivener. "Lord Worth is a good man who will find a way to keep you safe."

She didn't have the heart to tell Walter that she didn't care anymore about what became of her life or her future. Ever since sailing away from Dawson and leaving him behind for dead, she'd been dead inside herself.

The only thing keeping her going was the flicker of hope that maybe Dawson hadn't died, that maybe he'd revived. Or maybe Lord and Lady Wilkin had paid a ransom to get him back from Uncle and had been able to tend his wounds.

Joanna dismounted from the horse they'd shared for the journey overland from Dover. Walter had secured the extra horse for them and had also agreed to accompany them to Reider Castle, especially since he was familiar with the Weald and could lead them through the miles of wilderness and avoid the busy thoroughfares where anyone might recognize them and pass the information along to Uncle Hugo.

Uncle would come looking for her. 'Twas only a matter of time. Undoubtedly, he'd already sent men along the eastern coast, stopping at each port to investigate her whereabouts. How long before he learned she'd landed in Dover? How much longer before he realized Sybil Worth was her sister-in-law? Maybe Uncle was even now on his way to Reider Castle.

She assessed the regal fortress before her, its towers and embattlements rising around a central keep and protecting the thatched buildings that lined the walls—storerooms, stables, bunkhouses, and more. In the late afternoon, the servants were still busy at work, some in the gardens beyond the keep, others carrying cauldrons of water through a lower door that led to the kitchen, and stable hands tending to the livestock.

All was at peace. And her presence here was a liability. She should have insisted on traveling directly to the Low Countries and losing herself there rather than bringing peril to Sybil and everyone else who lived at Reider Castle.

But she'd come anyway. Selfishly. Because she was praying that miraculously Dawson had survived and would somehow find a way to escape from her uncle. Whenever he was healed and ready to make the journey, then he would know where to find her.

In addition, he'd asked her to wait for him, and she'd told him she would wait for him forever if necessary. She couldn't break her promise, had to be patient, had to give him time to return to her.

Joanna slipped an arm around Philippa's waist, holding her up. The simple act of kindness reassured her that she wasn't alone.

"You are a blessing, Cousin." Philippa squeezed back. Even if she'd been angry with Joanna during the remainder of the ship voyage for her part in leaving without Dawson, she'd forgiven her cousin. Joanna had only done what Dawson had wanted—to keep her away from her uncle at all costs.

They were both weary and dusty and hot from their travels. And hungry. Thank Providence and all the saints for Walter's assistance. Philippa couldn't imagine how they would have gotten along without him. Lady Wilkin had been the one to suggest reaching out to the scrivener who was a friend of the Worths.

Philippa turned to Walter, wanted to thank him again, but the keep door opened, and words fled at the sight of a young woman stepping out—a woman who resembled Lady Wilkin in coloring and in almost every feature but was years younger.

This had to be Sybil, Dawson's sister. Devoid of a head covering, she wore her dark-brown hair in a long braid that fell over her shoulder. Even though she was attired in a simple slender-fitting gown, she had a sword belt upon her waist and wore heavy, manly boots.

Philippa's heart gave a swift and certain beat, as if somehow this woman connected her to Dawson. She didn't know how, but she could feel an energy that linked them all.

Sybil took another step forward, her gaze raking over her and Joanna and Walter. Her scrutiny, the intense expression, the hardness was exactly like Dawson and brought swift tears to her eyes.

Philippa missed him with a sharpness that stole the air from her lungs.

Sybil focused on her, not seeming to miss even the tiniest detail. Again like Dawson.

Philippa felt as though she already knew the young woman. "Lady Worth, 'tis my pleasure to meet you."

"To what do we owe the honor of your visit?" Sybil remained on the top step and didn't bother with the usual curtsey.

When they'd arrived at the gatehouse of Reider Castle, Joanna had informed the guards that Lady Neville requested an audience with Lord and Lady Worth. Philippa hadn't reminded Joanna that her name had changed to Huxham. After all, word of her marriage wouldn't have reached Kent yet, particularly this remote country estate.

"Your mother, Lady Wilkin, gave me leave to take shelter with you."

At the mention of the name, Sybil's eyes narrowed. "And why would she think you need shelter with me?"

"'Tis a long tale, my lady."

"Give me the short version." Sybil's directness resembled Dawson's.

Philippa's throat closed up with unbearable grief. She loved Dawson. Yes, she loved him more than she'd ever believed possible. And, once again, she didn't know how she could endure life without him.

"My lady," Joanna started, her voice full of censure. "We have had a long and difficult journey. Perhaps we can partake of a respite before we discourse."

Sybil was silent.

Even the silence was similar to Dawson's, and the tears spilled over before Philippa could stop them. Being around Sybil would be torture, making her miss Dawson worse than she already did. "'Twas a mistake to come here." She swiped at her cheeks and broke away from Walter and Joanna, then stepped toward the mount.

"'Tis no mistake, my lady," Walter said kindly. "You can ask for no better place than this."

She shook her head. The only place she wanted to be was with her husband.

Joanna grabbed her arm to keep her from going. "This is where Dawson wanted us to come."

"Dawson?" Sybil's tone rose with a note of surprise.

"Yes," Joanna answered curtly. "Dawson Huxham. Your brother."

Philippa glanced over her shoulder to find that Sybil's eyes had rounded. She was not yet privy to the knowledge that her brother had visited recently in Norfolk. What would she think when she learned of it?

Dawson had shared his regret over the way he'd parted with Sybil. He'd wanted a chance to make things right with her. Would he yet get that opportunity? Or had it slipped by him?

Even if Dawson couldn't be here and share his regrets and apologize, Philippa could do so on his behalf, couldn't she? She could at least stay until she had the opportunity to make amends the way he would have wanted.

"Exactly how do you know my brother?" Sybil directed the question to Philippa, clearly sensing that she was the connection to Dawson more so than Joanna.

"My lady." Philippa shifted and bowed her head. "The reason I know your brother is because I am Lady Huxham. His wife."

Sybil stood unmoving, her mouth partially open. "His wife?"

"Yes, we were married."

"To my brother?" Sybil's tone echoed with disbelief.

Philippa had to think of a way to convince this woman that she wasn't fabricating the story. What means did she have to prove herself? She twisted at the diamond-encrusted wedding band on her finger before holding up her hand. "I wear this ring Dawson gave me on our wedding day."

Sybil trotted down the steps, took hold of her hand, and examined the ring.

Philippa used the occasion to study Dawson's sister more closely. She was stunning. 'Twas no wonder she'd captivated the heart of Lord Worth, whom she'd helped to save when she arrived.

Sybil let go of her hand. "Where is my brother now? And why isn't he with you?"

Philippa glanced at the servants nearby, who were now watching the exchange. "I would speak privately with you, if I may."

"You may speak openly."

How much did everyone here know about the time-crossing capabilities of the holy water? Perhaps they were well aware already. "He only came for five days."

Sybil visibly swallowed. "And . . .?"

"And I pray he has crossed time back to his own era, but I cannot be certain what has become of him."

This time Sybil gave a curt shake of her head, her eyes filling with a warning not to communicate anything more about the time crossing.

Philippa nodded.

Sybil took a step toward the keep. "You're correct. You do have a long tale. One I'd like to hear as soon as possible."

"And I should like to tell it to you." Philippa could only hope that in the telling, together they'd find a way to bring Dawson back.

~ 29 ~

As PHILIPPA OPENED THE MISSIVE, her hands shook. She lowered herself to the garden bench to keep from collapsing.

Thankfully, Sybil had given her some privacy after delivering it, and now the young woman leaned casually against a low wall, a bow slung over her shoulder and a quiver belted at her waist next to an arming sword.

Over the past sennight ensconced in Reider Castle, Philippa had learned that in spite of the brusque demeanor, Sybil was a kind and lovely woman. They'd spent many hours their first day together as Philippa had shared every detail of her time with Dawson, from the initial overlaps, the placement of the holy water in the alcove underneath the priory, and then all that had transpired during Dawson's visit. She withheld nothing, not even her love for Dawson. When she finished, tears had wet both their cheeks.

During the ensuing days, Philippa had spoken at length with both Nicholas and Sybil regarding the threat her uncle posed, especially now that he'd gained the king's involvement in her union to Godwin.

Nicholas had many contacts throughout Kent tasked with bringing him tidings of any importance, but none delivered news of happenings in Norfolk. Thus, they'd tarried without knowing what had become of Dawson and how the siege of Barsham had ended.

Philippa had been consoling herself that somehow Lady Wilkin had been able to find a way to save Dawson. But now, as she unfolded the parchment that had arrived from Lady Wilkin, she wasn't sure she was ready to learn of his fate. At least in her ignorance, she could hold out some hope.

The midday July sun seemed to pour out its heat and wrath upon her bare head. She bent her shoulders against the punishment. Then with a deep breath she dropped her sights to the sheet and read Lady Wilkin's first line.

"*We regret to inform you that Dawson has passed out of this life from injuries he sustained. Lord Deighton kept him a prisoner, offering to bargain if we betrayed you. As we felt certain Dawson valued your safety above all else, we could not in good conscience make that trade.*"

Tears clouded Philippa's vision. But she blinked them back and continued to read. "*John was able to speak with one of Lord Deighton's guards who was with Dawson in his last hours and learned that Dawson was unconscious and never awoke. I believe that means he returned safely to his other home. I regret that you did not get more time with him, for 'twas clear he loved you deeply.*"

The tears flowed freely down her cheeks now. Unbearable anguish pushed into her throat. She'd lost him. Dawson was gone. And now hundreds of years separated them.

Lady Wilkin had several more paragraphs outlining how the siege had ended and that Lord Deighton had retreated once he'd realized his efforts at Barsham were coming to naught. Philippa only glanced at the words to reassure herself that at least Lord and Lady Wilkin were safe. Then she lowered the letter and moved it out of the range of her dripping tears.

Sybil laid a hand on her shoulder.

Philippa held out the missive, unable to speak.

Sybil hesitated, then took it.

Philippa could only close her eyes. But even behind her darkened lids, the images of Dawson filled her vision, so many pictures of him and their time together—their walks in the garden, the meals they'd shared, the night stargazing on the turret, their wedding morning, and so much more.

After waiting all week for him to surprise her and spontaneously show up, she simply couldn't fathom never being with him again. The prospect of a future without him was too bleak to consider.

In fact, she wanted to shrivel up and die like one of the blooms that had wilted in the July heat. She might have wealth and lands and youth and beauty. But what did any of it mean if she wasn't free? Because ultimately, whether she gave herself over to her uncle's plans or continued to run away from him, she'd never truly be free. She'd always be bound by her circumstances.

"I'm sorry," Sybil said quietly. "I know how much you wanted Dawson to come back."

Philippa opened her eyes to respond but still couldn't formulate words. Instead, she swallowed a sob that pushed for release.

Sybil folded the parchment carefully. "As hard as this is, we can be grateful he's still alive in the present era."

Grateful? The word pummeled into Philippa. She'd always prided herself on staying grateful. But maybe she'd maintained a cheerful perspective because she'd never truly experienced the depths of despair like now?

Yes, she'd faced challenges, like when she'd lost her parents and then again when Robert died. But nothing else had ripped her apart the way this separation with Dawson was doing.

Maybe she'd been naïve to think a person could always find beauty in any circumstance. Maybe the lessons she'd given Dawson were nothing more than simple ramblings. Or did she yet have to learn that even the darkest moments had to be lived and accepted and embraced?

The tears came swiftly again, and she let them flow down her cheeks. She allowed the sobs to rise and escape too. She didn't know how she'd ever be able to see any beauty in losing Dawson. She didn't know how she'd ever be grateful for living apart from him. But maybe if she grieved for all the heartache and loss, she'd eventually find glimpses of beauty again.

~ 30 ~

THE DOOR OPENED, and Dawson closed his eyes, pretending to be asleep.

He didn't have to see to know Chloe was coming to check on him again. He'd heard her enter the flat, her tentative footsteps in the kitchen, and then her light knock against the door.

Even though she meant well, the helplessness simmering deep inside him was too near the surface, and he was afraid he would explode.

"Dawson?" Her whisper was cautious, as though she expected him to yell at her.

He didn't move and bit back angry words so that he didn't take out his frustration on her. This wasn't her fault. And it wasn't Acey's either. They'd been tremendous. He couldn't ask for better friends.

They'd been there with him through everything—his blindness, Sybil's death, the exploring at Walsingham, finding the holy water, his stay in the hospital, and the fight against the Hamin. They'd even saved his life that night in London when they'd been waiting for the counterterrorism agents to close in on the Hamin.

Apparently, he'd fallen unconscious to the floor in their private room. His heart had stopped beating, and Acey started CPR while Chloe administered the second dose of holy water. It had only taken five minutes, and Dawson was revived. He'd been groggy and tired and had slept for hours. By the time he'd woken, the agents had been back with news that they'd discovered the Hamin's bunker under the mosque and captured a handful of men there. They'd also arrested several more at the cottage by the sea.

Dawson was relieved the mission had been successful. The Hamin were being charged with kidnapping and murder—not just of Mum but of two other agents. He and Acey and Chloe didn't have to live in fear or secretiveness any longer. At least, they hoped they'd seen the last of the threats by the Hamin.

The first thing they'd done when returning to their flat in Canterbury was debug the place. The second thing Dawson had done was attempt to create an overlap with Philippa—had even gotten special permission to go into Reider Castle where he'd attempted it.

After having no success, he'd returned to the flat, fallen onto his bed . . . and he hadn't gotten back up. Not to shower. Not to talk to anyone. Not to eat anything other than takeaway.

He just wanted to be left alone. Didn't want to be bothered.

"I brought you a few groceries."

Dawson clamped his teeth together to keep from saying anything he'd later regret.

"You have to eat something, Dawson."

His hands fisted with the urge to pitch something against the wall. His mind flashed with the memories of the last time he'd done that very thing—the night Sybil had brought him the bottle of holy water. She'd delivered groceries too, had only wanted to help him.

But instead of responding in love, he'd been a total jerk. He'd told her that he wished she'd gone missing instead of Mum.

Fresh shame burned through Dawson as her silence replayed in his mind. His comment had been horrible. He had no excuses for saying it, for hurting her, for pushing her away. *God, forgive me. I love Sybil and miss her. And I wish I'd been the one to go missing instead of either Mum or Sybil.*

He couldn't hurt anyone again . . . not Chloe or Acey. Not any of his buddies.

But how could he make his way through the darkness that had settled around him? He wasn't blind anymore, yet the blackness was worse than ever. His whole life spread out before him as a long, empty tunnel, and he didn't want to get up and move forward. Not after losing everyone all over again.

He'd had a grasp of his mum again, and he'd had a grasp of love and a future with Philippa. The security and happiness of those relationships had been his for a few brief days, giving him hope that he had a fresh start.

What was wrong with him that he couldn't hold on to what was important? That he was always losing everyone he loved?

"I know being here is hard, Dawson. This isn't what you wanted." Chloe's words wobbled with emotion. "But I want you to know Acey and I will always be here . . . that we love you."

Acey and Chloe loved him. And he loved them in return. That meant he hadn't lost *everyone*.

Heat stung the backs of his eyes. Philippa had believed it was possible that anyone could experience beauty when life brought darkness. He had to push past this new kind of blindness—the losses, the hurt, the loneliness—and he had to start looking for the beauty.

Chloe took a step back and began to close the door.

"Chloe." He forced her name out, his voice hoarse.

She froze.

He shifted so that, through the shadows of his room, he could see her standing in the doorway. Her shoulders were slumped, her head down, and she stared at the floor.

"I love you and Acey too." The words were so soft that he hardly heard them himself.

But she sucked in a heart-wrenching breath, one laden with sobs. And she nodded.

Could he really do this? See the beauty? It seemed impossible. But somehow his words had meant something to Chloe, had been just what she needed to hear. And maybe they'd been what he needed too. A tiny ray of light in the blackness.

If he could keep on cracking the door wider, maybe eventually he'd let in enough light that the blackness would no longer seem so consuming. It was worth a try, wasn't it?

~ *31* ~

"LORD DEIGHTON IS ON HIS WAY HERE." Sybil's words broke through the fragile calm Philippa had been working to maintain.

Philippa dropped the embroidery and stood so quickly the basket of sewing supplies toppled, spilling glass-headed pins, thread winders, leather thimbles, bone needles, and the small pouch of beeswax she used for strengthening thread.

Her uncle was coming for her, had finally figured out where she was hiding. Even though she'd known this day was inevitable since getting Lady Wilkin's missive a fortnight ago, her pulse raced with cold dread anyway. "We must go, Joanna."

Joanna pushed up from the cushioned chair positioned near the large window in the great hall that afforded them sufficient light on the overcast day.

Sybil hesitated in the doorway, her hair windblown, her cheeks flushed with heat, and her simple gown strapped with her sword. She'd obviously just returned from a ride with her husband, Nicholas. The two oft left for long periods, sometimes even a day or two as they traveled around Kent and the Weald.

Philippa had tried to make sense of all that Nicholas and Sybil did during their travels. The couple had privately conceded that they had recently given some of their land in the Weald as a village to outlaws—outlaws they believed had been wrongfully accused. When Sybil and Nicholas weren't assisting the outlaws in their village, they were seeking evidence that could help vindicate the outlaws and bring about justice and mercy.

The two kept so busy that Philippa had rarely seen Nicholas. On the occasions he had been at Reider Castle, he'd been respectful and amiable. He was indeed a handsome man, dark-haired, dark-eyed, and strongly built, much like Dawson. But, of course, Dawson was more striking than anyone else. Even Joanna had admitted as much.

Philippa grabbed a fistful of her skirt and started to cross the great hall, heedless of anything but the need to get far away from Reider Castle and the good people here before she could bring them danger.

"Nicholas and I have spoken at length about your situation." Sybil stood in the doorway, her feet braced in a way that said she couldn't be moved. "We have agreed that you should continue to reside under our protection."

"No." Philippa didn't falter either in step or thought. "This time, I refuse to bring anyone else into the web my uncle is weaving around me. I must go and fight this battle by myself."

Sybil only widened her stance and crossed her arms, blocking Philippa's way.

Philippa wasn't a forceful person, didn't know how to even begin to thrust her way past Sybil. So she halted, unable to keep her shoulders from drooping. If she couldn't make herself stand up to a woman, how would she be able to defy Uncle when she faced him? Because face him she must if she had any hope of putting an end to the conflict.

"You are family, Philippa." Sybil's tone gentled. "We won't let you fight against your uncle alone."

Philippa's throat closed up as it was wont to do. Every day without Dawson was a struggle, and she was allowing herself to grieve losing him, losing their newfound love, losing the future with him she'd so hungrily wanted. She wasn't pretending the hurt didn't exist, although at times that might have been easier.

Yet, through the difficult days and even more difficult nights, she was reteaching herself the lessons on beauty that she'd shared with Dawson—slowing down to notice creation, doing what she could to serve within the castle, and practicing prayers of gratitude.

Now, however, 'twas time for her to stop prevailing upon the goodwill of others and learn new lessons. "I thank you for your hospitality. You and Nicholas have been a godsend—"

"And we'll continue to offer you our protection."

"No, 'tis too perilous. I shall embark at once to the Low Countries and tarry there next."

Sybil was quiet for a long moment, her green eyes intense and reminding Philippa too much of Dawson. "You haven't done anything wrong, Philippa. You should be able to live freely wherever you want."

"The only place I want to be is with Dawson." The words slipped out before she could censure them.

Sybil didn't budge from her spot in the threshold of the

door, and her gaze only narrowed.

"I am truly grateful for everything—"

"Is being with Dawson really the only place you want to be?"

"Yes." Philippa's voice cracked, and she had to rapidly push back the swell of emotion that was always close to the surface.

"What would you give up to be with him?"

She could readily answer that. "Everything."

"Everything?" Sybil's voice took on an edge Philippa didn't understand.

"He is all that matters." She twisted at the diamond band she still wore. After Robert died, she'd divested herself of his ring almost immediately. But she couldn't imagine taking Dawson's off, not even if her uncle finally forced her to marry Godwin.

Joanna now stood by Philippa's side, her pretty face creased with worry. "What do you have in mind, my lady?"

Sybil stepped into the passageway outside the great hall. "Follow me."

Philippa was surprised when Sybil led her and Joanna to the dungeons. She'd never had a need to visit the dungeons at Robert's estate and her uncle's home. And now as they descended a narrow stone stairway into a small holding area, she hung back and clutched Joanna's hand. "Why have you brought us here?"

Sybil was in the process of unlocking a heavy wooden door that led to the cells. "I want to try something."

"Do you intend to lock us up to prevent us from running away?" Joanna's grip on Philippa's arm tensed.

Sybil released a scoffing laugh. "Of course not." As the door swung open and she stepped inside with a torch, she removed something from her pocket. A tiny glass bottle.

Philippa's pulse hopped in her chest. Dawson had spoken of a tiny glass bottle containing the holy water that had healed him of his blindness. Did Sybil have holy water? And was she planning to attempt to connect somehow with Dawson?

But why would he be here in the dungeons of Reider Castle?

Philippa couldn't fathom the possibility that he was locked up during his era. Even if he was, all that mattered was the possibility of getting to see him again. Her feet carried her swiftly after Sybil until she was standing beside her in the long passageway between the cells.

Sybil had placed the torch in a holder on the wall, and it was casting flickers of light over the cells, revealing mildew, dampness, even flecks of dried blood.

"Let's try an overlap." Sybil was carefully removing a cork.

Dawson had used the word *overlap* to describe his initial interactions with her before he'd completely crossed to the past. "Do you think he will be here that I might speak with him?"

Unplugging the cork, she held the bottle out. "No. But I want to test something."

"Test?"

"Whether you can envision the year that Dawson lives in during the twenty-first century."

"Do you think 'tis possible?"

"I haven't heard of anyone who has overlapped with the future—except for prophets, including the most famous transport to the future that happened with the Apostle John when he wrote the book of Revelation."

Joanna took hold of Philippa's arm and tugged her away from Sybil. "Perhaps you should attempt the experiment for yourself instead of suggesting Philippa do so."

"I have and confirmed that a person who's died in one era can no longer create an overlap. The holy water doesn't work the same way."

Philippa shifted away from Joanna and took the bottle from Sybil. "So Dawson will never be able to communicate with me again via the holy water?"

"Right."

"But I might yet be able to do so with him?"

Sybil waved at the bottle. "Wet your finger, dip it inside, and give it a go."

"No." Joanna's expressive eyes registered fear and even frustration. "'Tis a terrible idea."

Before her cousin could stop her, Philippa wiped her finger around the inside of the bottle. Then she stuck her finger in her mouth at the same time she pictured Dawson and silently told herself the year he'd mentioned.

In the next instant, a gust of wind blew through her, as though to clear her mind. And she found herself blinking at the sight of a strange new place. Red lights glowed on the wall above the door. The wall had become a row of tables with several chairs with small wheels. On the table stood glossy mirrorlike items. The alphabet was spelled out on black squares in front of each mirror.

Slowly she pivoted, taking in the room around her. What

had happened? Where was she? Was this how the dungeons at Reider Castle appeared in Dawson's year? Or was she someplace completely different?

Gone was the staleness of the dungeons. Instead, a strong medicinal aroma permeated the room. There were no cells, only one large room with walls painted a bright white and tall shelves filled with all kinds and shapes of bottles and items she couldn't begin to name. A single light burned from the ceiling—the kind of light that Dawson had told her about, one devoid of fire. It illuminated the room enough that she could see she was alone. Not another person was in sight.

A part of her heart fell. She'd so badly wanted to connect with Dawson that she couldn't hold the disappointment at bay. But he wasn't here, and even if she could overlap to Dawson's time period again, how would she ever be able to figure out where he was located at any given time so she could be there to intersect with him?

She made a slow circle around the room, touching a firm raised bed, a strange box on a wheeled pole, and a moveable table. She crossed to a glass pot that had dark brown liquid inside but was cold. She fingered several polished mugs with interesting words on them like: *Don't talk to me until this cup is empty* and *Mondays were made for coffee.*

What was coffee?

Even as she took in more of the strange items, she felt herself waver, as if the room was beginning to shift. The torchlight flickered in the holder, the dark stone wall with the mildew reappeared, and Sybil stood but a foot away.

Philippa closed her eyes and then quickly reopened them,

trying to glimpse the different time period again. But she found herself standing in the dungeon passageway, the other place gone as if it had never existed.

"What did you see?" Sybil's intense gaze locked with hers.

But even as Philippa tried to speak, her knees buckled. Joanna, as faithful as always, was at her side, holding her up as a strange tiredness swept over her, almost as if the vision had drained her of energy.

As both Sybil and Joanna helped her up the stairs, she tried to explain what she'd experienced in the minute or so she'd overlapped with Dawson's era. The more she explained, the more animated Sybil's face became.

"You've described everything exactly how it was when I left." Sybil had surprising prowess and was practically carrying Philippa by the time they reached the hallway that led to the guest chamber.

Philippa's eyelids were heavy with exhaustion, and even with Sybil and Joanna assisting her, she stumbled into the room. As she fell upon the bed, she needed to know one thing before she gave way to the slumber that waited to claim her. "Will I be able to visit Dawson the next time?"

Sybil must have sensed her eagerness, for she replied with a squeeze to her hand. "I think that not only will you be able to visit, you might even be able to go there and live with him."

"Oh, please." Eagerness and desire for her husband filled Philippa so keenly, she wanted to weep. "Say 'tis true."

"When you are rested, we'll leave for Canterbury." Sybil's expression turned grave. "If we can't find a way for you to reach Dawson, then we'll go to the Weald where you'll be safe from your uncle for some time."

As Philippa drifted to sleep, she prayed earnestly that Sybil was right and that she might yet find a way to be with Dawson.

~ 32 ~

THIS WAS IT. She was leaving.

Philippa knew she ought to be anxious, but every nerve in her body was alive with anticipation.

"I think his home is right here." Sybil stopped her pacing behind several tenements and planted her feet before surveying the area more carefully. At the evening hour, the alley was deserted, since most families were inside their homes supping. Travelers and pilgrims to Canterbury were likewise filling the taverns and inns around town. Shops and businesses were closing.

Nicholas waited at one end of the alley, peering out onto the main road while his companion, a tall man who went by Ralph, stood guard at the other end of the narrow thoroughfare. Attired in their chain mail and armed with swords, they made imposing figures. Few would dare to question their presence in Canterbury.

Even so, Nicholas had gotten news earlier that her uncle and a retinue of fighting men had been spotted in Kent near Rochester. It was possible that by now they were near Canterbury, and Nicholas was taking every precaution not to be ambushed. He'd ushered them into Canterbury using a lesser-traveled gate and had kept to the quieter streets. And now that they were in the place Sybil believed Dawson lived, they needed to make haste lest they find themselves in a skirmish with her uncle.

Philippa wrapped her arms across her chest to hold back a shudder. Maybe she was a little nervous after all.

If all went as planned, they would be leaving Canterbury before the gates closed at the fall of darkness—or at least her body would be leaving Canterbury. She prayed her spirit would be with Dawson in a new time and place.

But first, Sybil had to locate the exact place where Dawson lived. Philippa needed to overlap there so that Dawson would find her during those initial hours when she would remain asleep and unconscious.

Sybil didn't want her to go to the wrong home or building or yard or street for fear that someone else would find her. But if that did happen, Sybil had coached Philippa through all the possibilities, trying to help her understand what to do and how to navigate in Dawson's time.

Sybil brushed her hand along the timber beam of the wattle and daub of the tenement. She counted half a dozen more paces before spinning and walking back, studying every inch of the ground.

"We cannot linger much longer"—Nicholas spoke tersely over his shoulder—"or we shall risk drawing attention."

Sybil squatted and ran a finger along the ground, her brow furrowed.

At the same moment, Philippa felt a strange pull, as if Joanna was tugging on her, except that Joanna was several steps away.

"What is it?" Joanna whispered.

Philippa smiled at her cousin then drew her into a hug. "I shall miss you."

Joanna embraced her tightly in return, her willowy body too thin after the past weeks of traveling and hiding. "I shall miss you more."

Philippa feared what punishment Uncle would deliver to Joanna if she ever returned home. Surely he would partially blame Joanna for helping Philippa run away. "Perhaps you shall consider joining me some day."

"If I could find someone like Dawson, maybe I would consider it."

"I shall search for such a man."

Joanna pulled back and blinked rapidly, clearly trying not to cry. "I believe Dawson is a rare man, and you are wise to risk everything for him."

Tears stung Philippa's eyes now too. Joanna had been a faithful servant and companion over the past weeks, even months before their running away. She would miss this friend. "I shall pray for you, Joanna."

"And I, you."

Philippa was already praying for her cousin, that she would remain safe during the coming days. Sybil had invited Joanna to remain at Reider Castle for as long as she wanted. But Joanna wasn't sure what she would do yet or how demanding her father would be in requiring her to return home with him.

"Ready?" Nicholas tossed the clipped word down the alley in their direction, his face shadowed.

"Almost." Sybil followed a line as it curved to the side of

the building. "I think this is a good spot."

Philippa approached, trying to imagine what she would find when she awoke. From everything Sybil had explained—in addition to all that Dawson had already told her—the new era would be shockingly different. Regardless, Philippa had already decided that if Sybil could adjust to living in 1382, where her life had radically changed, then she could do the same to be with Dawson.

Sybil tugged one of the dainty glass bottles from a pouch at her hip. She'd already explained how she'd discovered the miraculous holy water—that it, too, had once come from the priory in Walsingham. She and Nicholas had a small amount left in a flask that they intended to save for the future. But they were more than willing to give Philippa the required tablespoon that would help transport her to Dawson, since Philippa would need to save the two that Lady Wilkin had given her to survive the time crossing.

As Sybil uncorked the bottle, she nodded to the spot beside her. "Sit right here."

Philippa took a step, then halted abruptly as a room took shape just ahead and she caught sight of a man with curly red hair sitting at a table with a blond-haired woman. A box was spread out between them, and they were both eating flat, triangular pieces of bread.

The room around the two contained the same white-painted walls as the lab, the same strange fireless lighting, and many unexplainable items sitting atop cabinets that appeared to be built into the walls.

As much as she wanted to explore and admire the various

oddities, her gaze went straight to the man's leg. He was missing the lower half.

This had to be Acey, the friend Dawson had mentioned he lived with, the one who had served beside him in the army and had lost his leg during the same accident that had cost Dawson his vision. And the woman—was she Chloe? The one who'd also helped Dawson with his trips to the past?

The sight of them meant that Sybil had brought her to the correct place. But where was Dawson? Had he not lived after all? What if he wasn't there? What if she crossed time only to find herself alone?

"Where is Dawson?"

The moment she spoke, both Acey and Chloe glanced at her, their eyes widening with clear surprise.

But even as Philippa blinked, the couple disappeared. Her sights were instead focused on Sybil, who stood in the same place as previously, her intense gaze studying Philippa. "You saw something?"

Philippa nodded, her heart racing and her mouth suddenly dry. "I had a glimpse of Acey and Chloe."

"You're sure?"

"A man with curly red hair who is missing part of his lower leg? And a woman with shoulder-length blond hair?"

"That's them."

Philippa stared, trying to make the couple reappear. If she could do so, then maybe she'd be able to discover more about Dawson, where he was, if he was even still alive. But the tug of energy was gone, and she sensed that no matter how long she stood and tried to conjure the image of the two, she wouldn't see them.

JODY HEDLUND

"How did the overlap occur?" she asked. "Since I had none of the holy water as I did in the dungeons."

"From everything I learned, once a connection is established with a certain time period, the molecules have a quantum particle association."

Philippa had no idea what Sybil was talking about.

"My guess is that because you already made a connection with Dawson, the bond is pulling you toward him."

This time Sybil's explanation made more sense. "But he was not present in the room. What if he did not survive the crossing back after all?"

"We have no guarantees of anything." Sybil's eyes radiated a gravity.

Philippa hesitated. Was she willing to cross over with so many uncertainties? Especially not knowing if Dawson would be there? If he wasn't, what would she do?

"Even if he is still alive," Sybil continued, "what if he lives only another month, another week, or another day? None of us knows how long we have, which is why we must cherish each moment."

Never had truer words been spoken. Philippa nodded, then pulled Sybil into a hug. After but a moment, Sybil embraced her back. Then with Joanna's assistance, Philippa lowered herself to the ground. As she situated her skirt, Sybil held out the bottle.

"Thank you for all of your help." Philippa took the bottle gingerly, awed by the prospect that in just an instant her whole life would change forever—at least, she prayed it was so.

Sybil gave a curt nod. "Tell Dawson I forgive him and that I love him."

Philippa had already shared how much Dawson regretted his angry treatment of Sybil, how he'd wanted to ask for her forgiveness but hadn't had the chance. Sybil had listened to her graciously but at the time hadn't said much. Now, her words wrapped around Philippa's heart and warmed her. "I shall most certainly tell him. Such forgiveness will indeed be a blessing to him."

Nicholas called out something and removed his sword. Ralph spun and began to race toward Nicholas, his expression severe and his sword at the ready.

Sybil cast a glance toward the main road and then her features tightened. "You must go now."

Philippa didn't need anyone to spell out what was happening. She already knew. Her uncle had discovered her whereabouts and was closing in.

She brought the bottle to her lips and met Joanna's gaze one last time in a silent farewell. Then she tipped the holy water into her mouth. As she swallowed the tasteless liquid, she prayed to be taken to Dawson. An instant later, the world around her faded and disappeared completely.

~ 33 ~

DAWSON'S CHEST HURT, but he forced himself to look up at the stars anyway and continue to whisper the many things in his life he was thankful for.

All he really wanted to do was go inside his mum's town house—now officially his town house—curl up on the bed, pull the blanket over his head, and give way to despair. That's all he'd wanted to do since moving to Fakenham several weeks ago.

Even if it hadn't necessarily gotten easier to force himself out of bed each morning, the days were starting to pass without such extreme torture. His army intelligence work with the counterterrorism agency in London was interesting and even fulfilling. And though he had to drive into London to the office once or twice a week for meetings, he was working remotely from home while he kept an eye on terrorist movements in Walsingham.

He'd also started volunteering with a vision-impairment group in King's Lynn, putting into practice Philippa's lesson number two, that beauty was easier to see when serving others who were less fortunate. Doing so had helped put his life into perspective, teaching him to be grateful for all he had instead of what he was missing. A sense of joy came when he put aside his own selfish needs to focus on others.

The progress he was making was slow, but he was learning to see the beauty of life, even if only in tiny glimpses.

He let his gaze linger over the stars. The lights coming from the windows of the other town houses kept him from being able to view the stars as brilliantly as he had that night with Philippa on the turret at Barsham. But it was still an inspiring sight . . . and made him feel connected to her.

"I miss you," he whispered into the sky. "And I pray you've stayed safe with Sybil and that you'll be happy there."

He wished he could communicate with her. He'd tried to overlap recently, using his clearance with his new job to return to Reider Castle. He guessed she was still staying with Sybil, but no matter how hard he'd attempted to create a connection, nothing had happened, not even the slightest feeling.

He didn't want to stop trying, but he'd met with Harrison Burlington last week and ended up sharing everything about Sybil's and his adventures, including the fact that his mum was now living in the past. He told Harrison about his hasty marriage to Philippa and how much he loved her. Dawson had hoped Harrison would have suggestions on how to connect with her again, but the nobleman confirmed what Dawson had already suspected—that once a body was dead in one era, it would never be able to go back, not even in overlaps.

"I'm stuck here, Philippa," he whispered. "I'm sorry now for telling you to wait for me. If you do, you'll have to wait forever." He didn't want her to be as miserable as he was. He wanted her to find happiness and love again with someone else—at least, in theory he did, even if his heart rebelled against her being with anyone but him.

His mobile vibrated in his pocket. He'd turned it on silent mode when he'd stepped out of the town house a short while ago. He'd been too restless, unsettled, and had needed to calm himself and find a measure of peace before going to bed. He wasn't sure he was there yet. But he could admit that each time he did the hard work of pushing through the darkness, he seemed to see more clearly.

He pulled his mobile out. Acey's name and picture showed on the screen.

Dawson heaved a sigh. He wasn't in the mood to talk to Acey tonight. Hadn't been since the wedding close to two weeks ago. He was happy for his friends. He really was. They deserved to be married and have the entire Canterbury flat to themselves.

But seeing them together at the wedding had brought back a flood of memories of his wedding to Philippa. Even though she'd been attired in a sheet and nightgown, no other bride could compare to her. She'd been stunning.

He shoved his mobile back into his pocket, took a deep breath of the balmy August air, and then stared up at the stars again.

The vibrating ceased.

He started to relax his shoulders, but then another call came through. He waited. What if something was wrong? Why else would Acey phone him twice instead of leaving a message?

As his mobile went silent again, the soft buzz of texts started to come through. Then another call.

This time Dawson grabbed his mobile and opened the call in the same motion. "What's wrong?"

"Hey, man, you need to come to Canterbury." Acey's voice was threaded with an excitement that Dawson didn't understand.

"Something happen to Chloe?"

"Chloe's fine."

"You?"

"I'm fine too."

"Then what?"

Acey was silent for several long beats. "Dawson, I think I met your wife."

Dawson shook his head. "What are you talking about?"

"Your wife. Chloe and me, we were eating dinner and a woman showed up like a ghost. Scared the living daylights out of us."

The protest and frustration growing inside Dawson silenced abruptly. In its place came a tentative tremor of anticipation. "Why do you think she was my wife?"

"She asked where you were."

"Then she saw you too?" The tremor quavered again.

"Yes. She was there for a few seconds, then disappeared."

"Long light-brown hair, freckles on her cheeks and nose, and grayish-blue eyes?"

"That's her."

Dawson turned and entered his town house. If Acey and Chloe had seen her, then maybe he could too. He had to at least try. It didn't matter that he would arrive in Canterbury well into the early hours of the morning. And it didn't matter if he'd wake up his friends with a visit at the ungodly hour. If somehow Philippa had orchestrated an overlap with them, he was going there and wasn't leaving until he saw her.

"I'll be there in a few hours." He grabbed his keys from the counter and headed across the room, not bothering to pack anything.

"Wait, Dawson." Something in Acey's tone stopped Dawson. There was more. But was it good or bad?

"What?" He braced himself for the news.

"I was putting out the rubbish and locking up for the night. Stepped out into the yard for just a second . . ."

"And you saw her again?" Had he missed a second overlap?

"Yes—"

"Next time you see her, tell her to wait for me, and pick a time for a meeting." The overlapping wouldn't happen indefinitely. None of them knew how long the connection would keep happening, but eventually it would stop.

"I won't need to do that."

"Do it." Dawson started forward again, opening his door with more force than necessary. "Please." He tried to gentle his tone, but his plea was still terse.

"I won't need to because . . . she's still here."

Again, a tremor shot through Dawson, this one like a mild earthquake. "Still here?"

"Yeah, man. We don't know exactly how long she's been here, but at least thirty minutes, and she hasn't disappeared. Chloe thinks Philippa crossed time completely."

Somehow Dawson made it to the car—Sybil's Ford Focus—started it, and directed it to the road south to

Canterbury. All the while he drove, he spoke with both Acey and Chloe about how they'd discovered her lying unconscious in the backyard near the shed. The moment they'd noticed she was wearing Dawson's dog tags, they'd known who she was.

Acey had carried her inside and placed her in Dawson's old room in the bed they'd left for him to sleep in whenever he came back to Canterbury to visit. Apparently that's where she still was.

"Stay right by her side." He didn't care that he was speeding. "And if she wakes up, tell her that I'll be there soon."

"She's sleeping soundly, Dawson." Chloe's voice was calm and steady over the car speaker connected to his mobile. "You don't have anything to worry about."

Even with Chloe's assurances, he could do nothing but worry for the next three hours as he drove like a maniac. His thoughts pinged with every possible scenario, and the one he kept landing on was that Philippa had crossed time to be with him in Canterbury, probably with help from Sybil.

He tried not to let his hope rise too high. And he told himself over and over that he'd take whatever time with her he could get, even if it was just an hour.

By the time he parked on the street in old Canterbury in front of the flat, he could hardly wait another moment without going mad. He didn't bother to knock. As he burst in, Acey bolted up from the couch where he'd clearly been trying to get some shuteye.

"Is she still here?" Dawson didn't stop as he veered toward his old room. He'd told his friends to phone him if anything changed. And he'd talked to Chloe less than fifteen minutes ago. Even so, his heart thudded hard against his rib cage.

He didn't give Acey time to answer. He was already entering his room, his sights bypassing Chloe in a chair beside the bed and going straight to the person lying there—to the beautiful face he'd given up hope of seeing again.

It was her.

In three strides he reached the bed. He dropped to the mattress beside her and reached for her hand at the same time he bent and pressed a kiss against her forehead. Though she didn't respond, the warmth of her even breathing greeted him.

She was here. With him.

Tears flowed over onto his cheeks. He didn't care that Chloe was watching him and witnessing him crying. All that mattered was that they had this opportunity to be together again. He didn't know for how long. But for now, he'd find the beauty in this moment and cherish it as long as he could.

~ 34 ~

THE NOISES WOKE PHILIPPA. Noises unlike anything she'd ever heard before—whirring and rustling and beeping and too many other sounds she couldn't distinguish.

She couldn't make sense of the scents—a combination of various foods mingled with sweet floral aromas. And the textures surrounding her were strange too—softness and silk and coolness.

Her mind tried to put the pieces all together. Where was she? What had happened?

She scrambled to remember the last thing she'd done before falling asleep. What was it? She'd ridden to Canterbury with Sybil and Nicholas to cross time so she could try to be with Dawson. They'd congregated in an alley. She'd had the vision of Chloe and Acey. Then she'd taken the holy water.

'Twas her last memory.

Had she traveled through time? And if so, had she ended up with Chloe and Acey? Or had someone else stumbled across her?

Her body tensed even as her eyes flew open, and she found herself staring up at a white ceiling. She was inside a home. But whose?

She started to shift, only to discover that her hand was being held by a masculine hand that was both strong and gentle at the same time. She'd learned that touch, and it belonged to none other than Dawson.

Her pulse kicked into a wild, almost-delirious race. She turned her head sideways to find that he was stretched out beside her on a bed—one with a very firm mattress. His head rested on a pillow beside hers, and his eyes were closed.

Joy overwhelmed her so that she could do nothing for a long moment but simply stare at him in all his beauty—his hard chin and jaw, the light covering of dark scruff, the defined cheekbones, his incredible mouth, his angular nose, and his dark lashes resting against his cheeks.

He was here. Beside her. They were together.

He was fully clothed and lying atop the sheets, while she was underneath and seemed to yet be attired in the dress she'd worn into Canterbury—although her slippers were gone.

She shifted just slightly again, and as she did so, Dawson's eyes shot open. In the next instant his eyes met hers. Deep green that glistened with relief and love and tenderness.

"Hi," he whispered. "How are you feeling?"

All that mattered was that she was with him. The pleasure of seeing him again after being apart, the relief at making it to his era, the desire to make the most of every second with him before they were ripped apart again—she didn't know how to express all of her feelings save one way.

She leaned in and touched her lips to his. She meant to give him a sweet and gentle kiss of welcome, but the moment her mouth met his, her passion for him rose like a creature coming out of hibernation, famished and forceful. She raised both her arms around his neck and deepened the kiss, letting their mouths mesh with need born of desperation.

Time lost all meaning. All that mattered was being with Dawson. She wanted to spend eternity with him like this, their bodies molded together and his hands gliding over her as though he had to reassure himself of her presence.

But at a throat clearing from across the room, she broke away. Her chest heaved up and down in tandem to his. He was half on top of her and one of his legs tangled between hers.

The very nature of their position should have made Philippa gasp with mortification, especially because someone had caught them engaging in such intimacy. But as Dawson rested his forehead against hers, his nose touched hers, his breath mingled with hers, and his hands glided across her shoulder and down her arm, she didn't want him to move, didn't want him to go anywhere at all.

"Hi," he whispered again, his lips brushing hers and sending delicious shivers all through her body.

At his slight smile, she couldn't contain a smile of her own.

The throat clearing sounded again.

"Acey." Dawson lifted his head and glanced toward the door. "Would it be okay with you and Chloe if I introduce you to Philippa later? I need to talk with her first."

At a manly chuckle, Philippa's face heated.

"Right. Take all the time you need to *talk*." With that, the clicking shut of a door told Philippa they were alone. Yes, she was eager to meet Acey and Chloe, and she was eager to find out more details about her time crossing—who had found her and where. But for now, all that mattered was this reunion with Dawson.

She lifted a hand to his cheek and feasted upon his handsome features again.

"You must be tired," he whispered.

"I fare well, Dawson. You need not worry."

His brow furrowed.

"And I shall not go away this time. I am here to stay."

"But the holy water needed to keep you alive—"

She stopped his question with a soft kiss. She didn't linger, even though she wanted to. "Sybil gave me a dose from her supply of holy water to allow me to cross time. I also had the two your mother gave me—the two meant for you. Sybil and I placed them in the hiding place at Reider Castle."

"You did?"

"We considered that I might keep them with me in a pouch, but since we were not certain where I might cross or who would find me, we decided to store them in the castle."

"Good, then." He breathed out a sigh of relief.

She rose and let her lips fuse with his again, unable to get enough of him.

He was still halfway on top of her, his body so solid, so real, so alive.

She glided a hand over his arm and up to his shoulder, feeling his muscles ripple, luxuriating in the hardness and strength this man possessed.

"Then you really are here to stay?" His voice held a hint of despair, enough to know the battle to see beauty in the difficulties they'd faced had been just as challenging for him over the past weeks apart as it had been for her.

"I shall never willingly leave you again."

His fingers caressed her cheek and then slid to her neck as he angled down. "Am I dreaming? Tell me I'm not dreaming."

She smiled. "I would much rather show you than tell you." And she did.

- 35 -

A DELUGE OF WEAKNESS HIT PHILIPPA, so much so that she grabbed on to Dawson with both hands to keep from falling onto the beach.

His arm was already around her back, and now he halted. "What's wrong?"

"I think 'tis finally happening." Water lapped against her bare feet, burying them in a layer of sand. She breathed in deeply, letting the rhythmic tossing of the waves, the squawk of the gulls, the trill of insects in the grass soothe her.

She'd been in Dawson's era for a whole week, and no illness had befallen her. Of course, Dawson had gone directly to Reider Castle the day after she arrived and had retrieved the two ampullae she'd left there. He wasn't taking any chances, wanted to have them ready for whenever her body in the past began to die. They believed she'd last for a few days in a coma there at most.

But when day three had come and gone without any ill effects, then days four and five, Dawson had begun to worry. He'd speculated that someone was desperately trying to keep her body alive in the past, and the only one who would do that was her uncle.

Dawson kept the ampullae on him at all times, had even brought both with him to the beach along the shores of the North Sea where they were staying in a little cottage nearby for the weekend.

He'd promised her a honeymoon after the transition to his era was complete. But as far as she was concerned, he'd already given her a honeymoon over the past week since they'd returned to his town house in Fakenham. He'd spent nearly every moment with her, cherishing her more than she'd ever known was possible.

Mostly they'd stayed in his town house to allow her to slowly adjust to the strangeness of modern life. She'd found everything as different as he'd warned and even more so. At times the changes were frightening and overwhelming to her senses. The rush of the automobiles, the loudness of the TVs, the many devices that rang and beeped.

Fakenham had been quieter and calmer than Canterbury, the rhythms of life slower. And now, their getaway at the shore had been just what she'd needed to fill her soul with the simplicity she'd always known.

Although the magnitude of technology was beyond her grasp, she was getting quite accustomed to the indoor privy, the running water, the instantaneous lighting, and the ability to control the temperature within the home at the press of a button.

She hadn't been sure she'd like the clothing, but before leaving Canterbury, Chloe had helped her purchase ready-made skirts and dresses. Philippa wasn't brave enough to try on the trousers men and women alike were wearing—even half trousers called *shorts*—but she had allowed Chloe to fit her into outfits with shorter sleeves than she was accustomed to. Some skirts were even slightly higher than her ankles, like the billowy one she'd donned for the beach.

Strangely enough, most women wore their hair down, even the married women. No one wore head coverings, except a few men who donned caps. Without a servant or companion like Joanna to assist her, Philippa was learning to brush and style her own hair, which wasn't without challenges, although Dawson loved when she left her hair loose, so she'd taken to doing that more oft. Even then, she wore the hairpin that had once belonged to her mother, grateful that it had traveled with her so that she might have something from her old life.

She wasn't sure she'd ever get used to a grocery store and the abundance of food choices. And since she'd never needed to make food for herself—had always had servants to do it for her—so far Dawson had cooked, or they'd gotten meals from places that did the preparation for them.

Although the way of life was strange and new and scary, she was facing every challenge with Dawson by her side. He helped her to see the beauty in his world, and she knew that eventually she'd grow to see it for herself too.

At least, she hoped she'd live a long life with Dawson and maybe someday soon have his children . . .

"We should rest." Dawson began to lead her back to the blanket they'd spread out in the sand where they'd packed a simple fare.

She let him guide her, but only got halfway before the weakness hit her again. This time her legs gave out.

Dawson swept her off her feet and into his arms. "Let's sit for a spell."

She wanted to wrap her arms around his neck and nuzzle the scruff at the base of his chin. He'd promised her that she would enjoy the marriage bed as much as she enjoyed his kisses, and he'd been right. Oh, so very right.

But as he carried her toward the blanket, dizziness washed in to take the place of the thoughts of kissing and caressing him. "I'm dying, Dawson."

"You won't die. I won't let you go." His voice was low and fierce.

As he knelt on the blanket, she clung to him and kissed him fiercely in return. But before she could finish the kiss, the pain in her head and chest radiated so that she cried out. In the next instant, everything disappeared, leaving her in a blackness so deep and wide she didn't know how she'd ever escape.

• ● •

"There's naught more to be done, my lord." Joanna's voice came from above Philippa. Far away, as if in a dream.

"The holy water did not provide the miracle?" Uncle asked, tension in his voice hovering near her.

"'Twould appear the water you purchased was not authentic holy water."

Joanna was working with her father to bring Philippa back to life in the past? Why would Joanna do such a thing?

Philippa could feel Joanna holding her hand—at least, she felt a hand. Maybe it was Dawson's.

A gentle squeeze was followed by a kiss against her cheek. "He will never know I switched the water," Joanna whispered in her ear. "Now go. Be free."

Philippa's heartbeat stuttered. How had she ended up back in her uncle's clutches? Had it happened that eve in Canterbury when she'd drunk the holy water and fallen unconscious? Had Nicholas and Ralph been overwhelmed and unable to save her?

If so, Joanna had likely stayed with her and worked religiously to take care of her—which accounted for why she hadn't died sooner. And now, when faced with giving her holy water that her uncle had likely purchased at a great cost, Joanna had tricked him and given her a different water instead.

Philippa tried to clasp Joanna's hand back to thank her. But instead, she awakened to Dawson's hand within hers.

"Please, Philippa." Dawson beckoned her earnestly.

She could feel that she was sitting in his lap, and he was holding her tightly.

"Please, God. Please give us more time. I won't ever ask You for anything else. This is all I want, to have Philippa."

She was all he wanted. He said sweet things like that from time to time, things that made her swoon for him.

She cracked open her eyes. They were still on the beach. From what she could tell, not much time had elapsed. One of the ampullae was discarded on the blanket, the cork askew. Dawson had given her a dose of holy water to keep her alive here with him.

And now he waited and watched for her to revive. He wanted her more than anything else. She, likewise, could ask for naught else than to spend her life with a man like him.

"You are all I want too, Dawson." Her voice came out breathless.

He pulled back, his green eyes wide with fear. "You're back?"

"Yes. This time forever and always."

"You're sure?"

She nodded. She was still weak and tired. But as her life ebbed in another time and place, she could feel the energy infusing her here with him, the only place she wanted to be.

Joanna was right. Here she was finally free. Even though she'd still have many adjustments to make and would have much to learn, she'd been liberated to live and love. With Dawson.

That was truly worth everything.

She lifted her face and offered her lips to him. He was learning her signals well and needed no further urging to bend down and kiss her, fusing his soul to hers. For eternity.

Author's Note

Hi, friends!

I hope you enjoyed Dawson and Philippa's story! In plotting and planning for this time-travel story, I decided I wanted to do something a little different and bring someone from the past to the present day. And yet, at the same time I wanted to give you a trip back to 1382, the era for the other books in this series, so you could get a glimpse into what was going on with characters from previous books.

But bringing a character to the present age was a huge task to accomplish and created special challenges, not only in the logistics for making the time travel work (and having enough holy water for surviving the trip), but also in having the story timeline believable. You'll have to forgive me for the accelerated romance that happened between Dawson and Philippa. I don't advocate people falling in love so quickly, but in this story I didn't have an extended time to work with.

As always with my time-crossing stories, I tried to weave in true history so you get a blend of fact and fantasy. During the reign of King Richard II, there really were men who were plotting to overthrow him and put into place a different king, someone they believed was older and wiser and better able to run the country. In making Philippa's uncle part of the group hoping to do this, I wanted to give you a feel of the tumultuous political climate.

I also wanted Philippa to have plenty of motivation to leave her life in 1382. Obviously, as a woman of that era, she wouldn't fight too strongly for her right to choose her own spouse or have control over her wealth. Some women, especially widows, did gain autonomy and ended up having power and influence. But most often that was an exception. The large majority of women had few rights and lived at the whim of the men in their families.

Again, I hope you loved this book! Time-traveling stories are among my favorite to write. If they're among your favorite to read (and if you enjoyed this series), be sure to tell others about it. If there's enough interest, I might be persuaded to write more time-crossing books!

To stay up-to-date on all my book news, please visit my website at jodyhedlund.com or check out my Facebook Reader Room, where I chat with readers and post news about my books.

Jody Hedlund (www.jodyhedlund.com) is the bestselling author of over 40 historical novels and is the winner of numerous awards, including the Christy, Carol, and Christian Book Awards. Jody lives in Michigan with her husband, busy family, and five spoiled cats. She loves to imagine that she can really visit the past, although she's yet to accomplish the feat, except via the many books she reads.

BOOK 1 of the
Waters of Time Series

Come Back to Me

Scientist Marian Creighton was skeptical of her father's lifelong research of ancient holy water—until she ingests some of it and finds herself transported back to the Middle Ages. With the help of an emotionally wounded nobleman, can she make her way back home? Or will she be trapped in the past forever?

BOOK 2 of the
Waters of Time Series

Never Leave Me

Ellen Creighton's outlook on life is bleak as she comes to grips with the final stages of an inherited genetic disease that also took her mother's life. When her longtime friend Harrison Burlington locates two flasks of holy water he believes will heal her disease, can he convince her to take it—especially when she believes the holy water led to her father's and sister's deaths?

When dangerous criminals enter the equation, Ellen soon learns they will go to any length to get the powerful drug—including sending her back into the past to find it for them.

BOOK 3 of the
Waters of Time Series

Stay With Me

As a private investigator, Sybil Huxham has seen her fair share of strange occurrences. But nothing in her career has been more perplexing than the miracles she's witnessed as a result of people drinking ancient holy water. When she discovers more of the rare holy water, she experiences strange overlaps with a nobleman in the Middle Ages who is languishing in a dungeon, accused of treason, and condemned to die. To save his life, she finally crosses to the past completely.

Connect with
JODY

Find Jody online at

JodyHedlund.com

to sign up for her newsletter and keep up
to date on book releases and events.

Follow Jody on social media at
Twitter: @JodyHedlund
Facebook: AuthorJodyHedlund
Instagram: jodyhedlund
TikTok: @authorjodyhedlund